# The Side Hustle

a 509 Crime Story

by Colin Conway

Original Cover Design by Zach McCain
Updated Cover Design by Rob Williams

First Edition – 2019, Second Edition – 2023

ISBN: 978-1-961030-04-6

Original Ink Press, an imprint of High Speed Creative, LLC
1521 N. Argonne Road, #C-205
Spokane Valley, WA 99212

Visit the author's website at www.colinconway.com

# What is the 509?

Separated by the Cascade Range, Washington State is divided into two distinctly different climates and cultures.

The western side of the Cascades is home to Seattle, its 34 inches of annual rainfall, and the incredibly weird and smelly Gum Wall. Most of the state's wealth and political power are concentrated in and around this enormous city. The residents of this area know the prosperity that has come from being the home of Microsoft, Amazon, Boeing, and Starbucks.

To the east of the Cascade Mountains lies nearly two-thirds of the entire state, a lot of which is used for agriculture. Washington State leads the nation in producing apples, it is the second-largest potato grower, and it's the fourth for providing wheat.

This eastern part of the state can enjoy more than 170 days of sunshine each year, which is important when there are more than 200 lakes nearby. However, the beautiful summers are offset by harsh winters, with average snowfall reaching 47 inches and the average high hovering around 37°.

While five telephone area codes provide service to the westside, only 509 covers everything east of the Cascades, a staggering twenty-one counties.

Of these, Spokane County is the largest with an estimated population of 506,000.

This story is dedicated to those who
lose sleep to make their dreams come true.

*Good things happen to those who hustle.*

—Chuck Noll, four-time Super Bowl
Champion coach of the Pittsburgh Steelers

# The Side Hustle

# MONDAY

## Chapter 1

"How long have you been driving for Uber?"

"Seven months," Kirby Willis said. Using the rearview mirror, he looked at Anthony, his passenger, who was in his early thirties, with a fifty-dollar haircut, tailored blue suit, and unnaturally bright white teeth.

The Uber app had announced his name before Kirby picked him up. It was one of the reasons Kirby liked working with the company. Everyone was immediately on a first-name basis. Sometimes the people in the backseat forgot that. Anthony loosened his tie as he watched the scenery pass.

Kirby guessed Anthony's next question was either going to be about how Uber worked or if he knew where to get something illicit. It seemed it was always that way with this type—amped-up and in a thousand-dollar suit. Kirby liked the conversations about the ride-sharing service, but he hated the questions about anything illegal. In the past, he'd been asked for prostitutes, drugs, and even a gun once.

"Do you know where I can score?" Anthony asked.

*There it is*, Kirby thought. He shook his head, not looking back. "Sorry, no."

"You don't even know what I want."

"Again, I'm sorry."

Anthony made eye contact with Kirby using the rearview mirror. "What if I wanted some weed? Would you take me to a weed store? That's legal in this backwater city, right?"

"Yes, sir," Kirby said, becoming extra professional. "Do you have an address?"

Anthony flicked his hand in Kirby's direction. "I don't want weed."

Kirby looked at the GPS on his phone, which tracked the remaining time to his destination. Three minutes. Three long minutes. *Keep him occupied*, thought Kirby.

"Want to hear some music?"

"Are you kidding?" Anthony said. "I want some coke, and you're asking me if I want music? You're the worst driver I've ever met."

Kirby turned his attention to the road and ignored his passenger as he melted down in the backseat with a series of expletives. "I can't believe this," Anthony yelled and pounded the seat with his palms.

The car rounded the corner to Spokane's most exclusive and high-end hotel, The Davenport, and coasted into the loading zone. A valet hurried to the car to unload the passenger's bags. Anthony exited the vehicle but leaned back in before closing the door.

"I'm going to one-star you, man. You royally suck." He slammed the door.

Kirby lowered his head and took a breath.

*** 

Monday nights were a crapshoot at closing time. Some nights he'd get a handful of fares. Others, he'd strike out completely.

His phone dinged, calling him to Borracho, a busy nightspot and one where he often picked up customers.

His fare's picture showed up. She was a pretty redhead named Felicity.

It was a quick trip to the bar, as he was only a few blocks away. People milled around outside the various clubs along the street. He spotted her from the corner as she walked with an unsteady gait toward his car. Felicity reached out for a signpost to stabilize herself. She closed her eyes and inhaled deeply. She wore a light summer dress and flip-flops. With a breath of renewed confidence, she opened her eyes, released her grip on the pole, and hurried to his car. She pulled open the door and slid in.

"Take me home, Jeeves." She smelled of alcohol, and her words slurred together.

"Yes, ma'am," Kirby said, smiling politely.

He knew better than to engage her in conversation. For several minutes, she watched the city pass by outside her window.

Kirby's thoughts were broken when she said, "Hey."

He looked in the rearview mirror to see Felicity studying him through unfocused eyes. "Yeah?"

"Have we made it before?"

"What?"

"You and me. Have we hooked up?"

"No."

"Are you sure?" Felicity asked, a drunken smile on her face.

"I'm positive."

"If you say so," she said and turned back to the window.

A couple of quiet minutes passed before she said, "Do me a favor and stop."

"Why?"

"Please stop!" she begged, her voice now full of panic.

Kirby yanked the wheel to the right, bouncing the car into a mattress store parking lot. Felicity pushed open the door and tumbled from the rear seat to the ground. Kirby turned and watched her.

She regained her footing but stayed bent over at the waist, heaving. Nothing came out. Finally, she stuck her finger down her throat and vomited.

When Felicity finished retching, she jammed her finger into her mouth a second time. After the new torrent of vomit was through, she wiped her lips with the back of her hand and climbed into the car.

"That's better."

Kirby just stared at her.

"Drive, Jeeves!" she shouted with a laugh and returned to watching the city pass by her window.

At Felicity's destination, the Bear Creek Apartments, she climbed out unsteadily and held on to the door. "Hey, Jeeves?"

Kirby looked back. She swayed as she held on to the door; her dress had twisted around her and gathered at her waist. Her eyes were unfocused, and her smile drooped. "I bet you wanna come upstairs with me," she said in slurred words.

With a scrunched face, Kirby said, "I think I'll pass."

A pouty look passed over her face. Then she stood upright and slammed the door. As Kirby drove away, Felicity was bent over, sticking her finger down her throat again.

\*\*\*

Kirby called it a night after that. He returned to his one-bedroom basement apartment.

It had been a long day, and he wanted to unwind before heading to bed. He powered on his computer, then headed into the kitchen to make a peanut butter and jelly sandwich. He poured a glass of milk, grabbed his plate, and returned to the computer.

The first stop was Twitter to check his feed. He followed everyone from *Budgets are Sexy* to *Mystery Money Man*. Personal finance was his obsession.

He ate his sandwich and read several blog posts recommended by *Rockstar Finance*. Then he went to *Coach Carson* for an article about investing in out-of-town real estate. Next, he visited *Guy on FIRE* to read his latest article about why he hated tax refunds.

Once he was done reading blog posts, he wanted to see how the night's live webinar went with his friend, Frugal McDougal. He had built a substantial following around his advice and cutting humor. Kirby was hoping to pick up a nugget or two of wisdom he could apply to his own life.

The message board on *In Frugal We Trust* was lit up with questions about why the webinar hadn't started and where was Frugal McD? It wasn't like him to miss a webinar.

Kirby was disappointed he wouldn't get to watch a replay of the session, but he would reach out to Frugal in the morning.

He put the plate and glass in the kitchen sink and went to bed.

# TUESDAY

## Chapter 2

The body lay crumpled facedown at the base of the stairs, partially wedged into the corner of the small lobby. The neck was twisted at an odd angle. His red T-shirt had pulled up above his hips, exposing the waistband and logo of his Levi's 501s. His white tennis shoes were Adidas.

The right arm of the deceased was behind his back, exposing the palm. The two smallest fingers of the hand were splinted and taped together.

The stairs were a dark hardwood, the same as the landing. They appeared to be freshly swept, possibly polished. A handrail ran the length of the stairs, curling at the base.

The walls were painted an off-white and brightened the lobby. A large tapestry hung on the wall opposite the staircase. It depicted a European city. The decoration seemed out of place for the building.

There was no damage around the lower wall where the body lay. No evidence of blood, either.

"Think he fell?"

Detective Quinn Delaney turned to look for the origin of the voice. Lieutenant George Brand leaned around him to get a better look at the body.

"Maybe," Quinn said, slightly annoyed. He stepped back to give the lieutenant room.

George Brand was a tall, rotund man with thinning hair and round, wire-rimmed glasses. He resembled an oversized papa bear. While he had never been very physically fit, Brand had packed on an additional thirty pounds in the past several years since his promotion. He liked being behind a desk and had no aspirations of going any higher in the department. He'd previously been assigned to oversee the department's administrative division; it was a job Brand thoroughly enjoyed and was suitably skilled to accomplish. Unfortunately, he had crossed the new chief of police over public reporting policy and found himself reassigned to the detectives' office at the start of the year. It was a poor fit for all involved.

"What about an accident?" the lieutenant asked, passing by Quinn to wipe his gloved fingers along the edge of a stair. "Looks like someone might have polished the stairs recently. They could be slippery."

Quinn grunted a noncommittal response as he returned his attention to the scene. He sniffed and smelled marijuana. He leaned in but didn't notice it on the body. It was coming from one of the apartments. Cannabis had been legal in Washington State for years, but Quinn still couldn't get used to smelling it so brazenly used.

"Could he have been pushed?" Brand asked.

"Possibly," Quinn said, struggling to hide the irritation in his voice as he watched Brand study the top of the stairs.

"If he were shoved, that would have been a hard fall." The lieutenant whistled as his eyes traveled the path of descent, imagining the fall the victim took. "Boom. Yeah, I think he was pushed." Lieutenant Brand nodded, happy with his assessment. He smiled at Quinn and patted him on the shoulder. "I'll be outside if you need me."

Quinn watched silently as the lieutenant exited the lobby. For a moment, he thought about saying an expletive, but he kept quiet and refocused on his work.

He wanted to turn the body over and get a clean look at the victim, but that would have to wait until the forensic team arrived. Until then, he had to examine it in place. He squatted, then stood, and finally leaned over the body to get a better viewing angle.

"Did the lieutenant come by to tell you how to do your job yet?" a female voice called from the top of the stairs. "Quinn?"

"What?" he said while squatting again to study the body.

Quinn heard her footsteps as she descended the staircase.

"What's wrong?"

"Besides the dead guy?"

Detective Marci Burkett hit Quinn's shoulder with the back of her hand. "You're a piece of work."

Quinn stood to face his partner. Marci was thirty-eight years-old and stood 5'7" in high heels. She wasn't supposed to wear them while on the job, but no one dared argue with Marci. Her temper was legendary within the department, and it was rumored she'd gotten into more fights with other officers than criminals. She wore a black pantsuit that stood in stark contrast to Quinn's jeans and colored polo shirt. He was outside the department's dress code, but he was pressing the issue due to the early call out.

"Seriously, Delaney, what's wrong?"

"The job," Quinn said, taking a pen and notepad from his back pocket.

"That's bullshit. The job never gets to you."

"It does today, so leave it alone."

Marci lifted her latex-gloved hands in resignation. "Whatever, man. You should see this guy's apartment."

Quinn tilted his head. "Is he a freak? He better not be a freak. I don't need that today."

"See? I knew something was wrong."

"I'm not feeling well," Quinn said, exasperation seeping into his voice. "I just want a nice clean accident. No muss, no fuss. We can write a quick report and be done. Now, tell me—this guy isn't a freak, right?"

"No, he's not a freak. He's just... different."

"Got an extra set?" Quinn said, pointing at her hands.

She shook her head. "Besides, mine would be a half-size too small." Marci tapped her temple. "Think, McFly."

Quinn smirked at her.

"You're off your game, partner. Want me to take lead on this?"

"Let's go," Quinn said and curtly waved Marci to lead the way up the stairs to the second floor.

They were in the former Geiger Mansion, a Spokane landmark that had been converted to apartments decades ago. The apartments were in the historic Browne's Addition, a neighborhood known for its eclectic and offbeat inhabitants.

An officer stood at the entrance of apartment #4.

"Got an extra set of gloves?" Quinn asked.

The officer reached into his back pocket and pulled out a pair of blue gloves.

"How many apartments are in this building?"

The rookie patrolman, clearly not having had much interaction with detectives, stood straighter and spoke with formality. "There are nine, sir."

Quinn read the patrolman's nametag as he spoke. "Relax, O'Keefe. I'm just a cop, like you."

O'Keefe smiled nervously. "Sorry, sir."

"It's Quinn, Delaney, or Detective. Not sir. Okay? Tell me, how do you know there are nine units?"

"I talked with the apartment manager after we verified the body. She was the one who called it in. She lives in apartment nine, the basement apartment around back."

"Did she hear anything?"

"No, sir. She just came up from her unit to do an early morning check and found the body."

"What time was this?"

"Shortly after six a.m."

Quinn checked his watch. It was now 7:17 a.m. "What did you do when you saw the body?"

"I checked him for vital signs. He was cold. I called for a supervisor. The fire department arrived only moments after me and verified he was dead. They left him as they found him. No one disturbed the body."

Marci said, "I'm surprised those goofs didn't flip the guy over and try to revive him."

Quinn ignored his partner. "What happened next?"

"Several people came out of their apartments to see what was going on," O'Keefe continued. "A woman from the second floor said the victim's apartment was left open. When another officer arrived, I had him secure the scene due to his experience and not let anyone else inside the building. I moved up here to protect the apartment."

"Did you clear it?"

"I did. No one was inside."

"Did you disturb the apartment in any manner?"

O'Keefe shook his head.

"Fine."

Marci raised her eyebrows. "Satisfied? I already asked those questions. Can we go?"

Quinn pulled the latex gloves on and nodded once to Marci. They stepped into the apartment.

"Let me know when you've taken it in," she said, standing behind him.

Quinn stood silently, scanning the main room. There was a small futon with no cover, pushed against a far wall. Directly across from the futon, hanging on the opposite wall, was a medium-sized flat-screen television. No other pictures were on the walls. There was no coffee table. Only the futon and the flat-screen TV were in the living room.

"Minimal," Quinn said.

"To say the least," Marci said.

Quinn moved to the kitchen and opened an upper cabinet. Two glasses, two mugs, two plates, and two bowls were the only things inside. He opened the cabinet next to it. It was bare. He pulled open a drawer and found a similar complement: two forks, two spoons, and two knives.

He turned to the refrigerator and opened it. It was full of vegetables, meats, cheeses, and a loaf of bread. He closed the door and put his hand on it. Nothing was hung on the outside: no magnets or other pictures.

"Smells like patchouli oil in here," Marci said.

Quinn grunted his response and opened a lower cabinet. An unopened box full of packaged ramen noodles took the primary position. Next to it was a box of cornflakes, a container of oatmeal, and a little box of sugar.

"Are you done? You're missing the good stuff."

Quinn straightened and glared at his partner. "If he's a freak—"

"Trust me, this is interesting." Marci headed toward what looked to be the only bedroom in the apartment.

Quinn followed her and stopped just inside the doorway.

In the middle of the room was a standing desk. On top of it was a large-screen iMac. Quinn stepped around the desk to get a better view. A large boom microphone was secured to the corner, its arm looping up and over the computer. The closet doors were opened, and two six-foot-tall bookshelves had been installed inside. Books lined each shelf. Quinn scanned the titles. *Think and Grow Rich* by Napoleon Hill. *You Are a Bad Ass at Making Money* by Jen Sincero. *Rich Dad, Poor Dad* by Robert Kiyosaki. Quinn continued to scan all the titles before he announced, "Business books."

"Self-help, to be precise. Personal finance. I've read the Jen Sincero book."

Quinn glanced at his partner, then back to the books. "Really?"

"Yes, I read."

"Yeah, but this type of book?"

"So what? It doesn't make me a weirdo. Besides, you're missing the bigger picture here."

Quinn turned around and noticed a logo on the wall. In bold green script were the words, *In Frugal We Trust*. An oversized fist with a wad of cash was underneath the lettering.

"Huh," Quinn said and stood before the logo, studying it.

"I know, right?"

Quinn turned and faced the computer. "What do you think he was doing? A show or something?"

"Whatever it was, it wasn't porn," Marci said.

Quinn clicked his tongue against the roof of his mouth.

"What?"

"Seriously, what's all this gear for?"

\*\*\*

Quinn and Marci soon returned to the lobby and the body.

Geri Utley from the Forensics team stood by with her camera. Utley was a tall, thin woman with a ponytail pulled through her baseball hat. She wore a Forensics windbreaker, blue jeans, and tennis shoes.

She had already finished photographing the body in position and was ready for the detectives to reposition it for further inspection.

Quinn looked at Marci, who shrugged. "You're the lead, buddy. Get to work."

He crouched and pulled a small, thin wallet from the back pocket of the victim, passing it over his shoulder to Marci.

She pulled several cards from it. "Just a driver's license, one credit card, and a library card."

"No cash?"

Marci held the small wallet in between her thumb and index finger. "Doesn't look like there's a place for cash."

Quinn touched the back of the deceased's head, moving his hair. "There's an abrasion here."

Utley moved her position and photographed the area that Quinn had exposed. When she was done, Quinn let the hair fall back in place.

Marci read the driver's license. "Jacob Russell Kidwell. Age twenty-seven."

Quinn carefully rolled the body over. Kidwell's eyes were open, staring at the ceiling. His neck remained at the odd angle. Abrasions were visible on the forehead and right cheek. An area around his left eye appeared to be reddened. His lip was cut.

Quinn stepped back and let Utley photograph the body from various positions. He removed the notebook from his back pocket and jotted several reminders in it before stuffing it away. He looked back up the stairs and then down to where the body lay before frowning.

"What's wrong," Marci asked.

He sighed before admitting, "Maybe the lieutenant was right."

"Well then," she said. "He'll really be impossible to live with now."

# Chapter 3

As Quinn pulled into the station's parking lot, he saw Marci lean against the trunk of her detective's car. She watched him park and slowly get out of his car.

"Now, I know something's wrong," she called to him.

Quinn shut the car door and headed toward the station. "What are you talking about?"

"How many years have we been partners?"

He shrugged and waved his hand dismissively. "I don't know."

"Three, Quinn." She held up three fingers. "Three. You know that."

"Ok."

"And in all those years, whenever we break a scene, we haul ass back to the station, and the loser buys lunch."

"I can't today."

Marci stopped and threw her hands in the air. "You didn't even try. What is wrong with you, man?"

Quinn kept walking. Realizing he wasn't going to stop, Marci ran adeptly in her heels to catch up with him.

"Listen, I'm your partner. You can talk to me. Is it women problems? Is Barbara back in the picture?"

Quinn stopped suddenly and faced Marci. His face reddened as he spoke. "Don't mention her."

"Hey, pal, you married her, not me."

"I also divorced her. Don't bring her up." He pointed his finger, thought better about saying something further, and turned to walk toward the station.

Marci muttered, "The ex-wife-who-shall-not-be-named," then hurried to her partner. "What is it then? Your health? Your family?"

"No," Quinn said, frustrated. He turned to her. "Maybe I'm on my period. Cut me a break, will you? I put up with you when you're on the rag and get all bitchy."

Marci's face turned red. "Are you kidding? I'm showing concern for you, you prick, and you decide to go full misogynist?"

Quinn rolled his eyes. "Oh, give me a break, Marci."

"No, you give me a break. I'm trying to show that I care about you, dumbass, and you're treating me like dirt."

Quinn's face felt warm and tingly.

"I should invite you on the mat right now," Marci said, pointing toward the Public Safety Building. "You can try out some of that misogynistic bullshit in there."

"You wish," Quinn said with a quick snicker. "Am I now officially the last guy to bite on your challenge to hit the mat? You're just wishing you could try to kick my ass."

Marci pulled back slightly, surprised at Quinn's tone. "You know I could," she said softly.

"In those shoes?" Quinn said with a sneer and a flick of his eyes to her high heels. "You're just lucky no one has tested you in them yet."

"Do you wanna?"

Quinn stared at his partner, fighting back his anger. He knew he was dangerously close to out of control but couldn't stop himself.

"Are you scared?"

"Of you?" Quinn's face was hot, and his mouth was dry.

"Then let's go. Show me how tough you are."

"Fine," Quinn said and stepped back into a fighter's stance, his hands up near his face.

Marci stepped back quickly and caught the heel of her right shoe in a small hole in the asphalt. The heel broke, and Marci stumbled backward a half-step.

Quinn dropped his hands and snickered. "That's what you get. Maybe you'll listen—"

Marci moved so quickly he was unprepared for it. She spun, launching a back kick at Quinn with the foot that had the broken-heeled shoe. It hit Quinn in the stomach, doubling him over. He stood there for a moment before collapsing to his hands and knees, sucking for air.

She put her hand on his shoulder and leaned down. "You okay?"

The door to the station flung open, and Patrol Captain Lafrenz ran out. "Stop! Stop!"

Marci stepped back from her partner, who was still trying to catch his breath and looked at the captain.

Lafrenz, a silver-haired woman, months from retirement, was known to have a low tolerance for unprofessional behavior. "What the hell was that?" she yelled.

A long silence passed before Lafrenz asked in a raised voice, "Well?"

"Nothing," Quinn wheezed, as he regained his footing. "It was nothing." His anger was slowly draining and was now replaced by a feeling of embarrassment.

"That's nonsense, Delaney. I saw you two fighting."

Marci's eyes moved between the captain and her partner.

"We weren't fighting," Quinn said.

"Then what was it?" Lafrenz asked, looking between the two detectives.

The partners glanced at each other.

Quinn cleared his throat. "I bet her she couldn't take down a man of my size while wearing high heels."

Lafrenz's attention turned to Marci's shoes. "Damn it, Burkett! You know you're not supposed to be wearing those. I thought I made that clear when I was your captain."

"Yeah, but Cap...he went down *fast*."

"That's beside the point."

"Is it?" Marci said with a shrug. "I thought the point of the 'no heels' rule was that female detectives can't fight in them. I fight in them fine. I just showed it, even with a broken heel. You know full well there are male detectives who can't fight in a karate gi on a mat, let alone slacks and dress shoes."

"We have rules for a reason," the captain said.

"Rules take care of the lowest common denominator, Captain. Why punish the winners?"

"You're skating on thin ice," Lafrenz said. "Change the shoes. And don't ever let me see that kind of bullshit in the parking lot again. If you two have a problem, deal with it like grown-ups or take it to the mat." With a final glance at each of them, the captain turned and walked back to the Public Safety Building, shaking her head as she walked.

The partners waited until the captain re-entered the building.

"So, what is your problem?" Marci said, still watching the PSB's entry and not facing her partner.

"I don't have a problem," Quinn said, rubbing his stomach.

Marci turned to study him.

"What?" he said.

"You threw me under the bus."

"The shoes? I did that to save us from a fighting beef."

"Whatever. I would have taken the heat for what I did. You don't have to save me. I can save myself."

"I know that, Marci. Everyone knows that," he said, a tone of condescension creeping into his voice. "You're a self-rescuing princess. We've heard it all before."

She shook her head. "Something really has crawled up your butt."

Without looking back, Marci headed toward the front of the building; her gait made awkward due to the broken heel.

Quinn went in the opposite direction. He needed a walk around the building to calm himself down.

\*\*\*

At his cubicle in the detectives' office, Quinn turned on his computer and tossed his notebook on his desk. He opened it and set about his initial report on the dead body known as Jacob Russell Kidwell.

Quinn's cellphone vibrated. He recognized the area code as a North Carolina number. He silenced the vibration, flipped it over onto the desk so he didn't have to see the call, and tried to clear his head.

He needed to get a basis started for the report. Soon, he would receive additional reports from the patrol officers that would include interviews of potential witnesses. With the new online reporting system, their reports could arrive as soon as that afternoon. He knew he should start his own report, but he didn't feel like it.

Quinn leaned back from his desk, rubbing his stomach where Marci kicked him and stared at the blank document on his screen. Marci caught the movement from the corner of her eye. She turned to him. "You done already?"

"Just thinking."

"Sorry about what happened in the parking lot," Marci said.

Quinn closed his eyes and nodded. "Yeah, me too."

"I kicked you pretty hard."

"Not that bad."

"Really?" Marci said, watching as Quinn's hand rubbed his stomach.

An embarrassed smile crept at the corners of his mouth.

"Still friends?" Marci asked.

"Yeah," Quinn said. His eyes went to her shoes, which were now a different pair of black heels. They were still high, but lower than the version that broke, and they were plain. "Where did you get the shoes?"

"My desk. Girl Scout motto, be prepared, right?"

"You were a Girl Scout?"

"Yes. You want to tell me what's going on with you?"

Quinn shook his head. "I'm good. Just cranky today."

"Okay, fine, I'll let it be. You start your report yet?"

"No."

"Well, make it snappy. Since you were late to the parking lot, you're buying lunch today, and mama's hungry." Marci turned back to her computer.

Quinn sighed and turned his chair back toward his computer. He took several breaths to calm the rising frustration inside him. When he finally had control, his fingers settled on to the keyboard, and he began to type.

\*\*\*

"Why'd you pick Jimmy Johns?" Marci asked.

"It's fast." *And cheap*, Quinn thought. He had twenty dollars in his pocket and didn't want to go to the bank.

"Are we in a hurry?"

"No."

"You wanted something fast, though?"

"Yes," he said, stuffing his sandwich into his mouth.

"You're weird today."

"Hmph."

"That's the most intelligent thing you've said all day."

Quinn shrugged.

"Thanks for lunch, by the way. Where should we go tomorrow?"

"About that," Quinn said, putting his sandwich down. "I was thinking. Maybe we should skip going out to lunch for a while."

A hurt look passed over Marci's face. "You don't like having lunch with me? Listen, I said I was sorry for kicking you."

"It's not that. I'm thinking—"

"Is it a cost thing?"

"No," Quinn said, his irritation returning. "Never mind."

"Are you tight on money?"

"No, not that." He scrunched his face and shook his head.

"Then what?"

They sat quietly for a few moments until Quinn said, "I was thinking about the calories."

"Seriously?" Marci said with a small laugh. "You're like Mr. Stud Runner Man."

"What does that even mean?"

"It means you're in shape, dude. You already watch what you eat. Calories are your friend."

Quinn studied his sandwich. "Yeah, I guess so."

"You sure it's not about money?"

"No, I'm good," Quinn said, not making eye contact. "We'll do lunch tomorrow."

Marci bit into her sandwich. "Great," she said through a mouthful. "So, where should we go?"

\*\*\*

21

Back at the station, Quinn lowered into his chair and powered on his computer. For his background image, a picture of New York's Central Park appeared. It was from a vacation he'd taken the previous summer with a former girlfriend. She'd been his first romance following his divorce, and they had spent two weeks in New York together. It was an act of freedom for him. He was celebrating his independence from the nagging Barbara had developed over the last couple of years of their marriage.

Barbara always complained about money. She was never happy about their lives, and Quinn hated that. His work was filled with death and sorrow, and when he went home, he wanted to escape. He didn't want to listen to her grumble about their finances. They had once been a happy couple, but after nine years of marriage, they were at each other's throats. The funny thing is that they didn't fight about the things other guys in the department fought about. He wasn't cheating, and neither was Barbara. They had remained faithful throughout their marriage, like that was some big accomplishment, which maybe it should have been given how rampant and accepted that behavior was within the department.

There was still a part of him that liked his ex-wife. Well, everything except that she had turned into a financial shrew, always nagging and lecturing him about money. That part, he hated with a passion.

When Quinn was sixteen, his father died from a heart attack. His mother passed from cancer when he was in college. As far as he was concerned, there was no need to worry about tomorrow when there was a great likelihood it would never arrive for him. "Money helps us achieve our goals today," Quinn said to Barbara one night during what seemed like a particularly harmless conversation.

"Tomorrow will take care of itself." She lost it after that comment. The fight escalated until she said she couldn't take living with Quinn anymore and wanted a separation.

Quinn escalated the fight with, "I want a divorce."

There was no coming back from that.

That's why the trip to New York with the yoga instructor, Amelia, was so special. It was two weeks of release. No concerns. Just pure enjoyment. They went to museums and plays, ate dinner out every night, and even saw a Yankees game. It was the best vacation of Quinn's life.

Of course, he and Amelia ended their relationship a few weeks after they got home. He knew it wouldn't last forever. He still had the memories, though.

And the credit card bill.

\*\*\*

"Jacob Russell Kidwell is a nobody," Quinn said to Marci an hour later.

She leaned back from the neighboring cubicle. "What?"

"This morning's victim. He's a nobody."

"No history?"

"Zilch. I ran him through all the databases and not even a traffic ticket."

"Fake name?"

"No, it's the real deal," Quinn said. "He's just clean."

"Nobody's that clean."

Marci slid forward to her desk, done with the conversation.

Quinn looked around. His initial report was complete, and his job on this case would now consist of waiting. He'd gotten a couple of reports from the first officers on scene. Not much there, but it was added to his report.

He hadn't gotten the photos yet from the forensic team. They would usually upload them quickly but not as fast as he liked. They'd be ready for review by tomorrow morning.

The autopsy wouldn't take place for a day or two. It would have to fit into the coroner's schedule, and they would be notified when it would occur. He wasn't required to attend that process, but it was something he tried to do whenever possible.

They were also waiting for the computer forensic team to finish the digital imaging of Kidwell's hardware before they could get into it and start snooping around.

As anxiety he wasn't used to suddenly washed over him, Quinn pushed back from his desk and went for a walk.

# WEDNESDAY

## Chapter 4

MICKEYD, Kirby texted his friend. YOU SICK?

Frugal McDougal hadn't responded to a couple of texts from him on Tuesday. It happened occasionally. The guy was busy. Heck, everyone was busy nowadays. Kirby glanced once more at his phone, then set it aside and considered the day ahead.

There was a freelance writing project he needed to finish. One of his Twitter followers, a real estate developer, had emailed him some notes and .wav files for a book he wanted to "write." The developer understood his own weakness as an actual author and had hired Kirby to ghostwrite his story. The developer had read Kirby's prose on *New Fashioned Hustle*, Kirby's blog about investing and living a life beyond what society deems normal.

They had agreed to $0.10/word. Kirby couldn't believe his luck. A fifty-thousand-word book would net him $5,000. He'd never ghostwritten anything before and thought this would be a great opportunity. However, the developer was a terrible communicator and a braggart. Kirby had to drag the book out of him. He was at twenty thousand words, and the draft was full of stops and starts. It had no consistent theme. He had to figure out where to go next with the story, but he didn't feel like working on it today.

He sipped his coffee and thought, *What else then?*

He would drive for Uber later and pick up some quick cash; that was an easy decision. He could bang out a fifteen-hundred-word blog post, but he'd just updated the site yesterday.

He needed to continuously monitor the social media aspect of promoting his blog and website, but his Buffer dashboard was full for the next couple of days, so he didn't need to attend to that right now. Due to his Buffer account, his Twitter updates would automatically post when they were scheduled to go out.

Kirby Willis had more than four hundred followers on his blog and almost twelve thousand followers on his Twitter account. His Pinterest account was a meager one hundred and fifty. He hardly did anything with Facebook and YouTube, but he had a smattering of followers on those platforms as well.

However, in real life, things were dramatically different.

Kirby's last girlfriend ditched him because he wasn't "normal." He was actually glad she did because he could see down the road that she would be expensive to maintain, both financially and emotionally. He wanted to avoid either type of payment. Kirby had occasional relationships with women, but they often ended after a few dates. He didn't want a long-term commitment, not while he was trying to build something. Most women didn't understand his lifestyle. Once they were exposed to it, they quickly went for something flashier. Kirby understood, but he was determined not to change himself just to keep a woman who couldn't, or wouldn't, see his plan.

As for friends, Kirby only had a single real one: Frugal McDougal.

Kirby rechecked his phone, even though it had been less than a minute since he last checked. Consciously, he knew it was a nervous action, but he found himself hoping for a text from his friend. There had been no new activity from Frugal on his site for almost thirty-six hours. There had been no responses to the new messages left on some of his posts. Frugal's social media accounts were still active, but Kirby knew he had his Buffer account and would have set his posts to update for at least a week out automatically. There were multiple responses from followers to those posts that Frugal usually would have quickly replied. The media blackout was unlike him.

He put down his coffee, grabbed his keys, and went for a drive.

*\*\*\**

Frugal McDougal's apartment was in the hipster neighborhood of Browne's Addition, just five minutes from Kirby's place.

*I should ride my bike*, Kirby thought as he slid behind the wheel of his Toyota Prius.

He quickly removed the thought from his mind and replaced it with an option to listen to a podcast while he drove. Windshield University, Kirby reminded himself. He synced his phone with his car's radio and started a *Money Peach* podcast. The topic was how banks beat you with the amortization schedule.

When he arrived at McDougal's apartment, he parked and hurried up to the white and green former mansion.

He pushed open the door, hurried through the small lobby, and jogged up the stairs. When he turned the corner, he stopped short and stared at the front door of apartment #4.

Yellow tape with the words DO NOT ENTER—POLICE crisscrossed over the door.

Kirby moved to the door. He thought about trying the handle but didn't want to get in trouble with the police.

"He's dead."

Kirby spun around to see a woman at the end of the hall. She stood in the doorway of her apartment, #3. "What?"

"He's dead," she repeated and moved away from the door, leaving it open.

Kirby walked toward it and, after a moment of hesitation, entered her apartment. The smell of marijuana hung in the air.

The woman was in her late twenties with her hair pulled into a bun. She wore denim shorts, a plain black T-shirt that had been cut above the waist, and a sweater jacket that fell to her knees. Her feet were bare and slightly dirty.

She curled up on a light brown couch, tucking her legs underneath her, and lit a cigarette. "Want one?"

Kirby shook his head. "He's dead?"

"Fell down the stairs yesterday. They think he broke his neck. I overheard the cops talking about it."

Kirby sat on the couch. "Oh, my God."

"I saw you around here a few times. Were you friends?"

"Yeah. You?"

She yawned. "We got high together."

"High?"

"Didn't you smoke with Jake?"

"Jake?" Kirby said softly. He knew his friend's real first name was Jacob, of course, but he preferred to call him by his screen handle. Frugal refused to be called

Jake. He'd told Kirby he hated it. He said only football players and politicians were named Jake.

"What's your name?" the woman asked, dreamily.

"I'm Kirby. Kirby Willis. You?"

"I'm Fonda Shay. It's nice to meet you, Kirby Kirby Willis."

Kirby reached out to shake Fonda's hand, and she stared at it, confused for a moment. He was embarrassed at his action and started to pull back just as she reached out. Finally, they touched hands. Hers was cool and soft.

"I didn't know that about him," Kirby said. "The getting high, I mean."

"Don't you?"

Kirby shook his head.

"You should," Fonda said, her eyes drooping. "You look like the type who could use it."

Kirby looked down at his jeans and flip-flops. He thought he presented a relaxed image. Shrugging off her comment, he asked, "Did you hear the police say anything else?"

Fonda leaned her head back against the couch. "A couple of them said he might have been pushed."

"Why would they say that? Do you think that could have happened?"

"Maybe. I heard arguing at his place occasionally, but he never told me that kind of stuff when we made it."

Kirby stared at her.

Fonda turned her head to look at Kirby, leaving it to rest on the couch. She must have seen the questions in Kirby's eyes because she explained, "Jake would visit occasionally." A frown appeared on her face, and she looked back to the ceiling. "He called me pretty when he wanted his way."

"Did you hear him fall?"

"No, I was out. Like, out cold. Have you ever tried peyote?"

Kirby shook his head.

"Well, don't. It messes you up bad. I'm not going to do it again. When I woke up, the cops were here. I stayed locked in my apartment because I thought they were here for me. When I realized they weren't, I chilled and listened to what they were saying. Some of them came and talked to me, but I couldn't help them."

It was an odd sensation to understand that his friend was dead, but not really know he was gone. Kirby felt disconnected from the news and was having trouble processing his emotions.

Fonda lifted her head from the couch and studied him. She looked him up and down. Finally, a lazy smile grew. "You're sort of handsome."

Kirby looked away from her, checking out the apartment. Plants grew in macramé hanging planters. Vibrant paintings with violent and sexual overtones hung on the walls. The couch sat in front of the windows, and a Papasan chair was nestled next to it. Underneath the chair, a black backpack leaned against its base.

"When I'm upset, I do things to help push the emotions down. Do you?"

She was attractive, in a hippie sort of way, and Kirby immediately knew what she was intimating. However, he didn't go for women who used drugs. They didn't fit in with his plan. "I need to go," Kirby said and stood.

"You don't have to," Fonda said, unfolding her bare legs from beneath her. "Hang out and smoke with me."

There was something in her voice that both excited Kirby and made him uncomfortable. That sensation was a signal something wasn't in sync with his plan.

"I have to go."

As he headed toward the door, Fonda muttered after him, "Goodbye, Kirby Kirby Willis."

# Chapter 5

Quinn Delaney read through the letter a second time before tearing it to shreds and throwing it into the trash can under his desk. He kicked the can away from him, loudly banging it against the back of his desk.

"A letter from your ex?"

Quinn looked over as Marci stood by her cubicle, a cup of coffee in her hand. Her eyebrows raised in a questioning manner.

"Junk mail," he said.

Marci dropped into her chair. "The geeks said they'd have an image of Jacob Kidwell's computer finished by the end of the day. They're backlogged, but they'll put a rush on it for us."

"For you."

"What's that mean?"

"You know what that means," Quinn said without looking at her. "They rush because you're you."

Marci smiled and batted her eyelashes. "Aww, you're saying I'm pretty."

"They're afraid of you," he said gruffly.

Her smile faded. "Excuse me?"

Quinn held up his hand, warding her off. "I don't want to get into it."

"Tell me what you mean by that, Delaney."

"No," Quinn said with a shake of his head.

Marci stood and walked over to her partner. She leaned down next to his ear. "Tell me what you mean by that."

Quinn looked up at his partner, his face warming. "Step back, Marci."

She hesitated for a moment, but then stepped away. "What's up your butt?"

Quinn stood and leaned his hip against his desk. He crossed his arms and tried to breathe slowly to calm himself down. He didn't know why he was getting so angry.

Marci crossed her arms and stared at her partner, waiting for him to speak.

"People can feel pushed around by you."

Marci shook her head, her black hair flopping from side to side. "Pushed around?"

"Intimidated."

"I'm half your size. I'm half almost everyone's size."

"I'm not intimidated by you. I didn't say I was intimidated. I was talking about the geeks and the office staff."

"The geeks and the office staff?" Marci's voice raised. "What are you talking about?"

Quinn's cheeks reddened further, and he closed his eyes.

"What's going on?" Captain Gary Ackerman said as he walked into the detectives' office. Ackerman was dressed sharply in a suit and tie. All investigation units fell under his command. He stopped next to Quinn and gave him a disapproving glare before turning to Marci. "Why are you two openly arguing in the middle of my department?"

Marci's eyes flicked to her partner before she said, "I asked his opinion on my outfit. He didn't like it."

Ackerman's eyes appraised Marci's pantsuit before he turned to Quinn. He focused on his jeans and button-up shirt. "You're out of compliance with the dress code, Delaney. You look like a farmer. Was there a call out I missed this morning?"

Quinn lowered his head and felt his face warm further. There was no use in arguing. He knew he was violating the dress code.

"Captain Lafrenz called to say you two had an altercation in the parking lot yesterday. Something I need to know about?"

The two detectives looked at each other, then back to their captain. "No, sir," they said in unison.

Ackerman frowned while he studied them. Finally, he said, "Carry on," and walked deeper into the detectives' office, on the search for someone else.

Marci said with a grin, "Farmer Quinn. Oh, man, that's classic."

Quinn sat at his desk, ignoring his partner. Marci pushed her chair back to her cubicle. It took several minutes for calm to return to him. When it did, he put his hands on his keyboard. With a few quick keystrokes, Quinn pulled up his report on Jacob Kidwell and reread it. The final patrol officer reports had come in. When he finished reading the overall file, he grabbed his cell phone to see if he'd missed any texts. He stared at it for a minute.

He went back to the report and pulled up the initial evidence log.

"Marci?"

She leaned back in her chair to look at him.

"Do you remember seeing a cell phone at the victim's apartment?"

She leaned forward into her cubicle, disappearing from Quinn's view. A moment later, she leaned back again. "No. Do you think we missed something?"

"I don't think so," Quinn said, turning to face her, "but a guy with that much technology in his apartment, you'd think he'd have a cell phone, right?"

Marci stood and grabbed her jacket. "Let's go."

***

Fifteen minutes later, they were back at Jacob Kidwell's apartment building. "If this is a wild goose chase," Marci complained, "you're buying lunch."

"I bought it yesterday."

Marci smiled. "I know, but I'm going for back-to-back."

"You can't do that."

"Already done," she said, climbing out of the car.

"You're a little bully," Quinn said, following her up the sidewalk.

"Who are you calling little?"

They walked up the stairs just as a late-twenties white male exited the building. He made eye contact with Quinn while Marci had bent over to dust off her shoes.

As Quinn held the door for Marci to enter the apartment, the white male continued down the stairs and walked to the street. He climbed into a blue Toyota Prius with an Uber sticker on the passenger side of the front window.

"What are you looking at?" Marci asked.

"That guy who just left the building."

"What about him?"

"Nothing, I guess. I don't know."

Quinn stepped into the lobby and stared at the corner where Jacob Kidwell's body had been discovered. Marci stood next to him.

The manager, Rosanna Toombs, walked out of the back hallway and into the small lobby. "Detectives," she said, "here's the key you requested." Quinn had called her before leaving the department.

Rosanna was in her early sixties with short, curly hair. Her bright blouse was tucked into her blue polyester pants. The chemical musk of too much of the wrong perfume almost made Quinn cough. He would have preferred the smell of marijuana, which he assumed was still present in the building but was masked by the manager's fragrance.

As he took the key, Quinn asked, "According to the officer who interviewed you, you didn't hear any commotion yesterday morning?"

Rosanna pulled her hair back from her left ear, revealing a hearing aid. "I take both of them out at night. I can't hear much of anything."

"But you could have felt the floor shake," Marci said.

"It was the middle of the night," Rosanna said, "or morning, I guess. I was out like a light. I talked to the other policemen about this already. Am I in trouble?"

"No, ma'am," Quinn said, "We're just working out what happened. Thank you for the key."

\*\*\*

In Jacob Kidwell's apartment, the search began.

"If you were a cell phone, where would you hide?" Marci said as she pulled drawers open from a dresser in the bedroom. There was a minimal amount of clothing in each drawer.

Quinn got on his hands and knees to look under the futon. He didn't find anything there. When he rocked back to his knees, he stared at the uncovered mattress. "He slept here, right? On the futon."

Marci walked to where Quinn was standing. "Yeah, that's what we figured."

"Where's the cover? And the bedding?"

They looked at each other for a moment, and each went in separate directions. A couple of minutes later, they met back in the living room. "Okay, so now we have a missing cell phone and bedding for a futon," Marci said.

"You're presuming he had a cell phone."

"And bedding?"

"Exactly."

"I'll make the leap, Sherlock," Marci said. "Look at the other room. The guy was a nerd. He had a phone."

"That means I have to make the leap and say he slept with at least a blanket and pillow, right? Probably a futon cover, too."

"Or a sleeping bag or something. I think those are two reasonable assumptions, right?"

Quinn nodded. "So, we're saying..."

"The phone and bedding are missing."

"Or they were taken."

"The phone could be in his car," Marci suggested.

"Does he have a car?"

Marci shrugged. "I didn't run an AVR. Did you?"

An All-Vehicles Registered report from the Department of Motor Vehicles would list all the vehicles, including boats and trailers, registered to an individual. But Quinn figured there was a quicker way.

\*\*\*

Rosanna opened her apartment door and smiled, seemingly happy to be talking with the detectives again.

Quinn handed the apartment keys back to her and said, "Two follow-up questions, Ms. Toombs. First, did Jacob Kidwell have a car?"

Rosanna shook her head. "He used to, but not anymore. He told me he got rid of it when he realized how much it cost him. He pretty much rode the bus or used the Uber thing."

Marci scrunched her nose. "He gave up his car?"

Rosanna nodded. "That's what he said."

"Weird," Marci said.

Quinn glanced at his partner before continuing. "Second question. Do you have a laundry room in the building?"

Rosanna nodded. "We do."

"Do you clean it daily?"

"I do."

"You cleaned it yesterday, right? What about today?"

"Both. I clean it every morning like I said."

"Did you find a futon cover?"

"A what?"

Marci held her hands out wide. "It would look like a big sack."

Rosanna nodded. "I did! It was sitting in the dryer, along with a pillow and a blanket. Someone hadn't come back for them. I pulled them out and folded them. They're probably still in there."

The manager grabbed her keys and led the detectives to the laundry room. She opened the door and walked in. Several washers and dryers lined the opposite walls. On a shelf, a multicolored futon cover sat folded with a pillow, its case, and a thin blanket on top. Rosanna grabbed the stack and handed it to Quinn.

"Is this what you're looking for?"

"I believe so," Quinn said.

*** 

At the car, Quinn opened the trunk and pulled out several brown paper bags marked Evidence. He shoved the futon cover into one, the pillow and its case into the second, and the thin blanket into the third.

"Coincidence?" Marci asked.

"That they were washed? Probably."

"Think the suspect did it?"

Quinn closed the trunk. "Who knows? Now that it's been washed and dried, there's probably nothing there for us to find."

"It's more than we had thirty minutes ago."

"The cell phone is still missing," Quinn said, moving toward the driver's door.

"Assuming he had a cell phone," Marci said.

"I'm still willing to make the leap that the guy had one. I'd bet a month's worth of lunches on it."

Marci's eyes brightened at that.

# Chapter 6

Kirby Willis sent a Twitter message to Luke Jennings, who ran the website *How Now Cash Cow?* Kirby had gone to college with Luke and followed with amazement as his blog took off. Luke was from outside Atlanta, Georgia, and had attended Eastern Washington University on a football scholarship as the punter. After college, he returned home and entered the world of stock brokerage. He soon quit and started day trading for himself.

*HNCC?* was one of the largest blogs in the personal finance sphere and was what had initially sparked Kirby's interest in the subject. Following Luke's website is what led him to read *In Frugal We Trust*. Luke and then his later friendship with Jacob/Frugal were what inspired Kirby to start his blog, *New Fashioned Hustle*.

FRUGAL MCDOUGAL IS DEAD, Kirby messaged Luke. CALL ME.

The financial blogosphere is a small world, and most everyone knew the big players. Luke and Frugal were moderately well-known names on the scene. Kirby was still building his brand, but, as Frugal always told him, it took time and hustle. He had plenty of both, so he wasn't worried. He knew someday he'd make it.

It took less than two minutes, and his cell phone rang. Kirby answered it after the first ring.

"Is he talking about quitting again?" Luke asked, irritation in his voice.

"What? No. He's dead."

"Dead? Like *dead* dead?" There was a pause as the reality set in for Luke. "How did it happen?"

"He fell down a flight of stairs."

"Shut up," Luke said with a laugh. "You're messing with me."

"No, I'm serious. It's not funny. The cops think he may have been pushed. Murdered. There's police tape covering his door."

"Really? Did you get a picture of it?"

"What?"

"Did you get a picture of the police tape on the door?"

"No, why?"

"Because that shit would go viral. My followers would eat that up."

"That's sick, man. Frugal's dead."

"Yeah, I'm sorry," Luke said. He was silent for a moment before saying, "Listen, I know he was your friend. If you go back to the apartment, though—"

"No!"

"Okay, okay."

"What are we going to do?"

"What do you mean?"

"Shouldn't we do something?"

"Why?"

"Because it was Frugal, man. He was cool."

"Meh."

Kirby felt his eyebrows scrunch over his eyes. "What's that about?"

"He was okay."

"You're only saying that because he was getting as popular as you."

"He's not *that* popular."

"Why are you hating on him?"

"He's an arrogant jerk. I guess I should say was."

"He wasn't arrogant to me."

"Maybe not, but to a lot of the community, he was a turd. Did I tell you what he did at FinCon last year?"

"I don't want to know."

"He offered to edit my writing before I posted. Can you believe that?"

"Maybe he was trying to be helpful."

"I have almost ten thousand subscribers, Kirby. That's subscribers, Kirby, actual email subscribers. Not Twitter followers. Not Instagram followers. That's people who actually have signed up and want to read my writing. And this nobody from Podunk, Washington, offers to spell check my work. Screw him."

"Are you done?"

"Yeah, I guess." There was a long silence before Luke asked Kirby, "Were you just calling to tell me he died?"

"I was calling for advice."

"I have none, especially if it concerns that guy."

"Man, what happened to you?"

"I grew up, buddy."

"I've got to go," Kirby said.

"Hey, wait!"

"Yeah?"

"Get me a picture of that police tape."

\*\*\*

Kirby was angry after talking with Luke. He felt out of the loop regarding Frugal's death and wanted to help somehow. He thought about talking with the police, but what could he offer them? He tried to imagine the conversation.

"Hi, I'm Kirby Willis. I write a blog about saving money and growing your wealth. My friend also wrote a blog about the same stuff, and he died. Maybe I can help with your investigation. I mean, I've got no training in police stuff, but I've watched a lot of cop shows, you know."

*Geez, how pathetic would that sound?*

When he finished mentally beating himself up, he realized he forgot the one person he should have sought out immediately.

She lived in a downtown loft apartment. Kirby parked at a meter and plugged a couple of quarters into it. He ran across the street and pressed the buzzer at the door to her building.

"Whozzit?"

"It's me, Kirby."

"Why are you here?"

"I need to talk with you."

"About?"

"Fru—I mean, Jacob."

Kirby waited several seconds for the magnetic door lock to release. He was about to press the buzzer again when it clicked. He grabbed the handle and pulled the door.

He bounded the stairs, two at a time, and quickly arrived at the second-floor landing. Just two apartments were on that floor, the only units in the building. Kirby lifted his hand to knock on apartment #2 when the door opened. A woman in jeans and a paint-covered white T-shirt looked at him. She held a paintbrush in her left hand.

"You've got five minutes," she said.

Kirby's smile disappeared.

Holly Reese had been Kirby's first real crush in high school. When he found out she was Jacob's girlfriend, he was jealous, but at least he got to be occasionally around her. When Jacob and Holly broke up, he never saw her anymore. She considered Kirby part of a life that she wanted to discard.

Holly turned and walked back to the canvas she was painting. The sun shone through the windows, giving

Holly natural light to create in. It also highlighted her sandy blond hair.

She glanced at Kirby with irritation. "Are you going to stand there your entire five minutes, or are you going to speak? Either way, I don't care, but your clock is ticking."

"Jacob's dead," Kirby said, immediately hating how he didn't preface it with something to ease the news.

Holly paused with her brush, considering what Kirby announced. With the back of the paintbrush, she moved a few strands of hair from her eyes. "Okay," she said and pushed the brush back against the canvas.

"Don't you care? He was your boyfriend."

"Was, Kirby, was. Not anymore."

"But you had feelings."

Holly turned to face him. "You keep talking in the past tense, Kirb. I'm over him. I have been. I'm sorry I ever wasted any time on him."

"Aren't you sad?" Kirby asked, still standing near the front door.

"Why? His life and mine no longer intersected. That's the way he wanted it."

"That's cold."

Holly carefully put her paintbrush down and looked at the clock. She walked over to Kirby, standing directly in front of him. "He harped on me for the way I lived my life, especially how I handled my money. That gets old after a while. I don't care if I save or not. That's my choice. How he wanted to live his life was his. He was the one who said we couldn't be together. I respected that and, therefore, I cut him out of my life."

Kirby stared at her, his face growing flush.

"Why did you care so much about us, Kirb?"

"I don't understand."

"Then I'm not going to point it out. Your five minutes are up," she said, turning and walking back to her canvas. "I've got work to do. Let yourself out."

Back at his car, Kirby replayed her question. *"Why did you care so much about us, Kirb?"*

*What the hell did that mean?*

\*\*\*

Frugal had an existence outside his website. Jacob Kidwell worked part time as a real estate agent for a small start-up firm, Home Town Realty. He occasionally handled properties for former clients, but he had stopped practicing full time about a year prior to focus on his blog.

Kirby stopped by the office of Home Town Realty, which was located on Sharp Avenue, within walking distance of Gonzaga University. The office was a converted house.

He hurried up the four steps to the porch and opened the front door, which caused a bell to tinkle as he entered.

A woman behind a receptionist's desk looked away from her computer. The name plaque on her desk read *Helen Erwin.* She was a middle-aged woman, with a dark paisley blouse, darker brown hair, and dark-framed glasses on her face. Her brown eyes smiled at Kirby when she asked, "May I help you?"

"Yes. Is there someone here that works with Jacob Kidwell?"

The smile faded from both her face and eyes. "What has he done now?"

"Nothing. He still works here, right?"

She pursed her lips. "Mr. Kidwell is no longer associated with our firm."

"Can you tell me what happened?"

"No."

"I'm a friend of his and—"

"Good day."

"Well, you see—"

"That means goodbye. I won't talk any further about Mr. Kidwell."

As he walked back to his car, Kirby thought, *Has the world gone upside down? Why has everyone turned on Jacob?*

# Chapter 7

Quinn parked the car and got out. "Let it go, Marci."

"You said I intimidate the office staff and the geeks."

They had parked along Sharp Avenue in the Gonzaga University district. Parking was always a challenge, even for a detective's car. Unless it was an active emergency, it was discouraged to park illegally. As such, they parked a couple of blocks away and were walking towards the office of Home Town Realty, Jacob Kidwell's employer. They got that information off his rental application from the manager of his apartment building.

Quinn enjoyed being in the Gonzaga neighborhood and the opportunity to walk a couple of blocks among the older homes and college buildings. Even though it was summer and the students had gone home, it still reminded him of his college experience.

"You're a buzz saw," Quinn said, a hint of irritation creeping into his voice. Why wouldn't Marci let this stuff go? Especially now, when he felt like the world was pressing in on him.

"A buzz saw?"

"Your lack of height just makes it more frightening."

"That sounds like a premade excuse for when I kick your ass."

Quinn sighed. "That's what I'm talking about."

"What?"

"You're dialed to ten. It's tiresome."

Marci grabbed his arm and turned him to her, stopping them both in the middle of the sidewalk. "That's not true. I'm not always hyped up. It's just that I have to be better than any guy out there."

"Marci, stop comparing yourself—"

"If I can't do the things I want because I'm a woman, how can I not compare myself?"

"You've got to get over not getting on the team. That was years ago."

"Years ago? I'm thirty-eight, and I could still do it if the qualifications didn't exclude me."

"I didn't write the height requirements, nor did I write the standards for the physical fitness test, Marci."

"How many women have been on SWAT?"

Quinn shook his head. "I don't know."

"That's bullshit, Delaney. You know because you were on the team. There's never been one. Not one," she said, holding up a single finger.

"Women have been on the Tactical team."

"Fuck riot control," she said. "You were SWAT, and you know what that means."

Quinn stared at his partner. When she was fired up, it had to run its course.

"Have you heard the jokes about women police officers?"

Quinn cringed.

"I've heard them, too. All of us women have. That macho, misogynistic bullshit floats under the surface every day, and we hear it. You know what my favorite is?"

He watched her silently, knowing it best to keep his mouth closed.

"There are three things a woman can't do," she said, holding as many fingers in the air. Her face was turning red. "Write her name in the snow when she pees, fuck with her jeans on, and be a cop."

Quinn had heard that joke told many times over the years. He was now never more ashamed for not standing up and saying something instead of joining in the laughter.

"Well, guess what, pal?" Marci said. "I've written my name in the snow, I've fucked with my jeans on, and I'm the best damn officer you've ever met. That's why I'll fight any male cop in the department to show them they can't take me. Even if I lose—which I never have, mind you—they will respect me for standing toe to toe with them."

She stood with her arms crossed, shaking her head.

Quinn knew the sexist stereotypes present in every police department. He spoke in a genuinely caring tone. "Marci, you're a great cop and a solid partner. You may even be the last, true friend I have."

Marci relaxed and lowered her eyes.

"Would you just do me one favor, though?"

She nodded, still looking down.

"Please don't ever tell me again about having sex with your jeans on."

She snorted and let out a small laugh.

"Let's go," he said and started walking. Marci fell in step alongside him, both in silence.

As they approached the office of Home Town Realty, Quinn saw a young man getting into a Toyota Prius farther down the block.

"What the—?"

Quinn bolted. Marci quickly looked around to determine what was happening. She shrugged and ran after her partner, trying to keep pace in her heels.

The Toyota pulled away from the curb and into the flow of cars.

Quinn left the sidewalk and jumped into the street to get a look at the license plate. A Ford F-150 slammed its brakes, barely missing Quinn. The driver honked the truck's horn and let the blaring continue for several seconds.

"Give it a rest," Marci yelled at the driver. She opened her jacket and pointed to the badge on her waist. The driver stopped honking and held up his hands apologetically.

"What was that all about?" Marci asked Quinn as they stepped back on the sidewalk.

"That was the guy coming out of Kidwell's apartment building this morning."

"You sure?"

"Sure looked like the same guy. Same car, too. A blue Toyota Prius."

"Did you get the license plate?"

"No, it pulled into traffic, and I couldn't see it."

"Huh," Marci said, turning to walk up the sidewalk to Home Town Realty. "Too bad you weren't faster. Just proves they've let slow white guys onto SWAT."

Quinn stopped and stared at his partner. It was going to be that type of day with Marci.

\*\*\*

A bell tinkled as they entered the converted house.

The receptionist looked away from her computer, clearly irritated. A nameplate on her desk read *Helen Erwin*. She looked over her monitor at the two detectives and asked, "Are you two here to buy a house?"

"In his dreams," Marci said with a smile and wink.

Helen grinned back.

Quinn moved so Helen could see the badge and gun on his belt.

"Oh," Helen said.

Marci opened her jacket, revealing her badge and gun.

"Oh," Helen repeated. "I guess you're not here for a house."

"No, ma'am," Quinn said. "We're here to ask about Jacob Kidwell."

"He's very popular today."

"What does that mean?"

"There was a young man in here just a few minutes ago asking about him."

Quinn glanced at Marci with an *I told you* so look.

"I didn't tell him anything, though," Helen continued. "That would have been inappropriate."

"Did this other man say why he was asking?" Marci interjected.

"No. He just asked if Jacob still worked here. When I told him no and that I wouldn't talk further, he left. He was a very polite young man, though."

"Jacob no longer works here?"

Helen leaned forward slightly and lowered her voice, even though they were the only three in the building. "His contract was terminated a few weeks ago."

"Contract?"

The receptionist leaned back, and her voice returned to its normal volume. "He's a real estate agent. They are independent contractors, not employees. They can come and go as they please. We technically can't fire them. We can only terminate our relationship with them."

"Why was the relationship terminated?"

"Well, you really should talk with the designated broker, Amy Tillerson, but she's on vacation. I don't want to give any confidential information away and then have Mr. Kidwell sue us for a breach of contract sort of thing."

"That's not going to be possible," Marci said. "Jacob Kidwell is dead."

"Oh," Helen said again, this time covering her mouth.

"We believe it was intentional, and we're trying to determine why."

"Well, then I guess there's no harm in telling you what I know." She leaned forward again and lowered her voice. "Jacob's work had always been good. His paperwork was okay—not great, but not terrible either. His clients were always happy. He did okay with his sales. But he cut down his hours about a year ago to work on his blog."

"Blog?" Quinn said and then glanced at Marci. She nodded in understanding.

Helen shook her head. "I don't get it. Somehow, he made money on the internet. He took fewer clients, but still did an occasional deal now and then. However, over the past few months, his paperwork was poor, clients called to complain that he wasn't focusing on them, and there was even a complaint filed with the Association of Realtors."

"What was the complaint about?"

"His ethics."

"Who filed the complaint?"

Helen thought about it for a moment and then pulled out a file. "I might get in trouble for this," she said.

Neither Quinn nor Marci said anything.

Helen flipped through the file, stopping when she found it. "Paula Fairbanks with Dream Living South Hill."

\*\*\*

As they walked back to their car, Marci asked, "So who do you think this guy is? The one who arrived before us."

"No idea," Quinn said, working the problem out in his head.

"Do you think he could be our suspect?"

"Possibly."

"What are you thinking about?" Marci asked.

"When I first saw him and his car, I noticed an Uber sticker in the corner of the windshield. When we get back, let's contact the company and see if we can get the driver's info."

"Good idea."

"The receptionist said Jacob Kidwell quit to run a blog."

"You know what a blog is, right?"

"I'm not a caveman, Marci. I know what a blog is. How the hell did he make money with it?"

Marci shook her head. "I have no idea. It definitely sounds like some weird shit was going on."

*** 

They arrived at the Dream Living office on Spokane's South Hill. Its branch catered to the city's wealthier clientele, and the office reflected it.

It was new construction with high ceilings and an open, modern design. Through the glass separating the lobby from the rest of the office, people could be seen walking around or talking with each other. Some real estate agents were sitting in a bullpen area at their desks and on their phones. A few offices could be seen through their glass walls.

The receptionist was a young woman with a hummingbird tattooed on her left wrist. Her blond hair was tied loosely in a bun on top of her head. As Quinn and Marci approached the large mahogany desk, she looked up from her magazine and said, "How may I help you?"

"We'd like to see Paula Fairbanks."

"Who, may I say, is asking?"

Quinn pointed to the badge on his belt. "Detectives from the Spokane Police Department."

The receptionist's eyebrows raised, and she quickly grabbed the telephone. She tapped three buttons on the phone and talked as quietly as she could. When she hung up the phone, she said, "Ms. Fairbanks will be right out."

Quinn nodded and stepped back from the desk. He watched the office activity through the glass wall behind the reception desk. People milled about, many talking loudly. The detectives' office was also an open bullpen, but they all had cubicles, and their work was conducted in hushed tones. For an outside observer, this seemed completely different—like a mosh pit at a rock concert.

"That looks noisy," Quinn said.

"I wouldn't want all those people seeing me pick my teeth."

Quinn's phone vibrated, and he pulled it out. Seeing who the caller was, he silenced it and put it away. He failed to hide his look of irritation.

"The ex?" Marci asked.

"Yeah."

A tall, skinny redhead in a tight black skirt and bright green blouse walked slowly toward the lobby. Her eyes were on the detectives as she walked. She pushed open the glass door, and an explosion of noise interrupted. It faded as she passed through, and the door shut.

"I'm Paula Fairbanks," she said, looking from Quinn to Marci and then settling back on Quinn. She gave him an up and down appraisal, passing quickly over the gun and badge, lingering too long on his black shoes before returning to meet his gaze. It was clear she was neither impressed nor intimidated.

"Mrs. Fairbanks—"

"Ms.," Paula said, interrupting Quinn. "I'm nobody's chattel."

Quinn glanced at Marci, who shrugged and smiled, enjoying her partner's discomfort.

"Ms. Fairbanks," Quinn said, to which Paula nodded politely. "We're here about your complaint against Jacob Kidwell."

Paula looked Marci up and down now, before returning to Quinn. "Why would the Association of Realtors send two detectives to investigate an ethics complaint?"

"We're not here on their behalf, although we are trying to figure out why you filed that complaint."

"Did she send you to intimidate me?"

"What?"

"Tell her I'm not dropping my complaint. I'll file one against her as well."

"I think you're misunderstanding—"

"If you want to talk with me any further, I want a lawyer present. I'm not going to stand for this harassment."

"*Harassment?*" Quinn sputtered.

Paula turned to the receptionist. "Call my attorney. When you get her on the line, notify me." She turned back to the detectives. "When my attorney gets here, we can continue this conversation. Until then, I will not be intimidated by you. I've done nothing wrong."

Paula spun around, grabbed the door, and stalked to her office. The glass door thudded shut in her wake.

Marci looked at her partner. "What the hell just happened there?"

Quinn shook his head. "I have no idea."

"Do you want to wait for the lawyer?"

Quinn was out the door without answering.

# Chapter 8

When the barista at Rocket Bakery handed Kirby his cappuccino, he returned to his table and laptop. He was already logged on and at Frugal McDougal's website, *In Frugal We Trust.*

It felt odd. Like his friend was still alive but simply unable to be reached. Maybe he was on vacation and out of cell phone range.

Kirby scanned all the recent activity on Frugal's website, and it was all comments he'd read before. Nothing new or groundbreaking.

He sipped his coffee and switched to Twitter. His account lit up. He had twenty messages. Most of them were from followers he kept in regular contact with. It was the same underlying message: *Did you hear that Frugal McDougal was dead?*

Cash Cow had told everyone.

Kirby switched over to Cash Cow's Twitter feed. He'd pinned a tweet to the top of his feed. It read, R.I.P. FRUGAL MCDOUGAL. OUR FRIEND WILL BE MISSED. RT YOUR THOUGHTS AND PRAYERS FOR HIS FAMILY. He attached a photo of Frugal McDougal's logo.

It was a cheap shot, and one meant only to attract traffic. There were already 77 replies and 131 retweets.

Kirby couldn't believe it.

He opened the replies and read each one of them. All of them were full of shock and sympathy.

Kirby went to Frugal McDougal's Facebook business page. Jacob Kidwell didn't have any personal accounts. He spent much of his time hiding behind the persona of Frugal McDougal. He didn't enjoy living life as Jacob

Kidwell. Kirby rarely checked out Frugal's social media accounts. He had his own accounts to worry about.

Kirby waded through the nice comments about how Frugal would be missed. He continued past the comments about his death coming too soon and moved into conversations from previous posts.

A comment had been posted several weeks ago that Kirby had missed. YOU ARE DIRTY, JACOB.

That was it. YOU ARE DIRTY, JACOB.

It was from Paula Fairbanks, a local realtor. Both Kirby and Jacob knew Paula; she'd acted as Kirby's agent once and had crossed paths with Jacob many times. He wondered why she would post something like that. Those two used to be friends. And why hadn't he told Kirby about the comment?

*\*\*\**

Kirby walked into the offices of Dream Living Real Estate and asked for Paula at the receptionist's desk. Paula smiled as she approached.

She hugged Kirby in the lobby. "Look at you, Mr. Four-Hour Workweek. Are you planning your work or working your plan?"

Kirby smiled. "I work a lot more than four, but I always work for myself."

She looped her arm in his and escorted him to a nearby conference room. "What brings you by? Business or social?"

"Neither, I guess."

"What is neither business nor social? Everything falls into one of those two categories."

"Jacob Kidwell."

Paula's smile faded. "Did she send you here?"

"Who?"

Paula watched Kirby for a moment before asking, "What about Jacob?"

"He's dead."

She blinked several times.

"The police think he was murdered."

Paula covered her mouth. "That's why they were here."

"Who?"

"The police. They were here."

"Why would they want to talk to you?"

"Because I filed a complaint against Jacob."

"You did? Why? He was your friend."

"Used to be. It's business."

"Tell me what happened."

Paula hesitated, studying Kirby.

"Please, Paula. I'm trying to find out something that will help me understand what might have happened to Jacob. Nothing makes sense so far."

She slowly nodded but didn't say anything. They sat quietly for a few seconds before Paula spoke.

"He approached a client of mine about a property I had listed. The listing was about to expire, but I was going to get it relisted. In fact, we had already discussed it. But when I took the paperwork to the client, he refused to sign it and said he wanted to let it cancel. He never gave me an explanation.

"I relented, pulled my sign, and went about my way. A couple of weeks later, I started hearing rumors the whole block was under contract. My seller had agreed to a deal with someone else. It occurred behind my back while I had it listed. It wasn't a big commission, but I should have been a part of the negotiation process.

"My client refused to talk with me, which blew my mind. I later ran into his wife at Costco. She was hard to pin down, but she finally said they had agreed to sell. She admitted they worked with Jacob Kidwell to get the deal done."

Paula's lip slightly curled, and she tapped the conference room table as she fought to control her emotions. Once she did, she pressed her lips together, inhaled deeply, and then continued speaking. "That sneaky bastard stole my listing and aced me out of a commission. And to think I once thought of him as a nice, harmless guy. Once I got her talking, she told me the whole thing. That entire block is now under contract."

"The entire block?"

"Yeah. Every house on the block."

Kirby stared at Paula, working the magnitude of that out in his head.

Paula watched him come to the realization, and she said, "It's a big deal."

"Who's the buyer?"

"I don't know. It sounded like an LLC that Jacob formed, but it's too big of a project for him to do alone. There's no way he could have pulled it off himself. He has to be acting as a strawman."

"What's a strawman?"

"A frontman, so to speak. He makes the offer, gets everything under contract, lines up the deal, and gets it ready for closing. At the last minute, he assigns it to the actual buyer."

"Why do that?"

"If the buyer is a big hitter, you don't want the seller to know because they'll either jack up the price or play some other version of hardball."

"And you don't know who the real buyer is?"

Paula shook her head. "No one is talking. Everyone is being secretive."

"Everyone else thinks it's Jacob? Wouldn't they want some sort of proof of funds? Something to show that he could pull this off?"

"That's the thing. Normally, yes. But with a deal of this magnitude, it's a different type of beast. They had a short due diligence period, and he's already removed contingencies. However, there was a one-hundred-day period before closing to allow financing to take place. Due to the complexity, I could see why they would want it, why they would need it."

"The wife told you all this?"

Paula smiled. "Until her husband came back from the book section. When he saw us, he abruptly ended the conversation. I tried talking with him, but he said there was nothing to talk about. He steered his wife away from me and gave her a tongue-lashing. It was clear he wasn't happy to see me."

"Jacob put that whole deal together?"

Paula eyed him. "I see he didn't tell you about it. I don't know anything beyond what his wife said. I'm speculating at this point."

"If we wait long enough," Kirby said, "we'll discover the buyer, right?"

"Only if Jacob assigned the contract prior to his death. If not, the purchase and sale agreement is going to be voided because he won't be able to carry it through."

"So, back to the cops coming to see you…"

Paula shrugged. "I filed a complaint against Jacob a couple of weeks ago. They must have found out about it."

"What did you say to them?"

Paula smiled sheepishly. "Talk to my lawyer."

"Really? Why?"

"Because I thought she was using them to bully me into dropping my complaint."

"Who is she?"

"Amy Tillerson, Jacob's designated broker. We have a long history."

"About?"

"About a lot of things, but mostly about work. She's stepped on a lot of toes to build her business."

"Do you think she could get the police to do that? Intimidate you, I mean?"

"I don't know. Probably not. Maybe I watch too much Netflix." Paula leaned forward slightly, smiling brightly. "When are we going to work together again, Kirby?"

"Soon," Kirby said. "First, I've got to figure this thing out with Jacob."

# Chapter 9

The computer forensic team had a scanned image of Jacob Kidwell's hard drive. If something unforeseen happened now, anything of evidentiary value would be protected. They had unlocked the password and set a new, simple code for Quinn to use.

The computer was reassembled in a backroom of the detectives' office reserved for situations like this. There were already four other computers hooked up in there. Quinn looked at the names of the detectives listed on them. Three of them were sex crime investigators. He shook his head as he imagined what might be on them. *Give me a good old-fashioned homicide any day over a kiddie molestation case,* Quinn thought. The men and women who handled those cases were the real champions of the department. He couldn't stomach the idea of working with whatever was on those computers.

Kidwell's computer powered up, and Quinn was greeted with a login screen. He typed in the password given to him by the techs, DELANEY, and was greeted with a background image, a picture of a young woman in shorts and blouse, leaning against a tree. She was a beautiful woman, standing in some park. She looked young, maybe twenty years old. It was hard for Quinn to tell the exact ages of young people anymore. *The trick of age,* he thought. The older he got, the younger everyone else looked.

The background image reminded him of the picture of New York's Central Park that he had on his computer. There must be some significance to it.

He studied the picture for a couple of minutes. It wasn't a professional photograph. There were other people in the background of the photo, showing its lack of professional setting. The woman was smiling, almost laughing. The arch of the land and the row of apartments nearby made Quinn believe it was taken at Coeur d'Alene Park in Browne's Addition.

Quinn pulled out his notebook, dated it, and began making notes. The first one was: *Who is the girl in the background image?*

For the next two hours, Quinn searched through the browser history, emails, and files of Jacob Kidwell.

When it was time for a break, he grabbed his notebook and went searching for his partner.

***

"I'm tired of talking to corporate drones," Marci said, pushing back from her cubicle.

"What?"

She pointed at her phone. "Uber. I'm tired of talking to them."

"What did they say?"

"Essentially? Get a warrant. They said they wouldn't release the personal information of their drivers. They wouldn't even tell me how many of their Spokane County drivers drove a Prius."

"Did we expect any less? That's how corporate America works."

"Well, it sucks," Marci said. "And it's not like a judge will give us a warrant because we stumbled into the same guy twice. 'Your honor, he might be a suspect, and he might not be. Wow! Let me sign the search warrant now.' He wasn't exactly interfering in an investigation by walking out of the victim's apartment building, was he? Asking about Kidwell at his place of employment isn't much worse. He wasn't acting scared. Wasn't doing anything furtive. We're going to need more on this guy than just a hunch, don't you think?"

"Yes," Quinn said, drawing out the word.

Marci lifted her eyebrows. "Okay, hotshot. What did you learn?"

Quinn grabbed his chair and pulled it next to Marci. "I found his website, *In Frugal We Trust.*"

"The words on his wall?"

"Uh-huh. It's a website about money."

"Money?"

"How to save money, basically. Spend less than you make type of stuff."

"Sounds boring."

"Anyway, there are some videos on his site. I watched a couple of them. The kid was photogenic. Presented well."

Marci spun her pen through her fingers while Quinn continued to speak.

"I also searched his files and didn't see anything that jumped out. I'll spend more time with the computer, but nothing looks dirty."

Quinn's cell phone vibrated. He looked at the number, silenced it, and shoved it in his pocket. He fought back a sense of irritation.

"Your ex sure wants to get a hold of you."

Quinn glanced up at her.

"Late with the alimony?"

He sighed. "Something like that."

"Avoiding her is only going to make it worse."

His jaw muscles flexed a couple of times. "I'll call her after work."

The smaller detective watched Quinn. He could see the distrust on her face before she said, "So, the website?" and turned to her computer. She put her fingers on her keyboard, and, in a moment, Jacob Kidwell's website popped up on her screen. She moved her mouse around, quickly clicking through pages.

"The page looks nice. Info is basic, though."

"Yeah," Quinn said, moving to look over her shoulder. "Basic."

"And you didn't see anything that could be of use?"

"I was surprised at how clean the computer was."

"Like physically?"

"Like there wasn't a lot of crap stored on it. You know how your computer ends up being a garbage dump of old files? Kidwell's is super clean. There wasn't a lot of extra junk on it."

"Huh."

"I mean, there didn't seem to be a bunch of extra crap on it. It seemed super organized and clean. All around this blog concept."

"Huh."

"You said that already. The only thing that caught my interest was his background image. It was of a blond woman in shorts."

"Of course, that would catch your interest."

A flash of irritation surprised Quinn, and he pulled back. Marci didn't see it register since she was looking at the monitor. "It looked like a picture he might have taken," Quinn said. "Like it was a girlfriend."

"There were no pictures of a girlfriend hanging in the apartment, right?"

"The picture on the computer was taken three weeks ago at twelve-thirty p.m. It looks like it was taken at the park in Browne's Addition."

"And that's relevant how?"

Quinn stared at his partner. "I'm grasping."

Marci leaned back in her chair and tapped her pen against the side of her desk. "Where to now?"

Quinn reached out and covered the tapping pen with his hand. "I don't know, but I'm going to call it a day and head home. You?"

"I've got class tonight."

"Feeling the need to knock someone out?"

Marci smiled. "Unless you're volunteering. Want to hit the mat?"

"Not a chance. Take that aggression out on your fellow students."

\*\*\*

On his way home, Quinn stopped by Subway and picked up dinner. Then he continued north to his house.

He thought about working out after eating or maybe going for a run, but neither held any real promise for him. It was still a bright day, and he sat in his backyard, eating his sandwich and drinking an iced tea. From his yard, he had a view of the Little Spokane River. Most days, it was a view he truly enjoyed. Tonight, it held little appeal.

It had been almost eighteen months since Barbara and he divorced. She wasn't mean during the process. Quite the opposite, in fact.

Quinn quietly ate and thought about his ex-wife. She had been on him to change. They had racked up significant credit card debt.

They had also bought a 3,500-square-foot house overlooking the river. It was Quinn's dream home, but it stretched their finances.

Both drove new cars. Quinn had a Dodge Ram, and Barbara had an Audi TT. Their home looked like something on HGTV.

The nagging began when Barbara started reading personal finance books. One of them was a book he saw on Jacob Kidwell's bookshelf.

He quickly lost steam for his dinner, the more he thought about Barbara. Whenever his self-pity reached a high point, he admitted that he missed her. He hated that about himself, that he couldn't move on from Barbara. He wondered if he would be forever stuck on his ex-wife.

His phone vibrated, and he ground his teeth, not wanting to see who was calling. Unfortunately, as a homicide detective, he was a slave to the phone. Whether it was another call out, a witness with important follow-up information, or an officer relaying some requested details, he had to see who was calling.

When he checked the caller ID screen, he muttered. "Shit," and threw the phone into the middle of the yard.

# Chapter 10

Kirby stood on the corner of Queen Avenue and Lidgerwood Street. If what Paula had told him was correct, Jacob had managed to get the entire block under contract. This was a double block and constituted twenty-four homes.

*Twenty-four!* Kirby thought.

That was a mind-boggling accomplishment. Even an extremely low estimate of $100,000 per home would make it a $2.4-million transaction. To him, it made no sense to assemble so many houses for the sake of keeping them as single-family rentals. It wasn't the highest and best use of those funds. He and Frugal had had conversations like this previously, hypothetical scenarios about where capital should be spent and where it should be saved. Had one of those conversations been a ruse to help him formulate his plan for this project?

Kirby turned around and stood in the shadow of North Town Mall, Spokane's oldest and largest retail shopping center. He could see Kohl's, Macy's, and Buffalo Wild Wings from where he stood.

He turned back to the various homes and wondered, *What were you planning to do? And why didn't you tell me about it?*

\*\*\*

Kirby returned home and made a sandwich for dinner. While he ate, he logged into his laptop to check how his website was doing. He'd had an uptick in visits, but no new comments on any of his blog posts. He was slightly disappointed.

He logged into Buffer, his social media scheduler, to check out how he was set for content. He only had two more scheduled posts to his Twitter account, and then his queue would be empty. His Facebook account, which he rarely used, was already dry.

Kirby spent an hour searching content and scheduling it for the next couple of days. He included several of his own posts to encourage followers to stop by his site. When he was done, he flipped over to Frugal's website to see if there was any new activity.

*In Frugal We Trust* was inundated with a flurry of "RIP," "Rest in Peace," and "We will miss you" style comments on various blog posts. It was depressing to read them. He checked the different social media platforms. It was the same story. No one could believe Frugal McDougal was dead.

Cash Cow's Twitter feed was active with continued reminders about how much he liked Frugal McDougal and how upset he was to hear about his death. *What a hypocrite*, thought Kirby. Cash Cow also sent Kirby a Twitter message pleading one more time for a picture of the front door to Jacob's apartment.

Kirby closed his laptop and stood. He grabbed his keys and phone.

He was restless and needed to think. Kirby always felt better driving for dollars.

\*\*\*

Kirby only drove for a couple of hours before shutting down his Uber app. Unfortunately, the driving hadn't settled him down. He was on the north side of the city and drove to the block at Queen and Lidgerwood again. He circled it several times before pulling into the parking lot at North Town Mall.

It irritated him that he didn't know about the big deal his closest friend was working on. Not that he wanted to be a part of it, but it sounded fascinating, and something Jacob would have talked about. Why hadn't Jacob trusted him enough to share?

Finally, he made up his mind and headed south.

It took less than ten minutes to make it to Jacob's apartment building. He hurried up the steps to the second floor. The police tape crossing the door was still there. He argued with himself for a moment before pulling out his phone. He was about to take a picture, just in case he ever wanted it but put the phone away. He couldn't see a reason for ever having a picture of the door. He tried the door handle, confirming it was locked.

He pulled out his keys and slipped in the one for Jacob's apartment. He opened the door, carefully stepped under the tape, and turned on the lights.

Once through, he experienced an odd feeling, one that wasn't familiar: that of breaking the law. He knew what he was doing was wrong. He stood for a minute at the entrance of the apartment, considering what he was about to do.

"You're already inside," Kirby whispered to himself. "What's a few more feet going to hurt?"

He walked inside and stopped when he saw the futon. Its cover and pillow were gone. Why would the police take them? Did something happen on the futon?

In the single bedroom, the one Jacob called "the studio," it looked surprisingly barren. The police had taken both the iMac and his laptop.

Why would they do that?

"You shouldn't be in here," a female voice said.

Kirby jumped at the voice and turned around. Fonda Shay stood in the bedroom's doorway. She was in denim shorts, and another cut off T-shirt, this one faded green and read *Weed, California.*

"What are you doing here?" Kirby whispered.

Fonda leaned against the doorjamb and crossed her arms. The droopy eyes had been replaced by brightness. "I think I should ask the questions," she said too loud for Kirby's comfort.

"Lower your voice. I came to see if I could find something about what happened to Jacob."

"You mean Jake," she said without lowering her voice.

"Whatever," Kirby said, both in frustration with the shortening of Jacob's name and her lack of awareness about her volume.

"And what did you learn, Kirby Kirby Willis?"

Kirby shushed her before saying, "The cops took both of his computers and the cover from his futon."

Fonda looked over her shoulder at the futon. "Huh," she said. "Depressing. Let's go." She turned and walked through the apartment and out the door.

Kirby followed her, turning off the lights as he went, carefully stepping under the police tape, and then securing the door. Fonda watched him until he was done.

"C'mon, Kirby. Let's go smoke."

The curiosity Kirby felt bothered him. Fonda was attractive, but her open drug use was unsettling.

"I've got to go."

Fonda faced Kirby. "What do you mean? You just got here."

"I didn't come to visit you."

"Of course you did."

"No," Kirby said. "I didn't. I came to see Jacob's apartment."

"You knew there would be nothing for you to find. You wanted to see me again. Let's not pretend. Life's too short. C'mon, let's go."

He wanted to follow her because she was attractive and obviously flirting with him. However, he knew she would not further his goals. Everything he did in life revolved around one basic principle: will this make my life better? Kirby didn't see how getting involved with Fonda would improve his life.

"I'm leaving."

Fonda put her hands on her hips and pursed her lips in thought. Her flat stomach pulsed with her breathing. She looked like a grown-up version of a spoiled, pouty child. "If you don't come to my apartment right now, I'll call the cops and tell them you were in Jake's apartment."

"You wouldn't."

Fonda shrugged. "Maybe I would."

"Fine," Kirby said. "I want to talk with them, anyway. I want to know what's going on."

"You're not coming to my apartment?"

Kirby shook his head.

She turned and walked away. "What's a girl gotta do?" she said just before the door to her apartment swung shut.

Kirby ran down the stairs and out of the building.

\*\*\*

At the corner of the block, a man stood next to a white Ford F150. A Hayes Construction logo was on the door. Kirby saw him as he approached his car. The man was tall and stocky. He pushed off the truck and moved to intercept Kirby, who walked quicker to his Toyota.

He opened the door to get in, but the bigger man shoved the door closed.

"Hey!" Kirby said.

"Why were you in his apartment?"

"What are you talking about?"

The man pointed to Jacob's building. "I saw you through the window. You were in his apartment. Why were you in there? What were you looking for?"

"I wasn't looking for anything."

He leaned in, looming over Kirby. When he sneered, Kirby understood the implied threat.

"He was my friend," Kirby said. "I wanted to know what happened to him."

The tall man studied him for a moment before taking his hand off the door. "What did you see when you were in there?"

"What do you mean?"

"I mean, how did his apartment look? I assume you'd been there before."

"Oh, yeah, well. It looked okay."

"Was anything missing?"

"I'm not sure."

"How about I punch you in the teeth to help you remember?"

Kirby held up his hands in a defensive position. He blurted, "It looks like the police took both of his computers and the cover from his futon."

The big man thought about what he said for a moment and then asked, "Why would they take the futon cover?"

"I don't know. I'm not the police."

"What's your name, smartass?"

"Bob."

The tall man clicked his teeth together as he examined Kirby's eyes. "You don't look like no Bob."

"Well, I am," Kirby said, trying to sound indignant, but he was afraid he sounded like a jerk.

"How about that punch in the teeth, but this time I take your wallet? Will your driver's license say your name is Bob?"

Kirby looked down.

"I'm Kirby Willis," he said and then added his address for good measure.

The man smiled. "I like you, Kirby Willis. You're a fast learner."

He turned and walked toward his truck. Kirby opened the door, turned the key, and started his car. He silently roared away from the confrontation as fast as his Prius would go.

# THURSDAY

## Chapter 11

Detective Marci Burkett walked into the detectives' office to find Quinn hunched over his computer, intently reading. She quietly approached him and leaned over his shoulder.

She read aloud. "'How eating dinners out destroys your budget'?"

He jumped at hearing his partner's voice.

"What the hell is that?" Marci asked.

"The kid's website. I'm looking for clues," Quinn said, cringing at his choice of words.

"Clues? Okay, Sherlock," she said, dropping into her own chair. "I'll take budget savings, in the bank, with the knife."

"He was a good writer," Quinn said, turning back to the monitor.

"I think you're reaching."

"How was your night? Choke anyone out?"

"As a matter of fact—"

"If you two are done with your morning chit-chat, how about a little action on that homicide?" Lieutenant George Brand said as he walked into the bullpen. Both detectives turned in their chairs to face him. "Captain Ackerman was hot and bothered this morning on where all my cases stand, and I had no answers from you two."

"Maybe you should come around and ask some questions now and then, LT," Marci said.

Quinn smiled at her.

"That's what I'm doing *now*, Burkett. I need something for the captain. What have you got?"

"Nothing," Quinn said.

"What?"

"Nothing," Marci reiterated with a smirk. It was clear to Quinn that she was trying to upset the lieutenant this morning.

"We should get the autopsy report today," Quinn said quickly to take the focus off his partner. "The geeks imaged the computer yesterday and we're working with that now, but so far we've got zilch."

"Maybe I was wrong in my early assessment, as were you," the lieutenant said. "Maybe it was an accident. Does it look like we can reclassify it as such and clear it?"

Quinn glanced at Marci before saying, "No, sir. We can't. I believe in my gut it's a homicide. Are you getting pressure to clear cases?"

Brand nodded. "The administration is chewing everyone's backside now. The mayor is on an efficiency push and, for whatever reason, the council has bought into it. We're all on the hot seat. If there isn't serious movement in cases, they'll make some changes."

"So, if we don't clear our caseload, you could be transferred out?" Marci asked, a mischievous smile spreading on her face.

Brand turned his full attention to Marci, and a wicked grin, full of maliciousness, grew on his face. "That's right, Burkett, I will be transferred out due to ineffectiveness, but here are a couple of things to think about. First, who knows what kind of bully they'll bring in to replace me? At least with me, you know who you're dealing with, right? I give you two muddlers a lot of leeway to do whatever you want."

Marci looked to Quinn and, with her smile still intact, said, "Muddlers?"

"Second," Brand continued, "if they transfer me out for being ineffective, what do you think they'll do to you when I tell them you sandbagged me? I'm betting a transfer to Property Crimes."

Marci's smile slowly faded.

"Maybe they would drop you into a liaison position with city hall. Imagine spending your days investigating the crazy letters the city council gets. They all need to be vetted, you know? Have you ever talked with Corporal Anderson to see how he likes his position? It's been two years since he's been assigned there, and not even a union complaint could get him free. Would you like to take over for him?"

"Are you serious?" Marci asked, her face suddenly pale.

"I may not be a great investigator, Burkett, but I'm the best damn administrative lieutenant you've ever seen. I can write a report so damning it will follow you your entire career. Think about that, hotshot. Anderson once thought he could get the better of me. He'll never challenge me again."

"I wasn't implying anything, sir," Marci said, her eyes wide.

"Well, I was, Burkett. I most definitely was. Have a good day, Delaney."

"You too, sir," Quinn said as the lieutenant walked away.

When the lieutenant was out of earshot, Quinn turned to his partner and said, "Holy shit."

Marci continued watching Brand as he walked down the hall.

Quinn smiled a little. "I can't believe it was Lieutenant Brand who took down the legendary Marci Burkett. With a threat of *paper*, no less."

Marci shook her head in disbelief before turning to her computer, the color slowly returning to her face.

\*\*\*

His partner was quiet the entire morning, which allowed Quinn to focus on the autopsy report that had arrived. It had been emailed, with photos included, to both Marci and him.

The cause of death was asphyxiation from a broken neck. When Jacob Kidwell landed, his neck snapped and cut off the airflow to his lungs. There was no way to tell how long he survived, but Kidwell may have lain there for up to twenty minutes before fully suffocating.

The report noted contusions and abrasions around the head and upper torso. The broken finger was also called out.

It appeared the contusion on the forehead was in the same area where the head would have struck the wall, forcing the neck to snap. There was an abrasion on the right cheek where he might have rubbed the wall during his fall. There was a split on the lip. No conjecture where that came from.

However, the upper torso had several bruises on it. Two of them—the two on the left rib cage—were the size of a fist.

Jacob Kidwell had been in a fight sometime before his death.

\*\*\*

"Ready for lunch?" Marci said. "It's my day to buy."

"I'm good." Quinn didn't turn to face her when he answered. Marci continued to stare at him until he did. "What?"

"Are you kidding me?"

"About?"

"You're good?" Marci asked.

"I brought lunch today."

"You brought a lunch? We've been partners for three years, and you've never brought a lunch."

"I felt like bringing one today."

She peered at him suspiciously. "It's that kid's website, isn't it?"

"No. I thought I've been getting soft lately and should start eating healthy."

"Let me see your lunch."

"Why?"

Marci stood. "Let me see it."

Quinn shook his head. "You're being a bully."

"Tsk," she said and walked away.

Quinn smiled, secretly enjoying that he had frustrated his partner.

\*\*\*

The fingerprint results came back from Jacob Kidwell's apartment. Five viable prints were found.

Kidwell's were there and excluded.

A neighbor's prints had been found. A name check on Fonda Shay showed she had been previously convicted for possession of a controlled substance a couple of years earlier. She'd be worth a visit. Her fingerprints were found throughout the apartment. She had been interviewed by one of the patrol officers and denied hearing or seeing anything related to Kidwell's death.

Fingerprints belonging to Amy Tillerson, the owner of Home Town Realty, were also found in the kitchen. Real estate agents were required to be fingerprinted. She was his employer. Perhaps she had a reason to be there.

There were two other sets of fingerprints.

Both were found throughout the house and had no match in the system.

Quinn thought about the fingerprints for a minute. His mind wandered for a bit until it landed on two unanswered questions.

*Who is the guy driving the Toyota Prius, and how do I find him?*

\*\*\*

The car pulled alongside the curb outside the Public Safety Building. It was a newer Chevy Volt.

Quinn leaned down to see the driver. She smiled and waved.

He opened the back door and climbed in.

After watching a YouTube video on how it worked, Quinn downloaded the Uber app for his phone. He entered his credit card information and then ordered a car. He put in a location, and the Chevy Volt arrived within three minutes. His driver was Jenny. She was in her mid-twenties and had a Spokane Indians baseball hat pulled over her brown hair.

"Good afternoon," she said. "There are bottled waters in the doors if you'd like one. Sit back and enjoy the ride."

"It's Jenny, right?"

"That's right," she said, smiling.

The Chevy carefully maneuvered through traffic as she headed toward the freeway. Quinn had selected the

Valley Mall so he could talk with an Uber driver for several minutes.

"How long have you been driving?"

"About six months now."

"Is it good money?"

"In Spokane? Not enough to go full time, but it's a nice way to pick up extra cash. My cousin lives in San Diego. She quit her job to drive full time."

Quinn watched as Jenny entered the freeway, dodging semis to move to the far-left lane quickly.

"This is my first time using Uber."

"I'm your first," Jenny said with a playful giggle.

Quinn ignored her double entendre. "What's the best time to drive?"

"Hands down, the best time is from midnight until a little after two. That's the bar scene. A lot of drivers focus downtown then. You can make good tips driving drunks home."

"Do you do that? Work the bar scene?"

Jenny shook her head and looked at Quinn through the rearview mirror. "Not anymore. I tried a few times, but every drunk that got in asked me if I wanted to go home with him. I decided I like banker's hours better. The money might not be as good, but the people are better. Drunks suck."

Quinn chuckled. "I agree."

They drove in silence for a bit.

"Jenny?"

"Yeah?"

"Do you know other drivers? I mean, do you communicate with each other?"

"Not really," she said. "There've been some guys trying to get together to unionize. Kind of like the Seattle drivers have been, but this is Spokane. I mean, c'mon. I just want to drive and be left alone. If they make me join a union, I'll quit and do something else."

"Why did you start driving?"

"I wanted my own job. I didn't want to work for anyone else. That's the American way, right?"

Jenny exited the freeway and pulled into the parking lot of Spokane Valley Mall. The Uber app charged the correct amount immediately to Quinn's credit card. He pulled out a five-dollar bill and handed it to her.

"Thanks for the ride and the conversation."

"You bet. Have a great day," she said and sped away.

Quinn pulled out his phone and dialed Marci. She answered on the second ring.

"Where are you? I came back from lunch, and you were gone, but your car is still here."

"I need you to pick me up."

"Where?"

"The Valley Mall."

"How the hell did you get way out there?"

"I'll tell you about it when you pick me up."

*** 

"Who are we seeing?" Marci asked as she pulled her car to the curb.

"Fonda Shay."

"Didn't one of the officers interview her the day of his death?"

Quinn climbed out of the car and closed the door. "Yes, but we didn't know she had been inside Kidwell's apartment."

"Fingerprints confirmed it?"

"Yes," Quinn said, walking toward the apartment building. "She came up with a prior conviction for possession of a controlled substance."

"What was the substance?"

"Psilocybin mushrooms."

"Dude, just say 'shrooms. When you talk like that, you sound like the lieutenant."

"He really got under your skin, didn't he?"

Marci stopped talking then, her heels clicking on the sidewalk in the silence.

Inside the apartment building, they climbed the stairs to the second floor, the smell of marijuana in the air. At apartment #3, they knocked several times.

Music played softly inside, and footsteps padded toward the door. "Oh, damn," a voice said from the other side.

Quinn knocked again. "Fonda Shay, please open up. This is the Spokane Police Department. We need to talk with you."

The footsteps hurried around inside the apartment. The music stopped, a window opened, and the voice called, "Just a minute."

A moment later, the lock turned, and the door opened. Fonda Shay stood in denim shorts and a cut-off Bob Dylan T-shirt. Her mouse-brown hair was pulled into a bun, but several strands were astray. She wore rose-colored glasses.

Marci smirked. "Aren't you a little young for Bob Dylan?"

"Aren't you a little short for a cop?"

Marci's eyes slanted, and her smirk faded.

"Fonda Shay?" Quinn asked.

"Yes."

"Can we come in and talk?"

"I'd rather not," she said, looking back into her apartment.

"Good enough for me," Marci snapped. "Grab your stuff. You're going to the station for an interview."

Both Fonda and Quinn looked at her with surprise. Quinn turned back to Fonda. "Ms. Shay, we do need to talk. It's important. It's either going to occur here or at the station. It's your choice."

Fonda thought about it for a moment and then stepped back, opening the door wider. "C'mon in."

The smell of marijuana was thick inside Fonda's apartment. A large, red water bong was on the end table next to the couch.

"Damn," Marci said. "I'm going to get a contact high just being in this room."

"Maybe it will make you nicer," Fonda said as she climbed onto the couch and crossed her legs.

Marci made a face of irritation toward Quinn, who mimed a calming down motion with his hands.

"What's this about?" Fonda asked.

"It's about your neighbor, Jacob Kidwell."

"I already talked to the other cops. I didn't hear anything that day."

"How could you not?" Marci asked. "The top of the stairs is right outside your apartment."

"I hear people all the time. You get used to it."

"What if there was a fight," Marci said, "and it was loud? Would you sleep through that?"

Fonda tilted her head. "Am I in trouble because I didn't hear Jake fall?"

"We're trying to understand why," Quinn said. "We're just looking for something reasonable. In your statement, you only said that you didn't hear anything. Based on the proximity of your apartment, we don't see how that's possible."

"I was coming down from an experience—"

"Experience?" Quinn asked.

"With peyote. It was my first time, and it totally tripped me out. I don't know what time I went to bed, but it was early afternoon. When I woke up, there were cops in the building."

"How well did you know Jacob?" Quinn asked.

"He was a friend."

"What kind of friend?" Marci asked, her words challenging.

"Yeah," Fonda said, her glare showing she understood Marci's insinuation. "He was that kind of friend."

"When you hooked up, was it in your apartment or his?"

"Both."

"How many times have you been inside his apartment?" Quinn asked.

Fonda shrugged. "I couldn't even count. We've both lived here for over two years. We occasionally hooked up when neither was attached."

"In all that time, you two never got serious?" Marci asked, this time with no challenge or malice. There was actual concern in her question.

Fonda studied Marci for a moment, then shook her head. "I don't think he saw me as girlfriend potential. I was okay with that."

"Did Jacob have a girlfriend?" Quinn asked.

"Not anymore. He did for a while, but they broke up."

"Why did they break up?"

"He wouldn't tell me. Jake was sort of secretive about things when he would come calling."

"Do you know the girlfriend's name?"

"Not really. Jake had a piece of art hanging on his wall once, and it was initialed, H. Reese. When they broke up, she came in one night and spray-painted die across it."

"*Die?*" Marci asked.

"Yeah. As in death. I guess she wasn't happy about them breaking up, and she wasn't going to let him have a piece of her art to remember her by."

"Why not?"

Fonda shrugged. "You'll have to ask her."

*\*\**

Around 10 p.m., Quinn went downtown. He knew it was a needle in the haystack search, but he wanted to be out. Besides, he could bill the department for the time.

For a couple of hours, Quinn walked along the various streets that made up bar row, occasionally stopping to talk with Uber and Lyft drivers to see if they knew the driver of a blue Toyota Prius. Each conversation was a strikeout. However, Quinn continued to learn more about the ride-share industry.

He made the mistake of talking with a taxi driver to see if he might have seen his missing Uber driver. The driver leaned against the front end of his car, and his arms crossed over his chest. His gray hair peeked out from under a newsboy cap, and his wild eyes appeared slightly larger than usual behind his glasses.

"Are you kiddin' me?" the driver asked.

"Excuse me?"

"Those guys don't have to go through our licensin' process, and it's cuttin' into our profits. First, it was the millennials usin' them apps, but now even my generation is doin' it. You cops should be doin' your jobs and gettin' them off the streets. They're essentially stealin' from us, from the city, know what I mean?"

Quinn said, "I'm not sure that's our job."

The driver turned and pointed at his cab. "Then what the hell am I payin' all these fees and taxes for? It's a racket is what it is, and those Uber and Lyft drivers are gettin' around being licensed. It's complete bullshit. The cops ain't helpin', and the city's turnin' a blind eye to it. Or worse, they're encouragin' it. I can't tell which it is. I just know the game is slanted away from us, and it ain't fair. Just ain't fair."

Quinn listened to his tirade for a few minutes before turning and walking away without ending the conversation. The taxi driver continued to yell after Quinn.

At 1 a.m., Quinn called it a night and went home.

# FRIDAY

## Chapter 12

The previous night's driving was a complete bust.

Looking back, Kirby should have expected it. He had envisioned it would be a terrible night of sales, and it turned out exactly that way.

Kirby never fully believed in the concept of visualizing success until a former girlfriend turned him onto it. She was a big believer in the book, *The Secret*. He had shined her on by agreeing to read it, so he could keep going out with her.

She was a successful attorney and a partner in her law firm at thirty. She liked hanging out with Kirby and claimed she understood his different view of success. However, she had dreams of her own, and they were reinforced every day by the vision board she had in her bedroom. Every morning, she woke up and carefully walked through each of the things she would receive in her life. As they came true, she exchanged them with a new dream.

She must have had a different vision of a boyfriend because she soon replaced Kirby.

They had clearly been on different paths. She wanted power and prestige, and he wanted freedom. Their dreams weren't aligned.

His vision last night, though, was of failure, and it proved exactly so. Maybe he should have read that book, after all.

The downtown core had been slow, so he moved to the airport to see if he could snag a big fare coming home from a business trip. He did get a fare. Unfortunately, it was to Airway Heights, the city the airport butts up against. It was the smallest fare imaginable coming out of there.

After that, Kirby gave up on the airport and floated around in north Spokane before finally calling it a night and returning home shortly before 1 a.m.

He pushed those memories from his mind, though. Today was a new day, he reminded himself, and he had chores to attend to.

First, he had some lawn maintenance to jump on for the apartment building. It was his responsibility to keep the property looking good, and he took great pride in it.

Second, he needed to bang out a blog post for next Monday. He was cutting it thin, but he had an idea pop into his head last night. It wasn't a home run but one he could play with and expound upon.

Finally, he was going to do a little door knocking and see what he could learn about the project Jacob was working on in north Spokane.

***

"I'm not sure what I can tell you," she said, "but come inside. It's a little warm out there."

It was after 2 p.m. when Kirby finally finished his lawn maintenance and blog post.

This was the third person to answer the door. The first two who opened their doors refused to talk with him and asked him to leave. He had knocked on five doors before someone finally spoke with him.

She had introduced herself as Joyce Faber. Her small living room was intricately decorated with tchotchkes and knickknacks on every shelf and available space. They sat in two red wing-back chairs with doilies hanging over the top of each. A fan whirred softly in the corner.

"What are you asking for?" Joyce said.

Kirby thought about telling her about Jacob and his death, but he held back. Instead, he said, "I was looking to buy a house nearby and heard a rumor that this neighborhood is going to be sold. That struck me as odd, so I'm doing a little homework," Kirby said. "Is it true the entire block is to be sold?"

Joyce's eyes widened. "Oh, yes, it was very specific in my contract that they all had to sell, or none would sell."

"Your home is lovely, Mrs. Faber. Why are you selling?"

She smiled. "It's just a house without my husband. He passed several years ago. It's quite a bit for me to maintain. My time would be better spent doing more enjoyable things than tending to house chores, don't you think?"

Kirby nodded. "Do you know what they're planning to do?"

She leaned in, her eyes gleaming at the prospect of sharing her gossip. "They've been very secretive about it, that's for sure."

Kirby studied the woman before giving her a sly smile. "You know something, though, don't you?"

Joyce grinned. "They were trying to be coy, but I was tending my garden out front. I heard them talking. They were talking about visibility issues for the surrounding neighborhood."

"Visibility?"

"I think it's going to be a high-rise apartment. I think they're worried about the other neighbors complaining."

Kirby pursed his lips. "A high-rise apartment. In this neighborhood. Really?"

Joyce shrugged. "I don't know, but I've thought about it a lot for the past week. It would be right across from the mall. There's lots of shopping and food there. The movie theater is there, too. Have you ever been to the mall?"

Kirby smiled.

"Also, we're within walking distance to the hospital."

"Holy Family," Kirby said.

"Yes. If it is an apartment building, I would like to live here. It would be close to my friends and all the places I go to."

Kirby and Joyce chatted for another thirty minutes before it was time to go. He stood on the sidewalk outside her house and looked up in the air, imagining a high-rise apartment. "Okay, I see the vision," Kirby said out loud to himself. "Why keep it a secret?"

Kirby turned and walked toward his car. He stopped about a hundred feet away from it. Leaning against his car was the man he had seen outside Jacob's apartment. His Hayes Construction truck was parked behind his Prius.

Spotting Kirby, the man yelled, "Hey!"

Kirby took a step back, and the man moved toward him. Kirby turned and ran down the block. He looked over his shoulder and discovered he wasn't being pursued. He slowed to a walk and kept glancing over his shoulder. A thought suddenly occurred to him that the man had returned to his truck and would soon come barreling after him in a two-ton missile.

Kirby again ran, this time with an extra dose of fear. He saw a For Sale sign a block away and ran into the yard. With one hop and the hope the house was vacant, he scaled the wooden fence and was in the backyard. A large black dog immediately barked from the opposite side of the yard and scrambled toward Kirby. Its teeth slammed together with each bark. Kirby spun, grabbed the fence, and jerked himself back over the top. He landed with a thud on the ground. The dog continued to bark wildly through the wooden slats. Kirby lay there for a moment, catching his breath. Then the memory of the man resurfaced, and the fear of his truck returned. He got to his feet and ran again.

*\*\**

Five minutes passed before the dread settled, and common sense took hold. Kirby regained control of himself and realized the man wasn't following him. He turned and made the long walk back to his car.

It took him fifteen minutes to get back to the block where he had parked. Carefully, he peeked around the corner to make sure the truck was gone. Seeing it was safe, Kirby quickly walked to his car, opened the door, and climbed in. On his window, pinned under his windshield wiper, was a note.

He got out of the car, grabbed the paper, and opened it.

Written in pencil was *Kirby Willis— I know where you live.*

# Chapter 13

When Quinn's phone vibrated, he looked at it. He muttered under his breath before muting it.

"You haven't called her yet?"

Quinn shook his head and turned to look back out the window.

"Dude, you should call her. Take it from me. We don't like to be ignored."

He glanced at his partner. "Yeah, I know."

Marci pulled the car to the curb and parked. They were in a part of downtown that was quickly gentrifying. Twenty-five years ago, it was ground zero for the homeless, prostitutes, and gangs. Now it was home to loft apartments, boutique shops, trendy restaurants, and craft breweries. The West End had gone hipster.

In front of a brick building, Quinn pressed the call button.

"Whozzit?" came through a speaker next to the door.

"Spokane Police Department."

Pause.

"What's this about?" asked the voice through the tinny speaker.

"We'd like to talk with you about Jacob Kidwell."

Marci grabbed the door when the lock buzzed and held it open for her partner. "Age before beauty," she said.

Quinn led the way up the stairs to the second floor. The door was open, and a woman stood in the doorway. She wore jeans and a River City Brewing T-shirt. Her hair was pulled back, and she had a plastic glass full of iced tea in her hand.

"Holly Reese?" Quinn asked as he approached.

"Naturally."

"I'm Detective Delaney. This is my partner, Detective Burkett. Can we come in and talk?"

Holly opened the door wider before turning to walk inside. The apartment was a large loft with open space. Quinn stopped to admire a piece of art hanging on a wall. In the corner of the picture was the signature *H. Reese.* His eyes finished scanning the apartment. There was an unmade bed in one corner and a small kitchen in its opposite. A small seating area was in the middle of the apartment. There was no television present.

They had located Holly Reese by using a simple Google search combining the words *H. Reese, painter,* and *Spokane.* When her name popped up, they ran it through the Department of Licensing and found her home address. At the time, Quinn shook his head in mild wonder at the fact that his first investigative stop was Google, rather than the police department's own resources.

"Would you like to sit?" Holly asked as she sat in the corner of the loveseat.

Marci sat on the edge of a hanging bubble chair. Quinn sat on the small sofa near Holly.

"We'd like to ask you some questions about Jacob Kidwell."

Holly sipped her iced tea.

"Are you aware he's dead?"

"Yes," Holly said and rolled the glass between her hands.

Quinn glanced at Marci before looking back to Holly. "How did you find out?"

"A friend."

"What friend?"

"Does it matter?"

"Yes, it does," Marci said and promptly fell backward into the bubble chair. She struggled to upright herself, the chair swinging and turning as Marci fought to gain control. When she did, she rolled out of the bubble and landed as gracefully as she could in the situation. She stood next to Quinn at the edge of the couch. Her face was beet red.

The bubble chair continued to swing gently while the conversation continued.

"It matters who told you," Quinn said.

"I only know him as Kirby."

It was surely a lie, but Quinn didn't press it. "What did Kirby tell you?"

"He said Jacob was dead. Then I asked him to leave."

"Why would you do that?"

"Because Jacob and I broke up. After that, I cut him out of my life."

"Why did you break up?" Marci asked.

"Is that relevant?"

The way she asked that question reminded Quinn of the Vulcans from the various Star Trek episodes he'd watched. "Yes," Quinn assured her. "All of our questions are relevant."

Holly considered his answer, then seemed to relent. "Jacob got into this financial kick. No debt, save a lot, plan for the future. That sort of thing, you know? That's great, but it made him super judgmental. He didn't approve of the way I lived my life or how I spent my money."

"What was his issue?" Marci asked. "You weren't married, right?"

"That's correct."

"Then what was his problem?"

"I have a trust fund, Detective. My parents left me money that would take care of me. It's not a huge amount, but it's enough. Jacob didn't like the way I spent it. He thought I should be more…"

"Frugal?" Quinn suggested.

Holly nodded. "What's funny, though, is that he didn't have a problem asking me to pick up a dinner check if we went out to eat. Or pay for a plane ticket if we went away for a quick weekend. He used my money when it suited him but then complained about how I spent it. Sort of hypocritical, don't you think?"

"Is that why you broke up with him?" Quinn asked.

"He broke up with me. He said he didn't want to be with someone with as poor financial habits as I had. He claimed habits were contagious. His arguments were weak. I figured he found someone else and was giving me a convenient reason to exit."

"Is that when you broke into his apartment and wrote *die* across a painting?"

Holly sipped her tea. "You've done your homework."

"We're detectives," Quinn said.

"I painted that picture for him. I obviously didn't want it back, and I didn't want to leave a piece of myself with him. He had already taken too much of me to begin with."

Quinn reflected on that statement while Marci asked, "Die is a harsh sentiment, especially for an ex-boyfriend."

"I might have had a few glasses of wine before I did that. Once it was done, he was out of my system, and there was no longer a need to communicate with him."

*Definitely a Vulcan*, Quinn thought. "Where were you on Monday night until Tuesday morning?"

"In bed," Holly said. "Right over there."

"Can anyone confirm that?" Marci asked.

"When I'm not in a committed relationship, I don't regularly hop into bed with a man just to confirm my sleeping habits. What kind of woman do you think I am?"

"It's a modern world," Marci said.

"I'm not that modern."

"Do you know anyone who would want to hurt Jacob?"

"I haven't talked or seen him since I broke up with him. Jacob could be irritating, though. I would imagine that angered a few people."

"What's Kirby's last name?" Quinn asked.

Holly sipped her iced tea. "As I said, all I know is his first name. I never knew him by more than that. I don't know where he lives or what he does for a living. He was a friend of Jacob's who stopped by with him one time to see my art. That's how he knew where I lived."

"If we find out you're lying—"

"You won't," Holly said.

Quinn and Marci looked at each other before standing. Quinn handed Holly a business card. "If you think of anything else, please call."

\*\*\*

Outside, Quinn leaned against Marci's car and looked up at the window to Holly's loft. "What did you think?"

"She's cold," Marci said.

"I liked her."

"Of course you did."

"What's that mean?"

"She's young, blond, and emotionally detached. She's your ex-wife, twenty years ago."

Quinn shrugged away her comment. "Do you think she could have done it?"

"No."

"Why not?"

"She cut him out of her life. Like a wart. She was done with him," Marci said. "The girl is fully realized. I'll give her that."

"Do you think she'll call that Kirby guy?"

"Without a doubt."

"I have a suspicion that's the guy I'm trying to find. If it is, he keeps showing up where he's not wanted. I'm going to find him and ask him why."

# Chapter 14

Friday nights were the best nights for driving, and Kirby was killing it. He'd already made several runs from downtown to the South Hill. They were quick trips with good tips, which helped improve his mood.

On his mind was a text he'd gotten from Holly. POLICE CAME BY. STOP BY WHEN YOU CAN.

When he dropped by her loft, she wasn't there. He figured he would visit in the morning to see what they said. He would prefer to see Holly in person, anyway.

The Uber app dinged an alert for a pick-up at Fast Eddie's bar. It was great luck, as he was already stopped right outside the bar. It happened occasionally and was one of the reasons why Kirby would sometimes park outside of the more popular bars on busy nights. The passenger was identified as Quinn. He accepted the call, and the rear door opened immediately.

A tall man climbed in. He wore a windbreaker and jeans. It was a bit warm for a windbreaker, but to each his own.

The destination address popped up on his GPS as 1100 W. Mallon Avenue. It was only a few minutes to drive.

"How's it going?" Kirby asked.

"Fine," Quinn said, his head bowed as he texted into his phone.

Kirby pulled into traffic. "Did you have a good night?"

The man looked up. "Huh?"

Kirby smiled at him in the rearview mirror. "Were the bars good tonight?"

Quinn thought about his question for a moment. "I wasn't at a bar tonight."

"Oh," Kirby said as they crossed the river and headed north.

"How's your night?" Quinn asked.

"Great," Kirby nodded enthusiastically. "Thanks for asking. Productive so far. Hope it keeps up."

"How long have you been driving for Uber?" Quinn asked.

"About seven months."

"Do you like it?"

"Yeah," Kirby said. "Works into my plan like a champ."

"Your plan?"

Kirby turned west when his GPS indicated to do so, and he headed toward the pre-selected address.

"It's my goal never to have a real job and to be financially independent by the time I'm thirty-five."

Quinn tilted his head. "How old are you now?"

"Twenty-seven," Kirby said with a smile, watching the man in the rearview mirror.

His passenger leaned back, his face confused. Kirby remained quiet. Often, when he told people his plans, it resulted in one of two responses. Either the listener was eager to ask questions, or they shut down, not wanting to hear any more because it clashed with their own life's decisions. Kirby thought the latter was occurring and dealt with it as such.

They drove in silence for several minutes until their destination neared.

Kirby looked in the rearview mirror. "Are we headed to the police department?"

"Yeah," Quinn said, not offering anymore. He seemed irritated now, different from when he first got in the car.

Kirby continued to drive. He'd driven people to jail, to the hospital, and to a funeral. Those all seemed slightly weirder than this, so he let it go.

When the Uber app showed he'd arrived, he pulled to the corner.

"I hope you have a good night," Kirby said with a smile.

"Do me a favor and shut your car off," Quinn said.

"Why?" Kirby asked. His heart raced, fearing that he was about to be robbed.

Quinn put his hand on the back of the passenger seat. In his palm was a badge. "Kirby Willis, correct?"

"Yes?"

"I'm Detective Quinn Delaney. I'd like to talk with you about Jacob Kidwell."

# Chapter 15

"That's fantastic," Kirby said. "I'd love to talk with you."

It wasn't the reaction Quinn had expected. He had texted a dispatcher the license plate number and learned Kirby's last name while he was driving. She texted him back that his record was clean. Not even a traffic infraction.

"It's okay to park here?" Kirby asked. "It says *Police Vehicles Only*."

"Just get out," Quinn said, annoyance creeping into his voice. "I'll take care of it."

Outside the car, Quinn put a business card under the windshield wiper.

"That's so cool," Kirby said admiringly. "Can I get a couple of those cards?"

Quinn rolled his eyes. "Let's go."

As they walked to the front of the Public Safety Building, Quinn wondered why he was irritated. Was it the kid's exuberance, or was it that he announced with such nonchalance he planned to be financially independent at thirty-five years old?

Quinn held his ID card to the front door, and it unlocked. They entered the building, which was eerily quiet. On a typical workday, it would be bustling with municipal court activity. Quinn and Kirby continued walking through the lobby until they reached the entrance to the police department. Another press of the ID card and Quinn was now in the hallways of the department.

Kirby's eyes were wide with excitement as he scanned the walls. There were awards on the walls, along with various photos of the department throughout the years. It was a view not many people would ever get to see.

"In here," Quinn said, opening the door to a small interview room.

Kirby stepped inside.

"I'll be right back," Quinn said and closed the door.

When Kirby heard a click, his smile faded. He grabbed the door handle, but it wouldn't turn. He was locked in the room.

Several minutes passed before the door opened and Quinn reappeared. Kirby was seated at the small table, his phone in his hand.

"What are you doing?" Quinn asked.

"Looking up an attorney's number," Kirby said.

"You're not under arrest."

"Really? That door was locked."

Quinn looked back at the door and realized what had happened. "I apologize. I didn't mean to leave it locked."

"You must think I'm stupid."

"I don't think that," Quinn said, his face warming.

"Most people your age do. Just because I'm in my twenties, I don't know my ass from a hole in the ground, right?"

Quinn held up his hands. "Hold on. We're getting off on the wrong foot."

"It seems that way. Listen, I'm happy to talk with you. I've wanted to, in fact, but if I get treated this way once more, I'll walk out of here, and I'll call your supervisor—"

That did it for Quinn. He was tired of the easy play. He slapped the table with an open palm. Kirby jumped.

"Do not speak to me that way," Quinn growled.

Kirby stared at him.

"I already apologized for the door. Don't talk down to me again."

Kirby opened his mouth, but Quinn cut him off.

"Do not say you're sorry. I don't want to hear it. We are going to start over from the beginning. Is that clear?"

Kirby nodded.

"Fine."

Quinn took a big breath through his nose and blew it out through slightly parted lips.

"Kirby Willis, I'm Detective Quinn Delaney. I already said that, didn't I?"

"Yeah."

"You are not under arrest. Is that clear? I sincerely apologize for leaving that door locked. It automatically does it, and I'm not in the habit of unlocking it. You are not being recorded. If you were, that light on the wall would be red. Do you understand?"

"Yeah."

"We're just talking."

"Okay."

"Before we begin, I need to get some basic information."

Quinn asked for his birthdate, address, and phone number, all of which Kirby readily provided.

"Besides Uber, do you work anywhere else?"

"I'm self-employed."

It was the most common answer of the unemployed. He'd heard it for years from almost every criminal he'd arrested. From Kirby, though, he wasn't sure how to take it.

"How do you know Jacob Kidwell?" Quinn asked, setting his pen down and crossing his arms over his chest.

"He was my friend."

"How did you find out about his death?"

"I went to see him at his apartment. There was police tape across the door. I knew something bad had happened. A woman across the hall—"

"Fonda Shay?"

"Yes. She told me he had fallen down the steps. She said she overheard the police say he might have been pushed. In other words, murdered."

"Where were you the night he died?"

"I was driving like when I met you. I drove until two when the bars shut down. I went home, did some computer work, then went to bed."

Quinn leaned forward and made some notes. When he finished, he said, "I saw you outside Home Town Realty. Why did you go there?"

"I wanted to find out what happened to Jacob, and I figured I would start asking questions."

"Why?"

"Because he worked there."

"No, why did you involve yourself?"

"He was my friend."

"You also talked with Holly Reese."

Kirby stayed silent.

Quinn smiled. "It's funny. Ms. Reese wouldn't tell us who told her that Jacob was dead, and you won't say you talked with her. Are you both involved with Jacob's death somehow?"

"No."

"Then what's the big secret about Ms. Reese?"

"There's no secret. I didn't want her to get in trouble with you."

"Why would she be in trouble?"

"She wouldn't be, but I'm sitting in the police station on a Friday night. This doesn't exactly feel like a party."

Quinn smiled. He was beginning to like the guy. "Fair enough. And I apologize for the ruse and bringing you down here so late. However, this was the only way I could find you. It took a lot of work to track you down."

"I give you credit, Detective. That was the most creative introduction I could have imagined. I never figured I'd have picked up an officer tonight."

"Have you learned anything regarding your friend's death?"

Kirby stared at him.

"I'm not trying to jam you up. If you've found out something, then I want to know. I promise. We want to figure out what happened to your friend."

"Okay," Kirby said, nodding. "Well, Jacob was involved in a big real estate deal. I don't know what it means because he never told me about it."

"Would he normally tell you about his deals?"

"Yes, and that's what makes this one so weird. He's got the entire block at Lidgerwood and Queen under contract."

"I don't understand. What's that mean?"

"It means that he got twenty-four homeowners to agree to sell their houses, all at the same time."

"And that's a big deal?"

"I think so," Kirby said. "I mean, yeah. Yeah! A huge deal."

"How did you find that out?"

"I asked."

Quinn smirked. "Who did you ask?"

"I visited a realtor who told me Jacob might have done something underhanded to get a seller to cancel a listing with her. Then he wrote up the offer directly. She gave me the scoop on the rest."

Quinn flipped through his notebook. "Was this realtor named Paula Fairbanks?"

"Yeah."

"We talked with her," Quinn said. "At least, we tried. She refused. Why did she talk with you?"

"We're friends."

"Friends? How did you know she might be involved?"

"She wrote a note on his blog's Facebook page that wasn't very flattering. I stopped in to ask her why. She told me about the listing and a rumor that the block had been sold. So, I visited some of the homes and started door knocking. I learned info that way."

"What else did you find out?"

"One of the sellers thinks they're going to knock all the homes down and build a high-rise apartment building."

Quinn looked up at the ceiling as he thought. "An apartment tower? You said Lidgerwood and Queen, right? That's next to North Town Mall?"

"That's right."

Quinn lowered his eyes back to Kirby. "Who would want to live there in a high-rise?"

"That's funny. I asked the same question. The more I've thought about it, I realized, who wouldn't? The amenities are what will get people there. Plus, there will be an awesome view of the city. It will have all the services nearby with the mall, plus you've got retail road less than a block away. Besides, a developer won't build to hold. Once they're finished, they'll get the building to an acceptable occupancy level and sell the property. Who cares if the mall stays around long term? It's not their problem."

Quinn tapped his lip with his pen, thinking.

"You should talk with Hayes Construction about this," Kirby said.

Quinn paused his tapping. "Why?"

"Because I've been threatened twice now by a guy in a Hayes Construction truck. Once when he saw me talking to the neighbors and the other time when he saw me in Jacob's apartment."

Quinn's eyes narrowed. "When were you in Jacob's apartment?"

Kirby stayed silent.

"Did you go in after the apartment was secured?"

"If I say I did, do I incriminate myself?"

"Well, you do realize that's a crime, right?"

Kirby closed his eyes and nodded.

"What were you looking for?"

"I don't know," Kirby said with a shrug. "I wanted to see what happened to his apartment. Everything looked the same except his computers were gone, and his futon bedding was missing. Then Fonda came in."

"Fonda Shay was also in his apartment?"

"Yes."

Quinn shook his head. "How did you get in?"

"I have a key."

"Do not go in there again," Quinn said, his voice stern.

Kirby nodded.

"How often were you in Jacob's apartment?"

"A lot."

"There are two sets of fingerprints we haven't been able to match yet. Would you mind getting printed?"

Kirby shrugged. "I've got nothing to hide."

# SATURDAY/SUNDAY

## Chapter 16

After he finished drinking the glass of water, he put it in the sink. He walked outside, locked his apartment door, and turned around. He didn't expect the punch that knocked him to the ground. Two large arborvitae trees on either side of the apartment's entrance hid them from onlookers.

"I told you I knew where you lived." The man from Hayes Construction stood over him.

Kirby lifted his hands to protect his face.

"What were you doing at those houses?"

"Nothing," Kirby said.

The man kicked him, his work boot digging into Kirby's side. He let out a breath of air and doubled up. He coughed as he struggled to regain his breath.

"That mustuf hurt, didn't it?" the man asked. "I'll do it again if you don't tell me what I want to know."

Kirby lifted his hand. "Okay," he said between coughs. "Gimme a second."

His mind raced as he tried to figure a way out. There was only one option for Kirby, and that was to run.

He suddenly pushed up from the ground and moved past the big man. He saw freedom out in front and knew he could outrun the construction worker and his heavy work boots. Kirby had run cross country in high school

109

and still ran occasionally to stay healthy. That vision of escaping vanished when his feet became entangled with each other, and he tumbled to the ground.

The man had kicked out at him and hit his ankle. A wave of pain shot up Kirby's leg, which was replaced by the weight of the man landing on him.

Two quick punches to Kirby's face sent his world spiraling.

The man put one hand around Kirby's throat and lifted the other fist in the air. "What were you doing there?"

"I was trying to find out what Jacob was working on."

"Stay out of it. You'll get yourself hurt."

"I need to find who killed him."

The man studied Kirby before punching him and rendering him unconscious.

*\*\**

When Kirby awoke, he was still in the side yard of the apartment building. He sat upright and looked around. He didn't know how long he'd been out, and no one had checked on him. He shook his head. If someone walked by, they might have thought he was drunk. So much for friendly neighbors.

He got to his feet and limped back to his apartment.

A text message was on his phone. Holly Reese had asked how things went with the police.

CAN WE MEET FOR COFFEE? he texted. COPS HAVE TALKED WITH ME NOW.

She accepted his offer, and they planned to meet in thirty minutes at Rocket Bakery.

Suddenly, the punches didn't matter so much.

In the bathroom, he cleaned the blood from under his nose. Bruises had started to form on his cheeks and forehead. Fortunately, he didn't get hit in the eye or directly in the nose. It could have been much worse. He took a quick shower and headed downtown.

***

"What happened to you?"

"It doesn't look that bad. Sort of manly, don't you think?"

"It looks like you fell into a meat grinder. You should contact the media."

"Why?"

"The cops assaulted you. They can't get away with this."

Kirby pointed at his face. "The cops didn't do this."

"Who did it then?"

"Some guy. I don't know who he is. He started following me when he saw me at Jacob's apartment."

"Oh, my God. Are you okay?"

"Yeah, it doesn't hurt."

Holly studied his face. "I don't believe you."

Kirby shrugged. "Okay, it hurts a lot. I'm trying to sound tough."

"It isn't working," she said with a smile. "The cops came by to interview me."

"That's what you said in your text."

"They asked about you, but I didn't tell them anything but your first name."

"I appreciate that, but it turns out I made enough noise by myself. I'm happy they found me, though."

"You are?"

"Yeah. I didn't know what was going on. Now I do. Sort of."

"I think I might be a suspect," Holly said, worry filling her eyes, "because of what happened when we broke up."

Kirby's brow furrowed.

"The painting."

"They found out about that?"

Holly nodded.

"They must not think much of it," Kirby said, "or they would have taken you in."

They sipped their coffees in quiet. Holly stared out the window, and Kirby felt a swelling in his chest. He knew what it was.

"Holly," he said, immediately regretting it.

She turned to him, lost in thought. "Hmm?"

"Nothing."

"What?"

He shook his head and smiled.

She looked dreamily at him for a moment before he blurted, "Would you like to have dinner with me?"

Holly's eyes focused. "What?"

Kirby immediately sensed danger. "Dinner?" he said, his words soft.

"Oh, Kirby. I don't think so. You're my friend. I'd like to keep it that way."

He nodded.

"Please don't be upset," she said and then broke into a long explanation of why she thought Kirby was special. He was so smart. A really sweet guy. Such a wonderful friend. It was excruciating for Kirby to listen to.

He grabbed his phone. "I'm sorry," he said. "I forgot I have an appointment. I've got to go. See you later." Kirby stood and hurried out of the coffee shop.

# Chapter 17

Sunday morning, Kirby repaired a toilet.

It wasn't a complicated fix, just a flush valve replacement. Ellie, the renter in apartment #5, had complained to him that the toilet continued to run. Kirby investigated and discovered the problem. A quick run to Home Depot, a twenty-dollar purchase, and the problem was solved.

When Kirby walked out of the bathroom, Ellie was in the kitchen baking cookies. Ellie was in her late twenties, roughly the same age as Kirby. Her baby was asleep in its bassinette.

"All fixed," Kirby said. "No more running water."

"You're the best, Kirb. Want to stay for some cookies? Chocolate chip."

Although he enjoyed the smell and knew the cookies would taste great, he needed to go for many reasons. First, he had a lot of work to do. Second, he didn't want to be hanging out in Ellie's apartment when her boyfriend showed up. While neither he nor Ellie had any intentions of doing anything inappropriate, her boyfriend was a rather large fireman with a jealous nature.

"I appreciate it, but I've got a lot of things to get done today. I'd love to have one when they're done, though."

"I'll bring a couple down."

Kirby put his tools away in the shed behind the apartment building and was locking it up when he heard, "You do the maintenance around here?"

Kirby whirled around into a fighting stance, his hands at the ready.

Detective Quinn Delaney took a step back, a smile on his face. "Whoa, didn't mean to startle you."

Kirby lowered his hands, feeling slightly foolish.

"What happened to your face?" Quinn asked.

"I had another run-in with that contractor I told you about."

Quinn leaned in and looked at Kirby's face. "When and where?"

"Yesterday morning. He jumped me outside my apartment."

"How did he know where you lived?"

Kirby lowered his eyes.

"You told him?"

"I overshared when he threatened me the last time."

"Look up," Quinn said.

Kirby did as directed, and Quinn took photos with his phone's camera. "These aren't official. I should have a corporal come out and take photos if you want to file a complaint."

Kirby turned around and finished locking the shed. Then he said, "Why are you here, Detective?"

"I was thinking about something you said at the department."

Kirby walked toward his apartment. "I need to wash my hands. Can we finish this inside?"

"Sure." Quinn fell in stride beside him. "You said you thought the police took Jacob's computers. Isn't that what you said?"

Kirby unlocked his basement apartment and stepped in. "Yeah, that's right."

"What did you mean, *computers*?"

Kirby turned on the kitchen sink and, while washing his hands, said, "I don't understand the question. You took both, right?"

Quinn smiled then. "No, we didn't."

Kirby looked to Quinn, drying his hands. "I see. Which one did you get?"

"An iMac. It was in the bedroom."

"The studio," Kirby said. "We referred to that room as the studio. The computer on the standing desk was for his website and video production only."

"Okay. What was the other computer?"

"It was a Toshiba laptop. I don't remember the model, but it's what Frugal—I mean, Jacob—used for his job. His real estate work."

Quinn looked around. "Speaking of job. Why didn't you tell me you were the maintenance man for this apartment building when I asked where you were employed?"

"I'm not the maintenance man."

"I saw you walk out of the front of the building with some tools. What were you doing?"

"I had fixed a toilet and was putting my tools away."

"That sounds like the maintenance man."

"Think bigger."

"Okay, so you're the apartment manager. Again, why not just tell me?"

"Detective, I own this building. I'm self-employed. I don't work for anyone but me."

Quinn stared at Kirby as it sunk in. "How many units are in this building?"

"Eight."

Quinn looked up at the ceiling for a moment, then back to Kirby. "How much is it worth?"

"When I originally bought it?"

"Yes."

"Five hundred ten thousand."

"How could...?"

"How could I buy an investment property at my age? Why wouldn't I? What was stopping me?"

"The down payment."

"Why would that stop me?"

Quinn was clearly trying to figure out how Kirby could afford to buy an apartment building. Finally, he shook his head and said, "But you're an Uber driver."

"And?"

"How can you save any money, essentially driving a cab?"

"You're thinking about a single stream of income, Detective. How many income streams do you have?"

Quinn didn't answer.

"You have one, right? It's okay. Most people do. I had seven last year."

"Seven?"

Kirby held up his hand, lifting fingers as he counted. "My apartment building, my website, Uber, freelance writing, I got paid to be an extra in a movie, I helped flip a couple of houses, and I did some outside handyman work to fill in the holes in my schedule."

"That's a lot of side jobs."

"They're called side hustles, and it's how you create more income for yourself, so you don't rely on one job."

"How much did you make last year?" Quinn asked, then cringed. "I'm sorry. I shouldn't ask that."

Kirby smiled. "Why? I love talking about money. Last year I made over seventy-three thousand. After taxes, I saved roughly fifty-two percent of my income."

"Shit."

"What?"

"That's almost as much as I made."

Kirby noticed Quinn did not say how much he had saved. Kirby nodded. "Jacob side hustled, too."

Quinn refocused. "His website, right?"

"No. His website used to be his side hustle, but it became his main gig. He went to part time in real estate. Real estate was his side hustle."

"Wait, he made his living on his website?"

"Jacob was clearing more than seven grand a month with his website."

"Are you kidding? How can someone make over eighty thousand dollars a year with a website?"

Kirby smiled. "You've got to open your mind, Detective. It's just a numbers game. There's a blogger over at *Making Sense of Cents* who's making almost a hundred grand a month. I don't know if she's even at the top. Some guys, like *Mr. Money Mustache*, don't even report their income."

Quinn stared at him. "You're jerking me around."

"I wouldn't do that. I take this stuff seriously."

"I'm... I'm blown away."

"I get it. It shocked me at first, too. Then you get used to it. It's like being around real estate investors. There are guys making hundreds of millions every year, and then there are some making a few thousand. Like I said, it's just a numbers game."

"Jacob was making money with his blog, though?"

"Yeah. He didn't report it on his site like a lot of others do, but he'd grown his site that big. His site was becoming one of the biggest brands out there in the personal finance community. A lot of it had to do with his Frugal McDougal persona."

"I've watched some of his videos and read some of his writing. It's pretty good."

"You read blogs? Have you read mine, *New Fashioned Hustle?*" Kirby felt the excitement spread into a smile. He rarely got to meet people face-to-face who'd actually read his work.

Quinn shook his head. "Sorry, I haven't. I only checked out Jacob's to see what was on his computer."

Kirby shrugged, trying to hide his disappointment. "That's cool. I understand."

"So, Jacob's main gig was his blog, and his side hustle was real estate, correct? Did he have any other side hustles?"

"He used to drive Uber, and he used to scour thrift shops for stuff to sell on eBay. That game has really dried up, though. I know he did some website consulting for some bloggers and vanity sites—the sites people do mainly for their own passion projects. I don't know what else he might have done. I always thought he was fairly open with me, but finding out about this big real estate deal has me questioning things."

Quinn studied Kirby for a moment before saying, "Tomorrow morning, I'm going to go out to Hayes Construction and see if I can find the guy who assaulted you. I'd like you to come with my partner and me."

"I don't want to confront that guy."

"You'll sit in our car. No one will see you."

Kirby thought about it for a moment. "Okay," he said finally.

Quinn moved to the door and turned to face Kirby. "Seventy-three thousand? Really?"

Kirby nodded. "I'll show you my tax returns if you don't believe me."

He shook his head. "Unbelievable."

# MONDAY

## Chapter 18

"Who is this guy we're picking up?" Marci asked, activating the turn signal a moment before she turned the steering wheel and accelerated, barely avoiding a collision with a speeding truck.

"His name is Kirby Willis," Quinn said, looking back over his shoulder at the truck, which had slowed considerably after the driver undoubtedly noticed the vehicle that cut him off was an unmarked detective car.

"Kirby. Sounds like a vacuum cleaner."

Quinn shrugged.

"Wait. Is this the guy who warned the painter you thought was pretty?"

"I didn't think she was pretty."

Marci let out a single laugh. "Oh my God, you did. Why won't you admit it? Are we taking him in for questioning?"

"No."

Marci glanced at her partner. "Why not?"

"I already questioned him."

"When did this happen?"

"Over the weekend."

"What the hell?"

Quinn laid it out for Marci as she drove, from the meeting on Friday night to the second contact on Sunday.

"It sounds like you like this guy," Marci said.

"What do you mean?"

"You've got a man-crush."

"I do not."

"Seriously, you're blushing now. It's a full-fledged bromance."

"Knock it off," Quinn said, suddenly getting frustrated with his partner. "We're picking him up for an identification. He was assaulted over the weekend."

"Really?" Marci said in mock concern before her tone turned hard again. "And how's that our job? That's a task for patrol."

"It's our job because it's connected with our case. I could have done this alone, you know?"

"It's Monday. I haven't seen you all weekend, and I want to catch up, but I think you want to hang out with this Kirby guy more than me."

"Seriously, Marci. You're pushing this too far."

"All right, all right. I'm sorry."

Marci pulled to the curb in front of Kirby's building. He came out of his apartment and locked his door. Then he walked toward the detective car, lifting his face to the morning sun.

"California cool," Marci said, softly.

"What?"

"Look at him. Faded untucked T-shirt, jeans, flip-flops. California cool. Doesn't look like he has a care in the world."

"Now, who has a crush?"

Marci glanced at Quinn, her eyes telling him not to push it any further.

Kirby opened the back door and slid in.

"Good morning, Kirby. This is my partner, Detective Marci Burkett."

"Nice to meet you, Detective."

"What happened to your face?"

"I got in a fight. Didn't do very well."

Marci studied Kirby for a moment before turning forward. "You look all right," she said and dropped the ignition into gear. The car lurched from the sidewalk.

\*\*\*

"How long have you two been partners?"

"Three years," Marci said.

Both watched as Quinn walked into the office of Hayes Construction. Marci and Kirby had remained in the car, parked a couple of rows away from the building.

"Do you like it?"

"Being his partner? Sure. He's a good guy."

"No, I mean, being a police officer. It seems like you could learn a lot in your job."

Marci turned fully in her seat to look back at Kirby, who watched her intently. "Are you messing with me?"

"What do you mean?"

"People don't usually want to talk about how much I've learned on the job. Either they want to know if I've shot someone or they want to tell me how much the police have screwed them over. However, you come at me with 'there might be a lot to learn.' That's new."

Kirby smiled. "I read a book—"

"How much do you read?"

"Every day. At least a book a week, sometimes two. I don't have a television."

"Neither do I," Marci said, studying Kirby's face again. "Go on."

"Anyway, I read a book once that said never to take a job for a paycheck. Only take it for what you can learn. For whatever reason, that concept resonated with me."

"Work for education?"

Kirby nodded. "The paycheck, therefore, is secondary."

Marci smirked. "That makes no sense."

"It makes all the sense in the world."

Marci furrowed her brow.

"I don't mean to pry, Detective. Is there something you'd rather be doing than this?"

"Not really. I like what I do. I think I have the best job in the world."

"Then, you're lucky. Stay with it."

"What about you? Do you like what you do?"

"More than anything," Kirby said. "However, most people don't. Actually, I think most hate their jobs. They're only in it for the paycheck. That's the wrong motivation. If you're in it for what you can learn, once you've reached the point of diminishing returns, you can move on to something new. Unfortunately, most people stay stuck in the rat race, chasing an imaginary piece of cheese they never catch, not knowing how to improve their situation."

Marci shook her head. "Where did you come from?"

"From here."

"Can I ask about the bruises? You said you lost a fight."

"Yeah."

"Does it bother you?"

"That I lost? Sort of, I guess. I'm more bothered by the fact that I was in a fight in the first place. Normally, I can talk myself out of any situation."

"I think most guys would lie about losing the fight."

"Why would I lie? He was bigger and a better fighter. Truth be told, I haven't been in a fight since second grade. I think I lost that fight, too."

Marci laughed.

He was about to open his mouth to continue talking, but there was a heavy tap on his window. He turned to look and came face-to-face with a very large man.

Kirby jumped across the backseat of the car.

"What's wrong?"

"That's him. That's the guy."

Marci saw the man staring at Kirby and was out of the car in a second. "Excuse me, sir. I'd like a word with you," she said from the opposite side of the vehicle.

The big man looked at Marci with confusion. "Why? I didn't do nothin'."

Marci moved quickly around the car, her high heels clicking on the ground, her long black pants whipping with the movement.

"Spokane Police. Move away from the car."

The big man looked Marci up and down, a grin spreading across his face. "You look like Hollywood Police."

"What's your name?" Marci asked.

"I don't need to speak to you."

The big man turned and headed toward the office building.

"Hey, dumb ass, I'm not done with you."

The big man whirled around. His face burned red. "Whadja call me?"

"Sir," Marci said, immediately shifting gears back into professionalism, "I'd like to speak with you about an alleged assault yesterday afternoon."

"You called me dumb ass," he said, balling his fists.

Marci lifted her hands in a submissive *I don't want to fight* posture. "Perhaps you misheard me. Fighting with a police officer will end badly for you."

"No bitch cop is gonna call me names."

Quinn burst out of the office and ran toward the confrontation, but it was too late. The big man moved. He threw a punch at Marci, but she slipped it easily. She punched him in the ribs and resumed a fighter's stand behind him. The big man doubled, caught off guard by the punch.

He chuckled. "You're a fighter. I like women who fight."

Marci ignored the bait, knowing what it was intended to do.

The big man feinted with his right and threw a looping left hand. Marci rode the first punch back and ducked the second. With all her force, she rotated her hips and punched the big man in the groin. He dropped to his knees and cupped himself with his hands.

Marci stood her ground, her hands at the ready for the big man to move again. "Lay on the ground and spread your hands out wide," she said.

The big man continued to moan as he cupped himself.

Quinn arrived and grabbed Marci by the shoulder, pulling her back. "Douglas Rafferty, you're under arrest for assaulting an officer," Quinn said.

\*\*\*

A short while later, a patrol car arrived and took Douglas Rafferty to the police station. Quinn rode along with the officer. Marci drove Kirby back to his apartment.

The initial few minutes were quiet. Kirby finally said, "That was impressive."

Marci remained silent, paying attention to the road.

"Did they teach you how to do that in the police academy?"

She shook her head.

Kirby left her alone in her thoughts for a few minutes before asking, "Do you not like to talk about it?"

Marci's eyes flicked to the rearview mirror to look at Kirby before focusing back on the road. "I've studied the martial arts since I was a kid. I started in Kenpo, still train occasionally with my original instructor. I've also trained in Krav Maga for some time. I'm working now in Brazilian Jiu-Jitsu."

"It shows. You're really good."

They rode in silence, before Marci asked, "So you've never trained?"

"In martial arts? No. It was never my thing, but you're excellent at it."

"A lot of guys are intimidated by it."

"Of the martial arts?"

"Of my skill in them."

"Why?"

"Because I'm a better fighter than most."

"That's funny."

Marci clenched her jaw, and her eyes flashed to the mirror. "What do you mean, that's funny?"

Kirby was looking out the window, so he missed her reaction. "People get upset over the craziest things. It's like kids who get upset when others say, 'my dad can beat up your dad,' know what I mean?"

Marci relaxed. "Sort of."

Kirby continued to watch the passing scenery. "It's like this. You are who you are. In other words, you're perfect. We're all perfect. You know what I mean?" Kirby turned to look at Marci, but she was now staring straight ahead. "Some things you're going to be better at than the partner you're with, whether it's your life partner, business partner, or detective partner, in your case. Some things you'll be worse at than them. Together, you should make each other stronger."

Her eyes softened as she looked back at him in the rearview mirror.

"Men are stupid," Kirby said, turning back to the window. "Women have the same issues at times, though. Maybe it's just the whole human race. We haven't fully evolved yet."

Marci pulled the car over in front of Kirby's apartment. He reached into the front of the vehicle to shake Marci's hand. "Detective, it was sincerely nice to meet you."

She smiled. "You, too, Kirby."

He climbed out of the car and walked back to his apartment.

# Chapter 19

"What were you doing at Kirby Willis's apartment on Saturday afternoon?"

Douglas Rafferty leaned back in his chair and stared at Quinn. He made a sucking sound between his teeth.

"You assaulted Mr. Willis—"

"You have no proof."

"We have photographs—"

"No witnesses."

"We have a witness."

"No, you don't."

Quinn leaned back in his chair. "You're right. I don't. I'm not sure why I even care. The most important thing in this matter is the assault of my partner."

"Assault? I never hit her. At best, it's attempted."

"That's not how it works. You attacked my partner, and we have two independent witnesses."

"You two are not independent."

"Independent means we weren't involved in the fight."

Rafferty leaned forward in his chair. "Your partner doesn't fight fair."

"Her job is to win. Not to fight fair."

"I'll remember that."

"That sounds like a threat."

Rafferty shrugged and leaned back. "It's not a threat. I wouldn't do that. I'm not that kind of guy."

Quinn opened his file. Before he came into the interview, he had printed off Douglas Rafferty's criminal history. "That's not exactly true."

"You callin' me a liar?" Rafferty said, leaning forward in his chair.

Quinn looked up from his papers, meeting the other man's glare. "In fact, I am. It says here you threatened an ex-girlfriend after she went to the police. You were arrested for assaulting her. Must have been bad. You were charged with second-degree assault."

"The papers you're lookin' at must show it was dropped to fourth degree. Wasn't that big a deal."

"You hit a woman."

"C'mon, man. You know how it is. She made me do it."

"It also says in here you were charged and convicted for malicious mischief ten years ago. What was that about?"

"Nothing."

"I'm going to pull the records on it. You can bullshit me and let me further believe you're a liar, or you can start to tell the truth."

Rafferty smirked. "A previous employer called it in. It wasn't as bad as they made it out."

"What happened?"

"They said I slashed a couple of tires after I got fired."

"And what really happened?"

"I only slashed one. The other was already flat." Rafferty laughed.

Quinn watched the big man until he was done. "What's your interest in Jacob Kidwell?"

Rafferty crossed his arms, watching the detective. "Who?"

"How are you connected to Jacob Kidwell?"

"I don't know what you're talking about."

"What about Kirby Willis? What about him?"

"Who?"

"You're connected to Jacob Kidwell's death somehow, and I'm going to figure it out."

"I didn't kill him."

"Who?"

"Him. Kidwell. I didn't do that."

"You said you didn't know him."

"Yeah, well, I didn't kill him either."

"Then why were you outside his apartment?"

"I was only supposed to find out what he was doing."

"Who hired you to follow Kidwell?"

Rafferty opened his mouth to speak, but a knock on the interview room door interrupted the conversation. It swung open with Marci in the lead and a woman behind. "Don't say anything further, Douglas," the woman said forcefully.

The big man's eyes slanted, and his jaw flexed at being given orders. Quinn wondered if it was because the orders came from a woman.

"I'm Wanda Acosta, your attorney, and he's done speaking with you." She was short and slightly overweight but had an attractive, round face. She wore an expertly cut pantsuit that revealed more about her level of success and power than a recent profile had in *Spokane Living* magazine.

Quinn had crossed paths with Acosta several times through the years, and the outcome was never good. She was one of the best criminal defense attorneys in town.

"I assume you have enough to charge him for the incident in the parking lot today?"

"We do," Quinn said.

"Then get to it," Acosta said, "because this interview is over."

*\*\*\**

Marci and Quinn stood in the bullpen as Acosta talked with her client. Rafferty stood with his hands cuffed behind his back.

"Well, that's interesting," Marci said. "Wanda isn't cheap, and she doesn't handle just anyone."

Quinn said, "I doubt Rafferty has the cash to afford a half-hour of Wanda's time."

"I'd like to know who made that call."

"Without a doubt, the call started from the construction company. Someone saw the arrest. They either called her or placed a call to someone who then called her. We just have to work it backward."

"I'll handle his booking," Quinn said. "You start the report."

"Sounds like a plan."

Wanda Acosta nodded towards the detectives, indicating the conversation with her client was officially over.

# TUESDAY

## Chapter 20

"I confirmed that he had all twenty-four properties under contract."

"Are you sure?"

"Yes," Kirby said.

Paula Fairbanks leaned back in her chair. They were at the Starbucks on 37th and Grand Boulevard. Kirby had texted her for a meeting, and Paula suggested a coffee.

"How do you know?"

"I talked with a woman who said her neighbors had agreed to sell."

Paula sipped her iced coffee. "Since our talk, I've had some time to think about this. I tried to remove myself from the equation and not get emotional about it. That's what blinded me to the whole thing."

"I can understand," Kirby said.

"Let me break it down so you can see where I'm at. Twenty-four lots are comprising a city block at the corner of Queen and Lidgerwood, correct? Do you know what the zoning is there? Until recently, it was classified as residential."

Kirby suddenly felt unsure of what he knew.

"A couple of years ago, it was modified to mixed-use—residential and retail. Do you know there's an interesting quirk to that mixed-use zone along that corridor? No? Well, neither did I until I started researching it. The city hasn't put a height restriction on it. I'm sure they meant to, but right now, there is none. So, if someone wants to do a monstrous tower, I'm sure the city would fight with everything they've got, but a smart developer could get in there and build a reasonably sized building and likely not get much pushback at all from the local powers that be. The neighborhood might have something to say, but you deal with them like anything else. You power through it until you're done."

Kirby concentrated intently on Paula's story.

"So back to the twenty-four houses. For argument's sake, let's say Jacob convinced all the property owners to sell at the same time."

"That would have required twenty-four separate negotiations, which in itself is a monumental task."

Kirby stared at Paula.

"I'm trying not to disparage Jacob's ability, but that seems really above his skill level. Don't you think?"

"Yeah, probably."

"It might even be above Amy's level. Do you know Amy Tillerson?"

Kirby shook his head.

"That's his designated broker. His boss, so to speak. I've always thought she was a bitch, but again, I'm trying to look at this rationally. She's good. I mean, she's still a bitch, but that doesn't stop her from being good at what she does. I wouldn't have thought she could have done a deal like this. You see, if someone could put together a deal like this, all twenty-four houses, it goes down in the county history books. It's that big of a deal."

"Yeah," Kirby said, trying to process their conversation.

"Here's the kicker, though—not only did they just get the property owners to sell, they have them set for a simultaneous closing."

"That sounds wobbly."

"Very. Imagine this. Transaction C can't happen until transaction A and transaction B happen first. Okay, that's not that bad, right? We can all fathom that because there are only three parts. In this scenario, we're talking twenty-four letters, which is X, right? I had to figure that out in advance. Anyway, A, B, and C must happen first along with all the other letters through W before X, the final house sale occurs. Do you know how many things can go wrong?"

"Wow."

"That's why they are trying to keep this quiet and under the radar. It will only take one person stepping out of line to blow the whole deal apart."

"What if one of the homeowners doesn't want to sell?" Kirby asked.

"The purchase and sale agreements will probably have an enforcement clause. The buyer can enforce specific performance."

"When we talked last time, you said if the contract was in Jacob's name or an LLC he owns, the deal is void upon his death."

"Yes."

"So, all of his work is for naught."

Paula tilted her head from side to side. "Maybe."

"What do you mean?"

"I also said to see if the deal was assigned."

"How do I know that?"

"Well, Amy will have a copy of the paperwork or the title company handling the transaction will. Have you talked with either of them?"

"No."

"Both will have a fiduciary duty not to divulge any information about a specific transaction. This would be a substantial transaction, so I doubt they would be willing to give you the slightest bit of info. The police, perhaps, could get that information with a warrant."

"Huh," Kirby grunted thoughtfully.

"Or you could speak with one of the people you talked with previously. They might know if it's been assigned. If it has, the title company will notify all sellers there has been a change in the buyer."

Kirby brightened. "There is a sweet old lady who might just tell me that."

\*\*\*

"I'm not telling you anything ever again," Joyce Faber said.

"Why not?"

"You got me in trouble," she said through her screen door.

"How did I do that?" Kirby asked. "All we did was talk."

"After you left, someone called and reminded me of the confidentiality agreement. I'm not allowed to talk to anyone about our deal."

"Who called you?"

"I can't say."

"There's a confidentiality agreement?"

She shook her head. "Even by saying that, I've said too much."

"Please, Mrs. Faber. I'm trying to find out what happened to my friend."

"I can't help you," she said. "Please, get off my property before someone sees you."

She shut the door in Kirby's face.

***

"Is it standard procedure to have a confidentiality agreement?"

Paula Fairbanks shook her head. "No. Definitely not. There's never been one in a deal I've worked on. Again, good for Jacob. I wouldn't have thought about doing something like that."

Kirby had driven straight back to the Dream Living Real Estate office to talk with Paula after Joyce had shut the door in his face. They were sitting in the conference room. He had thought about calling her but wanted to brainstorm the situation. Right now, he felt very alone working on Jacob's death, so getting to talk with someone in person allowed him to feel more connected to the universe—even if one of them was the real estate agent who helped him buy his apartment building.

Paula leaned back in her chair and looked up at the ceiling. "I've never seen a deal like this, let alone been a part of one. There had to have been a confidentiality agreement in place, right? It's obvious. A former boyfriend of mine is a commercial broker. They have them in their deals all the time. It's a different game than the one we play. He had to sign confidentiality agreements before he could represent certain tenants. They wouldn't want anyone knowing they were looking to move into the market. The more I think about this deal, the more sense it makes to have a lockdown on the information."

"How so?"

"In this case, I can see two scenarios. First, one of the homeowners wants more money. They start talking with the other homeowners and determine they're getting less value than their property is worth. They can rattle the deal by demanding more, claiming they won't sell."

"But there's a contract, isn't there?"

"Exactly. And if they have a confidentiality agreement, I'll bet the duty to perform clause is ironclad."

"Meaning they have to sell as long as the buyer gets to the table?"

"Correct. So, I doubt they'll worry about a homeowner stepping out of line."

"What's the second example?" Kirby asked.

"Here's why most developers want a seller to keep quiet. If another developer gets wind of a project, they'll start sniffing around. Some will even try to get in the mix and see if they can snake the deal."

"That doesn't sound ethical."

Paula shrugged. "Ethical or not, it's business. If what you said is true, if there's going to be a high-rise apartment building, that's a bold move for that part of town. It could seriously be a game-changer. A rival developer could taint the waters today to kill the deal so they can swoop in and get the project tomorrow. If they could do that, why wouldn't they?"

Kirby shook his head. "Twenty-four homes. That's a lot of people to keep quiet."

"I think it was Ben Franklin who said, 'Three can keep a secret if two of them are dead.'"

"Oh."

"Yeah. Best not to have secrets, Kirb."

\*\*\*

"Is Amy Tillerson in?"

Helen Erwin, the receptionist for Home Town Realty, looked up from her computer and studied Kirby. "Who should I say is asking?"

"Kirby Willis."

"You were here last week, asking about Jacob, weren't you?"

Kirby nodded. "Yes, ma'am."

"Did the police find you? They asked about you."

"Yes, ma'am, they did," Kirby said. "Everything is fine."

"Wait here."

Helen stood and walked into a back office. Kirby could see her talk with a woman who had short blond hair. The woman glanced at Kirby for a moment before looking back at the receptionist. They continued their conversation for several minutes.

Kirby shoved his hands in his pockets and looked around the office. There were several official posters on the walls about the duties and responsibilities of agents, along with beautiful promotional photos of houses.

The receptionist walked back out and stood in front of Kirby. "Ms. Tillerson isn't available right now."

"I can see her right there."

"She just returned from vacation and is very busy."

"I only need a few minutes of her time."

"If you give me your name and number, she will contact you later to schedule an appointment. She's getting ready for a meeting and can't be disturbed."

The finality in Helen's tone let Kirby know he wasn't getting past this gatekeeper.

He wrote his name and phone number down before leaving.

\*\*\*

Kirby stood in front of the front desk officer and felt strangely nervous.

"Who do you want to see?"

"Detective Delaney?"

"What's this about?"

"A case he's working on."

"Does he know you're coming?"

"No, ma'am."

The desk officer called Quinn's line and announced Kirby. A few minutes later, Quinn appeared from around the corner. After shaking hands, the detective asked, "What's up?"

"I found out some new things I thought I should tell you."

"You shouldn't be poking around anymore."

"I'm not going where I don't belong. I promise."

Quinn jerked his head toward the door. "Come on back."

Kirby nodded. He could have phoned Quinn with the information he learned, but he had an ulterior motive.

"Let me grab a notebook, and then we'll go to one of the interview rooms."

Quinn stopped by his desk, and Marci turned to see them. "Kirby Willis. It's nice to see you."

She had remembered his name. He struggled to contain a smile.

"Afternoon, Detective."

"Call me, Marci," she said.

"Marci," he said with a single nod.

A small smile appeared on her face.

"This way," Quinn said, ignoring their conversation and directing Kirby to an interview room.

Once seated, the detective asked, "What did you learn?"

"I'd recommend you contact Amy Tillerson at Home Town Realty."

"We already tried. She's on vacation."

"She's back."

"How'd you know?"

"She posted an update on her Facebook page. We friended each other long ago when Jacob started working there. I just stopped by her office."

"Her receptionist was supposed to call us when she returned."

"Amy refused to talk with me. I could see her in her office, but she still wouldn't come out."

"Is that weird?"

Kirby shrugged. "I don't know. We're Facebook friends, not friends in real life, so she doesn't owe me any special kindness."

Quinn wrote on his notepad while Kirby waited. "What else?"

"Remember we talked about the twenty-four homes being under contract?"

"Yeah."

"Well, I think the purchase and sale agreements might hold the key to what happened to Jacob. I stopped by Paula Fairbank's office again this morning. According to her, if the contract were in Jacob's name, it would become void upon his death. However, some purchase contracts will have an 'and/or assigns' provision in it. What that means is the buyer can assign it to someone else. Occasionally, the buyer will just assign it to an entity, like a limited liability company, that they create for themselves. Not a big deal, right? Other times, the buyer will assign it to another party when they realize they can't perform, but the property is still a good deal."

"Is that what you think Jacob did?"

Kirby shook his head. "I don't know. There's a third option, however. That's when the buyer is operating as a 'strawman.' Jacob could have put the contracts in his name, so everyone thinks he's buying the property. Then, right before closing, he assigns the contract to the real buyer."

"Why do that?" Quinn asked, writing as he spoke. "Why act as a strawman?"

"I asked Paula about the same thing. Here's how she explained it. Let's say I was a wealthy investor, and I came to you wanting to buy your property. You wouldn't negotiate very much with me, right? Because you would know I could afford it, you'd dig your heels in and behave differently. In the case of the properties involving Jacob, had the home sellers known who the real buyers were, they might have realized they could cash in on a much larger payday."

"Ah."

"A strawman—Jacob, in this case—comes in so he can portray the deal in a different light. Get a better price, more favorable terms."

"Can we find out who the buyer is and if Jacob was acting as a strawman?"

"It would be tough to find out if he was acting as a strawman. That's the point. You don't want people to know until it's too late. However, the buyer will be listed on the purchase and sale agreement. Amy Tillerson must have a copy of the contract in her office. If she doesn't share it with you, then there will be a copy at the title company."

"Which title company is it?"

"No idea."

"That's not a lot to go on."

"Is it more than you had ten minutes ago?"

Quinn looked at his notes and nodded. "It is."

"There's one other thing."

"What's that?"

"There's a confidentiality clause in those sale agreements."

"How do you know that?"

"I went back to talk with the nice older lady who first chatted with me. She wasn't so nice the second time around. Someone threatened her with the contract. She confirmed there was a confidentiality clause and wouldn't give me the time of day again. Basically, she told me to get lost and closed the door in my face."

"That's interesting how she changed."

"Not really."

Quinn looked up from his notes. "How's that?"

"Money. It changes people. Take Mrs. Faber, the old lady I spoke to. She was sweet as honey when she believed her deal was going to go through. She was counting dollars and imagining where she was going to move. As soon as someone threatened her money, though, her world turned upside down. She no longer was very nice. I don't ever want to be that way. Money should be a tool to help us get what we want. Fundamentally, it shouldn't change who we are."

Quinn studied Kirby for a minute until Kirby finally said, "Are you okay, Detective?"

"Did you grow up with money?"

"No, not at all. Why do you ask?"

"Your views on money are… different."

"I was raised by a single mom, Detective, and I never knew my dad. My mom did a great job, but we were lower middle class at best. She often was on public assistance. My grandparents are solidly middle class. Money was forbidden to be discussed whenever we were at their house."

"Then how did you learn so much so early? I mean, you're not even thirty yet."

"I read and paid attention, basically. I was hungry for it. A lot of the kids I went to school with were in the same situation. They were poor or lower middle class, and it seemed their families had accepted their lot in life. But I knew this one kid, Adam Boone, whose family looked like the rest of us. Except they did everything differently. He brought lunch every day that was better than the hot lunch the school gave out to those on assistance. His parents smiled when they picked him up at school. When I went over to his house to play, it wasn't overly nice, but it was clean and well kept. They respected their stuff. His mom stayed at home while his dad owned his own accounting business."

Quinn put down his pen, crossed his arms, and listened.

"They only had one TV, which was in the family room. Adam got one hour of screen time a day. He could choose to watch TV, play video games, whatever, but it was for only one hour a day. My mom used our TV as a babysitter. I get it. She was working her ass off, and she needed a distraction for me while she was trying to get stuff done, but I wasn't engaging my brain as much as I could have been.

"One day, while I was at his house, Adam said he needed a new toy. I don't remember what it was, but I do remember this. His dad stopped him and said, 'Do you need it, or do you want it?' Adam thought for a moment and said, 'I want it.' I believe that exact moment changed my life. Mr. Boone said, 'Perfect. How do you want to get it?' Adam looked around the house for thirty minutes, trying to find a job to make some money. I tagged along, not understanding what was occurring. When Adam found an idea, he finally made his dad an offer to pick up the leaves falling from the trees. 'For how much?' Mr. Boone asked. 'Twenty dollars,' Adam said. 'Are you doing the job alone, or is Kirby helping?' I remember my eyes widening in excitement. Man, I got to tell you, at that moment, if things played out differently, I might be somewhere totally different. Anyway, Mr. Boone said, 'If Kirby helps, it's ten dollars apiece. You won't be able to afford the toy you want, but you'll get the job done quicker.' My buddy looked at me and said, 'Want to help?'

"We went outside, and raked leaves that day, and I made ten dollars. Up to that point, I never had ten dollars in my life. While we worked, Adam told me about the chores he had to do that were considered his in the family, but if he found creative jobs to do around the house, his dad would pay him various amounts. Anything from one dollar to twenty dollars. Adam told me his dad was trying to make him an entrepreneur. We were nine years old when I learned what an entrepreneur was. I don't think there were two other kids in our school who could tell you what an entrepreneur was. I decided right then and there I would only work for myself. After that, Adam included me in his entrepreneurial jobs if I could help him find some. I worked hard to find jobs for us to do for his dad. His dad never once complained. He always encouraged us to keep going. We did so much work around that house until we were old enough to start working for the neighbors."

Marci opened the door to the interview room and stuck her head in. "How are things going?"

Quinn looked at Marci, his eyes slightly out of focus.

"You okay?" she asked.

"Yeah. Just thinking."

"That's all I had for you, Detective," Kirby said. "I'm going to take off if that's cool?"

Quinn absently nodded as Kirby stood.

"I'll walk you out," Marci said.

*** 

"Detective Delaney seems like a decent guy," Kirby said as they walked the hallway, their pace slower than usual.

"He is," Marci said. "He's a good partner, too."

"How are you after the fight in the parking lot?"

"I'm fine."

"It didn't bother you?"

"No, I'm good."

"You're kind of a badass."

Marci smiled but didn't look at Kirby.

"Where do you train?"

"On the Mat Mixed Martial Arts. It's up north."

"I've seen it. It looks like a busy school."

Marci glanced at him. "Why do you ask?"

"I was thinking maybe I should try a class."

"I thought you weren't interested."

"I wasn't before."

They pushed through the exit door into the lobby of the Public Safety Building. Marci stopped walking, and Kirby turned to face her. "Are you flirting with me, Kirby?"

"I'm trying."

"I'm ten years older than you."

He shrugged. "That doesn't mean anything. Like I said, you're a badass."

Before she could protest, Kirby turned and walked away.

After a moment, Kirby looked back and caught her watching. They both smiled.

# WEDNESDAY

## Chapter 21

Quinn's phone vibrated. He pulled it out of his pocket, checked the screen, and muted the call. A wave of irritation swept through him.

Marci looked at him, a smirk on her face.

"What?"

"You still haven't called her?"

Quinn shoved the phone back into his pocket.

"You're the worst liar I know," Marci said and pulled the car into a space.

They were in the parking lot of Hayes Construction.

"What's the play here?" Marci asked.

"We're going to pull the thread on Douglas Rafferty and see what we find."

"I know that. Let's try bad cop, good cop."

"We don't do that."

"I know, but let's try it for once and see if it works."

"It won't. Just be who you are. That freaks them out enough," Quinn said with a smirk.

"What?" Marci replied with a tone of indignation.

"Nothing," Quinn said as he opened the door to the office building.

Marci stood in front of him, her hands on her hips. "Are you saying I'm a bad cop or that I have a bad attitude? Careful how you answer, partner, because both of those are going to play poorly."

Quinn's irritation was at the surface, and he struggled to contain it. "Never mind. I was popping off."

She clenched her jaw as Quinn let the door go and stepped inside. She was forced to hop inside before the door swung closed on her.

Quinn walked up to the front desk and rang the small metal bell. A name placard on the desk read *Tommi*.

A young male with slicked-back hair hurried to the front. "Yes? How can I help you?"

Quinn pointed to the badge and gun on his waist, and Tommi raised his eyebrows in response. Quinn then thumbed toward Marci, who opened her jacket, exposing the gun and badge on her hip. Tommi nodded to her.

"Detective Delaney of the Spokane Police Department. This is Detective Burkett."

"Okay," Tommi said. "I've got it now. You were here the other day when I was at the doctor's. The fight in the parking lot, right? I'm sorry I missed it." Tommi took a quick look around before leaning in conspiratorially. "I've never been a fan of Mr. Rafferty."

"We'd like to talk with Mr. Hayes," Quinn said.

Tommi stood upright, regaining his air of professionalism. "That won't be possible."

"Why is that?"

"He's dead."

"Huh," Quinn said.

"It was years ago. I think you'd like to talk with Victoria. That's his wife. She runs the company now."

"Is she available?"

"She's in a meeting, but if you give me a few minutes, I'll get her for you."

"Thank you."

After Tommi left, Marci smiled at Quinn.

"What?" he asked.

"You assumed a man ran this company."

"Excuse me?"

"You asked for *Mr.* Hayes."

"Whatever."

"That was sort of sexist."

Struggling to contain his irritation, Quinn turned fully to Marci. "Why are you busting my balls?"

"What?"

"Is it so hard for you to be nonjudgmental?"

"I'm just saying, couldn't you just come in and ask for the owner?"

"Seriously? You're doing this here, now?"

"What do you mean, I'm doing this? You're the one who was sexist. You're the one who's been on edge lately. I don't know what's going on with you, man, but stop taking it out on me."

Quinn's mouth opened slightly to protest when a door opened, stopping their argument.

Tommi returned with a thin woman in dark slacks and a paisley shirt. Her salt-and-pepper hair was cut short in a style preferred in the 1980s. "Detectives, this is Victoria Hayes."

Quinn introduced Marci and himself before asking for a private place to talk.

"This way," she said and led them to a glassed-in conference room. On the wall hung a sizeable flat-screen TV. In the middle of the room was a rectangular conference table made of concrete. Seven chairs lined each side, and a single chair was at the head. Victoria took the seat at the head of the table. Marci and Quinn both sat with their backs to the outside wall, so they could see through the glass and watch anyone approaching.

"Thanks for meeting with us, Ms. Hayes," Marci said.

The woman nodded. "Victoria, please. I assume this has to do with Mr. Rafferty's assault in the parking lot."

"Yes, ma'am, it does, we're—"

"Mr. Rafferty is no longer employed by us."

"Were you the one responsible for hiring him?"

"I don't do the hiring of our employees. I have a human resources director for that."

"Do you do the firing?" Marci asked.

"I definitely do that. When I heard about the assault in the parking lot, I notified the HR director to terminate Mr. Rafferty immediately."

"Did you hire a lawyer for him?"

Victoria stared at Marci, not answering.

"His attorney, Wanda Acosta, is one of the best defense attorneys in town. Wouldn't you agree, partner?"

"She's fine," Quinn said.

Marci's eyes remained on Quinn for a moment before she said, "Fine? Really?" She turned her attention back to Victoria. "If Wanda were a man, he'd say she's the best."

Quinn's chin dropped.

Victoria shook her head and focused solely on Marci as she continued.

"Anyway, because she's the best, she can charge the steepest rates. Supply and demand, right? Douglas Rafferty doesn't seem to me to be in the position to pay her rates. He's going to need a benefactor. I'm guessing that's you. Or the company, at the least."

"We hired Ms. Acosta. And, yes, I agree she's the best."

"Okay," Marci said. "I can appreciate that you hired her for your employee."

"I didn't hire her for my employee. I hired her for my business."

Marci and Victoria stared at each other for a moment until Victoria said, "Perception, Detective. In this business, in this world, perception is reality. If my employee attacks a police officer and is found guilty, do you know what that does to my business?"

"It'll hurt."

"Of course it will hurt. My competitors will use that fact against me. They'll slander me and my business while we're bidding jobs. They'll make false accusations while attending city functions. After a while, Mr. Rafferty's actions will be seen as my actions."

"Were they your actions?"

Anger flashed over Victoria's face but was quickly replaced by calm. "No, Detective. Most certainly not. I would not advocate violence, especially against a police officer."

"Mr. Rafferty indicated to us that he was asked to follow Jacob Kidwell."

"Jacob Kidwell?"

"He was a real estate agent who put together a twenty-four-house purchase that your company is bidding to replace with a high-rise apartment building."

Victoria's face went flat. "That was supposed to be confidential."

"Nothing is confidential while we're investigating a homicide investigation."

"Homicide?"

"Yes."

"He's dead?"

"Yes."

"We did not ask Mr. Rafferty to follow Mr. Kidwell. Whatever he was doing, he was doing for himself. Let's make that clear."

"Were you bidding the project for Kidwell?"

Victoria looked down at her hands. "For him and his client, Michael Smith."

Quinn jotted the name down in his notebook. "Do you have a way of contacting Mr. Smith?"

Victoria shook her head. "We always dealt with Jacob. It wasn't until I saw Michael with Jacob one afternoon that I realized they were working together."

"You don't seem very fond of Mr. Smith."

"He had some previous troubles. Police-type troubles. You should be able to find out about him. But he served his time and is out now. People deserve a second chance, right? Kumbaya, and all that."

"Sure," Quinn said. "A second chance."

\*\*\*

Outside, Quinn dialed a familiar phone number.

The call was answered on the second ring. "Crime Analysis, this is Debbie."

"Debbie, it's Quinn."

"Hiya, kiddo, what can I do you for?"

"We need help finding someone."

"That's my specialty."

"I know. All we've got is Michael Smith."

"Not much better than John Smith."

"Tell me about it. The guy has some sort of criminal record. He would be affiliated with either the construction industry or the real estate industry. Beyond that, we don't have much to go on. Can you help us out?"

"How fast do you need it?"

"We're in the middle of a case, so it's got some time sensitivity, but it's not monumental."

"I'll get on it."

Quinn hung up and looked at Marci. "That's how nice people do business with other nice people."

"I'm nice," she said, climbing into the car.

\*\*\*

"We'd like to speak to Amy Tillerson."

Helen Erwin nodded, stood from her desk, and walked back to the office of her employer.

"Are you still mad at me?" Marci asked. "I said I was sorry."

"You called me sexist in front of a witness."

"It got her to open up."

"She was already talking," Quinn said, surprised by the whine in his voice.

"Maybe," Marci said. "But I don't know if you would have been upset by that a week ago."

"What's that mean?"

"Everything is getting under your skin right now."

"I'm not irritable," Quinn snapped.

Marci turned and faced him with raised eyebrows.

"I'm not irritable," Quinn repeated.

"Whatever," Marci said.

The two of them watched the conversation between Helen and Amy through the windows of Amy's office.

"Do you think people are really afraid of me?" Marci asked.

"Yes. Isn't that what you want?"

Marci shook her head. "You're not getting it."

Helen stepped out of Amy's office and waved for the detectives.

"We can continue this conversation at another time."

"Let's not," Marci said.

Amy Tillerson's office was a shrine to herself. The walls were covered with awards, plaques, and pictures proclaiming the greatness of Amy Tillerson. On the corner of the desk, a frame was facedown.

Amy stood and moved around the desk to shake the hands of both detectives. She wore a short black miniskirt with a muted floral blouse. After their introductions, she returned to her chair. She motioned for Quinn and Marci to sit in the chairs in front of the desk.

"How may I help you, Detectives?"

"We'd like to ask you some questions about Jacob Kidwell."

She covered her heart. "I heard. Terrible news."

"Yes. That's why we're here," Quinn said.

"You think it was deliberate? His death, I mean."

"That's what we're trying to determine. When did you get back to the office?"

"Yesterday," Amy said. "I always wonder why I leave. It's always so darn busy upon my return."

"How was your vacation?" Quinn asked.

A quick wave of sadness passed over Amy's face, and her eyes flicked to the facedown frame on the corner of the desk. "It didn't go as well as I had planned."

"Sorry to hear that," Quinn said.

"Me, too," Amy admitted.

"We asked your assistant to contact us when you returned," Marci said. "Was there a reason she didn't?"

"I asked her not to."

Quinn glanced at Marci before asking, "Why would you do that?"

"As I said, I'm busy upon returning. I told Helen, and you're more than welcome to verify this, to call you tomorrow to set up an appointment. I just needed some time to get caught up following my vacation. I've got a business to run."

"How well did you know Jacob?" Quinn asked.

"Well enough, I guess. He was a broker under my license. Beyond that," Amy shook her head, "I didn't know him very well. He kept to himself."

"There was a complaint filed from another broker…"

"Paula Fairbanks." Amy crinkled her nose. "She's a lousy agent."

"Why do you say that?"

"She didn't service her client. Jacob did, so now she wants to cry foul. I thought they were friends, but it happens all the time. People cry over spilled milk. Well, money. Spilled money? Lost money. You get what I mean. Anyway, I wasn't worried about her. Jacob did fine."

"Then why did you terminate your relationship with Jacob?"

"It had nothing to do with Paula's complaint. Quite frankly, his attitude had grown poor lately. I want a certain type of agent associated with my firm."

"How would you describe his attitude?" Marci asked.

"Demanding. Ungrateful. Occasionally demeaning. I didn't need that at my firm."

"Were you aware of a deal that Jacob had put together for twenty-four houses at the corner of Queen and Lidgerwood?"

Amy tightened her lips and inhaled quickly through her nose. She recovered and smiled. "Yes. Of course, he was my agent. I knew everything he was working on."

"Can we see the file on that?"

"May I ask why?"

"We believe it may have played a role in his death."

Amy nodded. She leaned slightly to look past the detectives and yelled, "Helen."

The receptionist hurried back to her office. "Yes?"

"Please pull the files related to Jacob's redevelopment deal up north."

Helen looked confused.

"What?" Amy asked, her tone demanding.

"Well—"

"Where are the files, Helen?"

"He took them with him."

Amy's cheeks reddened, and her jaw muscles flexed. Her voice was stern when she spoke. "He's not supposed to take any files out of this office."

Helen looked suddenly very flabbergasted. "But didn't we—"

"Don't make excuses, Helen. Just tell me what happened with the files."

Helen slowly nodded, understanding the gravity of the situation. "I argued with him not to remove them, but you were gone, and he said he only needed them for a little while. He said he would bring them back later that day. He could be very persuasive when he wanted to be."

Amy's face tightened and relaxed, and she struggled to appear calm as she spoke to the detectives. "Apparently, the files are gone. This is what happens when I'm not here." Amy's flash of anger toward Helen was the receptionist's signal to go back to her desk. "I'm sorry. I should control myself better."

"Why would he take the files?" Quinn asked.

"I don't know. He should have his own copies of those documents. That must be the reason. He lost his and wanted to copy ours. He could have copied them here, though. It doesn't make sense."

"What title company is handling escrow for that deal?"

Amy shook her head. "I'm sorry. I don't remember."

"Who was the original buyer on the sale contract?"

"It was Jacob, but under an LLC, he formed, I think," Amy said.

"Do you scan the files? You know, to put them on the cloud?" Marci asked. Quinn nodded at his partner's question.

"There is no state requirement to do so, at least, not yet. When they require it, we'll do it. Some firms do it now, but it's an extra cost, and we run on a very low-profit margin."

Quinn looked over his shoulder to the lobby. "I noticed there are only a couple of offices here. How many agents do you have?"

"I currently have thirty-one agents. They pay a monthly 'desk fee' that allows them to hang their licenses here, use an office when in the area, and the conference room when available, et cetera. Our business model is built around the idea that the agents will work remotely. The bonus is they get to keep one hundred percent of their commission."

"How much is this desk fee?"

"Eight hundred dollars a month."

"That seems steep."

Amy shook her head. "Quite the opposite. Some places take a percentage of an agent's fee. Even if the fee were ten percent, the agent would only have to bring in eight thousand dollars a month in gross commissions, which isn't much. Most bring in far more than that."

"How much was Jacob bringing in?"

"When he hustled, Jacob was earning over one hundred thousand a year."

Marci and Quinn looked at each other.

"However, he slacked off a lot lately. He had gotten involved with that strange little website of his. I don't get it. He would come in and do a deal or two, but his production was way down. He was only averaging a few thousand a month."

"This deal up north seems a bit out of step with how he's been working, right?"

"Quite frankly, yes. I didn't expect it from him."

"Why were you in his apartment?" Quinn asked.

"What?"

"Why were you in his apartment?" he repeated, his words slower than before.

"I wasn't."

"You were."

Amy looked between the two detectives, searching for an answer.

"Your fingerprints were found in his apartment."

Amy's eyes widened for a moment, and then she calmed down. "Oh, you mean before. I'm sorry. I was thinking you were accusing me of, well, you know. Yes. I went to Jacob's apartment to have him sign a document. An offer on a property. I can pull that file if you'd like."

"Was the document you had Jacob sign an assignment to the original purchase and sale agreements for the twenty-four houses?" Quinn asked.

"What? No. As I said, I have the file on that offer if you want to see it."

"If an assignment of the purchase and sale agreement shows up after his death, that could be seen as a motive."

"As far as I know," Amy said, setting her jaw and glaring at Quinn, "there was no assignment signed. Are you accusing me of something? Should I contact my lawyer?"

Quinn looked at Marci for a moment, then turned back to Amy. "That's all for now. Thank you for your time."

\*\*\*

In their car, Marci asked, "What do you think about her?"

"She's fishy."

"Yeah," Marci said as the car lurched away from the curb. A car honked behind them. "Do we need to go back at her?"

"I don't know yet, but how I see it, we've got two tasks."

"What are those?"

"Task one," Quinn said, "we need to find the title company where the original sale contract was recorded."

"Task two?"

"We need to look further into Amy Tillerson. Something's not right there."

# Chapter 22

Kirby was on the street, washing his car while wearing shorts and flip-flops. It was a beautiful summer evening as the sun started to set. Music from his cell phone pumped through a nearby portable speaker.

He thought about Jacob's death as he applied soap to the Toyota. Jacob had become distant recently, both in person and with his online activity. They were never the best of friends, hanging out every night, but they did see each other frequently. They shared a lot of what was occurring in each other's lives.

Kirby tried to remember if there was ever another period where Jacob had become distant. As he hosed down the car, Kirby remembered there was. It was when he first started dating Holly Reese. At first, Jacob didn't even know that Kirby had gone to high school with her. That wasn't why he grew distant, though. It was that he had fallen head over heels for her and was spending all his extra time and mental energy on her. When they broke up, Jacob became the friend he remembered.

Jacob had several other girlfriends before, but they never mattered to him the way Holly did. Therefore, he didn't go off the proverbial rails.

Kirby wondered if Jacob had met a new woman.

A motorcycle pulled up to the curb behind him, the noise drowning out the music from the portable speaker. Kirby turned to face the rider, who reached for the ignition key, turning off the engine. Calm returned to the neighborhood.

The rider pulled off their helmet, and black hair spilled out.

Kirby smiled with recognition. "Hey, Detective. What brings you by?"

Marci Burkett remained seated on her bike. She wore a black leather jacket, blue jeans, and black boots. "I was out for a ride and in the neighborhood. I saw you washing your car and thought I would say hi."

"Nice bike."

Marci studied Kirby for a moment. Kirby couldn't figure out what she was trying to decide. Finally, she asked, "Do you ride?"

Kirby shook his head and picked up his T-shirt. He pulled it over his head. Then he grabbed a towel to dry the car. "I took a class with a friend once. He was getting a motorcycle and told me about it. I thought it would be something new to learn, and it wasn't overly expensive," he said, wiping the towel back and forth across the roof. "It was a two-and-half-day course. You know what I'm talking about?"

Marci nodded.

"Anyway, my friend and I passed. He ran out and bought his motorcycle. I took the lesson and filed it away. I didn't want a motorcycle before the class, and I didn't want one after, but it was a good experience. I never have to look at a bike and wonder what it would be like to ride one now."

"You're an interesting dude, Kirby."

Kirby's smile faded. "Interesting?"

"In a good way," Marci said, her smile growing. "Want to go for a ride?"

Kirby looked at his flip-flops and then shook his head. "Not really."

They stared at each other until Kirby asked, "Want a beer?"

# THURSDAY

## Chapter 23

Marci was already at her computer when Quinn walked into the detectives' office.

"You okay?" he asked.

She leaned back in her chair. "What do you mean?"

"You're here early."

"It's eight."

"As I said."

Marci smiled and turned back to her computer.

"Now, I know something is wrong."

"What do you mean?"

"I gave you a perfect opportunity to bust my chops, and you didn't take it."

Marci shrugged.

"Did you choke someone out at last night's class?"

Marci's face changed. "I most certainly did not."

"Hey, I'm sorry. I didn't mean to—"

Marci stood and walked away without looking back.

"Way to go, Delaney," Lieutenant George Brand said as he walked into the detectives' bullpen. "I don't know what you said, but you upset Burkett."

Quinn watched his partner walk down the hallway until she disappeared into the women's restroom.

"Delaney."

Quinn shook himself back to the present and looked at the lieutenant. "Sir?"

"Update me on the case with the kid who fell down the stairs."

"Kidwell. He was pushed."

"I'm starting to believe you have no proof of that."

"We know he owned two computers—a desktop and a laptop. We recovered only the desktop. The laptop is missing."

"Maybe it was getting repaired."

"Unlikely."

"How do you know?"

"Because of the victim's friend. He said the laptop should have been there. The laptop was used for business while the desktop was used strictly for website-related activities."

"What business was conducted on the laptop?"

"Real estate transactions, mostly. There may be other businesses. I'm not sure."

"And you believe something with real estate is involved in his death?"

Marci stepped out of the women's restroom and started back toward the detectives' office. When she saw Lieutenant Brand talking with Quinn, she turned around and walked in the opposite direction. Quinn saw her pirouette in the hallway.

"Detective?"

"Huh?" Quinn said, returning his focus to the lieutenant.

"Real estate. You believe it's involved somehow?"

"Yes, sir. The victim was involved in a transaction we believe was worth at least two million dollars."

"To the victim?"

"No, sir. He would only earn a commission on that amount. However, to the developer involved with the project, it would be worth substantially more. We're still trying to get our heads wrapped around it."

"I'm sure it's very interesting. However, I'm still getting pressure from the chief. Since it seems this wasn't clearly a homicide, we could move this case very easily to an accidental death. Slip and fall sort of thing."

"I don't buy it, sir."

Brand stared at him for a moment. "It's your clearance rate, but it's also mine to a lesser extent since mine is blended among all detectives. Yours is going to look bad if you can't clear this one."

"I understand, sir." Quinn was going to continue explaining his stance, but Brand had moved away toward the captain's office.

He sat at his desk and turned on his computer. He had one primary task for the day: find out what title company was handling the transaction Jacob Kidwell was involved in.

Two hours later, Quinn leaned back in his chair. Marci still hadn't returned to her desk.

"Screw it," he muttered.

Quinn's phone vibrated, and he immediately knew it wouldn't be a good phone call. He pulled the phone from his pocket and saw the area code was from West Virginia. He muted the call.

He left the department and drove to Washington State Title Company on Fourth Street.

The receptionist smiled at Quinn as he entered.

"I'm Detective Delaney with the Spokane Police Department. I'd like to speak with Judy Huynh."

"Just a moment."

A couple of moments later, Judy Huynh walked out and smiled, her hand extended. She was a small woman, expertly dressed in a gray pantsuit. They shook hands as Judy said, "How may I help you?"

"I talked with your assistant while you were out of the office. I'm trying to locate a specific real estate transaction."

"May I ask why?"

"It may be related to a homicide. I'm not entirely certain yet. One of the leads that popped up in my investigation is a real estate transaction involving an agent. He was the homicide victim."

"Can't you get the file from his brokerage firm? They are required by law to keep a copy."

"We tried. However, they are claiming the agent took the file out of the office against their authority."

Judy's brow furrowed. "Interesting."

"Very."

"I'm not allowed to share any information with you, Detective. I hope you understand. We have a duty to all parties involved."

"I completely understand. Your assistant would not confirm or deny that there was a file in your office for that transaction. However, she strongly recommended I come down and speak with you in person. If you just confirm the existence of such a transaction, I will get a warrant for that file."

Judy considered Quinn's request for a moment before saying, "What's the file you're looking for?"

"It would involve twenty-four separate transactions for single-family homes. Each transaction is a standalone. However, we believe they must all be executed at the same time, so they will be intertwined somehow. It will need some sort of performance language. How that looks, I'm not exactly sure."

"North Spokane, correct?"

"Yes, exactly."

"We have that transaction."

"Can you tell me who the buyer is, so I can correctly fill out the search warrant?"

"I'm sorry, Detective. I can't do that. I've told you more than I should."

"I understand," Quinn said. "I'll be back with the appropriate warrant."

\*\*\*

Quinn hurried back to the department, and Marci was still gone.

He set about writing a search warrant for Washington State Title Company. While working to be as detailed as possible, Quinn realized he would have to list every seller separately. For a moment, he thought about listing just a single transaction, but that wasn't doing the job thoroughly, and the individual Purchase and Sale Agreements might not have the same information as the rest.

Quinn called up the city's geographic information system (GIS), which allowed him to use an online map to walk through any neighborhood. He could hover a pointer over a house and click on it, revealing the homeowner's information as per the tax assessor. It was an invaluable tool for him.

It took a few hours for him to complete the warrant.

In that time, Marci still hadn't returned to the office.

\*\*\*

Quinn got a judge to sign the warrant, then returned to the office of Washington State Title Company with it in hand. Judy Huynh walked out and smiled. "Back so soon, Detective?"

He held up the document. "Here you go."

Judy read the warrant and nodded. "It's going to take us some time to get this copied. You can either wait or come back in an hour."

Quinn looked at his watch. It was almost 3 p.m., and he realized he hadn't eaten lunch.

"I'll come back."

He drove to a nearby Burger King. A heavyset girl behind the counter looked at him with bored eyes. A tattoo on her neck peeked out from underneath her collar. "Can I take your order?"

"Whopper, small fries, small Diet Coke," Quinn said.

She entered it in the register with a few button presses and announced the amount. Quinn started to hand her his credit card, but she pointed at the machine in front of him. "You run it yourself."

Quinn inserted the card, and a moment later, one word popped up that caused his heart to race: DENIED.

"There a problem?" the girl asked.

"It says I'm denied. Maybe I can rerun it?"

"Won't change nothin'. Never does," she said with a smirk.

"I don't know how this could have happened."

"See it all the time," she said, the boredom returning to her eyes.

Quinn reached into his pocket and pulled out a couple of crinkled bills. "How much can I get for this?"

"A burger."

"I'll take it," he said with resignation.

The girl shook her head as she deleted the previous order and replaced it with the single hamburger.

"Can I get a cup for some water?"

As he ate, Quinn sat in the corner of the restaurant, watching traffic slowly drive by.

\*\*\*

He returned to the department with copies of the transactions. Washington State Title Company had carefully packaged each transaction into separate 8x14 envelopes, so there were twenty-four of them.

Marci was at her desk. She leaned back as he walked in. Her olive skin was flush like she'd just run a mile in the sun.

"Did you work out or something?"

"You don't look well," she said.

"I'm fine," he said with a shake of his head. "Just stressed."

"About?"

"Ex-wife issues," he said.

"You need to deal with it head-on, man."

Quinn felt like yelling at Marci but knew it was his problem, not hers. He dropped the files on the floor next to his desk.

"What have you got there?"

"Copies of all the transaction files from the title company."

"For the deals Kidwell was working on?" she asked excitedly.

Quinn grabbed the top envelope and tore it open. Marci picked up another and did the same.

Marci said, "Says here that the buyer is Marmot Territory, LLC."

Quinn turned to his computer and went to the state business license search. The state's database listed all members of any corporation. It was public record and didn't require a search warrant.

It took a few keystrokes, and Quinn spoke as he read from the screen. "Jacob Kidwell wasn't the sole member of Marmot Territory, LLC. He was involved with Michael Smith."

"Michael Smith? The same guy that Victoria Hayes told us about."

Quinn jumped to the criminal database to conduct a different search. "It's such a common name. The results are too numerous to weed out. We need to get him on the radar and track him down."

"Wasn't Debbie from Crime Analysis working on that for you?"

"She is, but I only asked her yesterday afternoon," Quinn said, irritated at Marci's question. "Give her time."

Marci looked up from the document she was reading. "We've got another hurdle."

"What's that?"

"The title company was only retained to insure title. They aren't closing the transaction."

Quinn looked at his partner. "Who is doing that?"

"The law offices of Desantis, Newell, and Acosta."

"Acosta? Wanda Acosta? She's a criminal defense attorney. Not a property attorney."

"Her law firm is full service, though," Marci said. "They'll have someone on staff that can perform this function. That muddies the water, don't you think?"

Quinn picked up the file he opened and stared at it for a moment. He then dropped it on his desk and stood. "I'm done."

"You okay?"

Quinn left without another word.

\*\*\*

When he got home, Quinn grabbed several letters from his mailbox and went inside. There was one from his bank. He sat at the kitchen table and opened it.

The title of the letter was *Notice of Foreclosure Proceedings*.

Quinn held the piece of paper in a trembling hand and paced the house. His face felt warm.

*How could it have gotten this far?*

*How did I get so far behind?*

His credit card was now maxed out, and he was behind one truck payment.

He and Barbara had always danced on the thin line of financial disaster when they were together. At any time, they were one paycheck away from ruin, but the two of them could handle it. Divorce changed everything. Quinn dug his heels in when he came over the top and demanded the divorce.

He wanted the house. Barbara relented.

He wanted the RV and boat. Barbara said okay.

She didn't fight him on anything he wanted to keep. The only thing she said was, *"If you want it, you get the debt."* Quinn was so angry at how she had been after him about money that he blindly said he wanted everything.

His attorney did what he was told and went after her. Her attorney clearly communicated she just wanted to be free. Barbara didn't want anything except to walk.

In the end, Quinn won. He got it all, including the debt.

Immediately, he couldn't afford the payments. The little extra money he had in the checking account was soon eaten up with monthly service payments. He worked additional duty when he could, but as a Major Crimes detective, he needed to be available at a moment's notice. Standing guard for a rock concert didn't make sense if he would be called off for a homicide. He was often passed over for the sensitive extra-duty gigs due to the demands of his regular assignment.

He soon skipped the RV, boat, and WaveRunner payments one month. Then he skipped a payment on the timeshare the next month to get caught up on the payments he skipped the previous period. Each month, the skipped payments got a little larger, until he was forced to skip a house payment.

He ignored the calls from his various lenders and paid the next month's payment when it came around, but he remained in the cycle of skipping payments to make ends meet.

Standing in the kitchen, he knew he should have stopped the cycle and sold something, maybe everything. In fact, at this moment, he wished he had sold everything and started completely over, but he didn't. He'd slowly drowned, dog-paddling in debt, skipping a payment here and there, then skipping others to make up for it. Then he had to skip a second house payment to get everything caught back up. He was two house payments behind with no savings. He had stopped contributing to his retirement account years ago. Besides, he'd already raided it when they wanted to buy the house; there was almost nothing left.

Letters soon arrived from his home lender, but he threw them away, unopened. He knew what they would say, and he didn't want to face the truth. He was embarrassed. More than that, he was afraid. Everything that he'd worked for and purchased had become an albatross around his neck, but he couldn't see a way to remove it.

If the upper administration at the police department found out how bad his finances were, he would be reprimanded. They would argue that it could subject him to potential influence from criminal elements. He knew he wouldn't compromise his integrity to help himself financially, but he was in way over his head.

Quinn stared at the heading of the paper. *Notice of Foreclosure Proceedings.*

Maybe Barbara was right. She had compared him to an alcoholic or someone with a gambling addiction. His lips twisted into a sneer, and he yelled.

Quinn crumpled the foreclosure notice and threw it into another room.

# FRIDAY

## Chapter 24

Quinn called into the department early and left a message for Lieutenant Brand that he needed a couple of hours off that morning. He promised he would be in later.

He'd spent the night reading *In Frugal We Trust* and then jumped over to Kirby Willis's website. The more he learned of Kirby's story, the more he realized he needed to talk to someone about his situation.

Quinn admitted to himself that he liked the guy and maybe opening up about his problems might help.

He called Kirby's phone, but he didn't answer. He figured he might be working on his apartment building. Suddenly, time felt precious, and he needed to act now.

Quinn drove to Kirby's apartment in his truck, a late-model Dodge Ram with several years of payments remaining, even though he was now behind one month. He thought about those truck payments as he drove.

When he arrived at Kirby's building, he pulled to the curb behind a motorcycle. As he walked to the front door, he turned and looked back at the bike. It looked familiar, but he shook it off and continued, excited to talk with Kirby.

He knocked on the door to the basement apartment. When he didn't hear movement immediately, he knocked a second time.

"Coming," he heard a yell from inside. A moment later, Kirby opened the door. He wore shorts and a T-shirt. "Detective?"

"Hey."

"You okay, Detective?"

"Can I come inside? I need your advice." Quinn stepped by him without waiting for a reply.

"Uh, wait."

"Is something wrong?" Quinn asked, once inside. "Want me to come back?"

"Well—"

"I'm in deep trouble."

"What do you mean?"

Quinn opened his mouth to speak, but he didn't know how to start. He stared at Kirby, his mouth still open.

"It's okay, Detective. What's going on?"

"I'm screwed," Quinn blurted. "I mean, really screwed. The bank is getting ready to foreclose on my house. The credit card companies have cut me off. I have no idea what I've done to my finances. I should be getting ready for retirement, but I'm going to be working security into my eighties if I don't get my act together."

Kirby held up his hands. "Maybe you should stop talking."

Quinn walked around in circles, his hands on his head. "I'm losing my mind, Kirby. I don't have anyone I can talk to about this. I read your blog last night, almost every article."

"I'm flattered," Kirby said, "but you really should stop talking."

"I want to bounce some things off you. Maybe get some clarity and then figure out how I can handle this."

"Please, Detective—"

"I don't have any friends that understand this stuff, and they'd judge me for screwing up so badly. I'd talk with my partner, but she wouldn't understand."

"Detective!" Kirby yelled.

"What?" Quinn said, lifting his head and focusing on Kirby.

"I wouldn't understand?" a woman's voice said behind Quinn. He spun around to see Marci standing in the doorway of Kirby's bedroom. She was putting on her leather jacket. "Why wouldn't I?"

"Marci?"

"Because I'm a woman? Or because I don't understand money?"

"What are you...?" Quinn said softly, looking from Marci to Kirby back to Marci.

"What's it to you?" she said.

"He's a witness."

"So? You're here asking for financial advice."

"It's not the same thing," Quinn said.

Marci walked by her partner, shaking her head. She stopped in front of Kirby. "Tonight?"

Kirby smiled.

Marci kissed him on the cheek and left without another word.

Quinn stared at Kirby before saying, "Why didn't you warn me?"

"I tried."

Quinn muttered, "Shit," and hurried out of Kirby's apartment.

# Chapter 25

"I thought you weren't going to be in this morning," Lieutenant Brand said.

"I changed my mind," Quinn said, not looking up from his computer.

"I was disappointed when I got that message. My impression of you is back in the favorable column now that you're here. Where's your partner?"

"No idea. I'm not her keeper."

"Are you two having a problem?"

"We're fine."

"Doesn't sound like it."

Marci walked into the office and tossed her keys onto her desk.

"Burkett," Lieutenant Brand said. "You're late today."

"I'm not late. I signed in with radio while driving in."

Quinn snickered lightly.

"What's your problem, Delaney?" Marci said.

"Yeah, Delaney, what's the problem?" the lieutenant echoed.

Quinn threw up his hands. "I've got no problem."

"Do you two need counseling?" Brand asked. "Do I need to have you in my office to work out whatever is going on here?"

Both detectives looked at the lieutenant and simultaneously said, "No!"

"Fine. Take care of your business and get refocused on this case. I'd like to have it resolved soon."

Lieutenant Brand turned and walked away.

"Where do you get off being mad at me?" Marci whispered and pointed a finger at him.

Quinn leaned back in his chair. "Are you kidding me?"

"My personal life is my own."

"What if he ends up being our suspect?" Quinn whispered.

"He won't."

"What if he is?"

"And you're going to him for financial advice? How fucked up are your finances, Quinn?" Her voice raised due to her anger.

"Keep your voice down, Marci," Quinn whispered, his face reddening.

"Seriously. Are you going to get jammed up on this?"

Quinn stood and walked away. Marci watched him until Quinn waved for her to follow.

They walked outside to a private area near the courthouse.

Quinn said, "I didn't mean for you to hear that."

"No shit, partner. I figured that."

"Quit being hostile, Marci."

"You haven't seen hostile yet."

Her eyes challenged him. Quinn looked away for several seconds before his eyes settled back on her.

"My finances are a disaster. They were a mess before the divorce with Barbara, and they've only gotten worse. I'm behind in my house payments. My truck. Everything. They just cut off my last credit card."

Marci stared at him.

"I'm screwed, Marci."

"How? We make a great living. We've got fantastic benefits."

Quinn ran his fingers through his hair. "I don't know. I thought everything was okay, and then suddenly it wasn't, and I don't know how to get out."

"Why didn't you get help?"

"I figured I could handle it. I'm a smart guy. At least, I think I am."

"This doesn't sound very smart."

Quinn closed his eyes.

"I'm sorry, Quinn," Marci said, touching his upper arm. "I didn't mean for it to sound that way. I'm your friend. I'm trying to point out what you've been doing isn't smart. It's the exact opposite of that. We can figure this out."

"We don't need to do anything. I will do it."

Marci dropped her hand. "Your macho bullshit isn't going to get you out of this problem."

"I know, Marci, but you helping me isn't going to work."

"Why not?"

"Because you're my partner, and I don't need you knowing my business."

"Well, that's nice. You were willing to tell Kirby your business."

"So what? You showed Kirby your business."

Her hand whipped out so fast that Quinn didn't see it. He only felt the slap across his face.

"Shit!"

"Don't talk about me like that."

"If you were a man, I'd punch you for that."

"If I were a man, you wouldn't have said that to me."

They stared at each other for a moment before Quinn asked, "Why did it… how did it… I mean, what were you thinking?"

"Seriously? He's cute, and he's not afraid of me. Mostly, he doesn't judge me."

"I don't judge you."

Marci's eyes softened. "Quinn, you're one of the worst."

Quinn tilted his head.

"You think I'm a buzz saw, which is cool, but you don't understand I'm still a woman. There are still certain things I want out of life. You never pay attention to the things I say."

He thought for a moment. "Are you saying you're attracted to me? Is that it? Did I miss something?"

"Sometimes you're a moron," she said and walked away, leaving him standing alone in the courtyard.

\*\*\*

Back at his desk, Quinn found a folder with a yellow sticky note on it waiting for him.

The note read, *Sorry for the delay. I think this is your guy—Debbie.*

Quinn opened the folder and found several pages of data for Michael Alan Smith. Thirty-nine years old.

He had been arrested for possession and distribution of methamphetamine. He spent almost three years in prison and was released eighteen months ago. He wasn't on probation or parole. He'd served his entire time and was not currently under Department of Corrections supervision.

There was no current address on file. They may not have had a way to find Michael Smith, but at least they knew who he was.

# Chapter 26

Kirby rode his bike to Vessel Coffee House. He brought a small notebook in his backpack, along with his tablet.

After he ordered an iced mocha, he sat at a table to make general notes. Occasionally, he did this to let the creativity flow. He would generate business ideas, story concepts for his blog, or to-do lists. Everything was on the table.

Kirby flipped back and forth between pages as new article concepts popped up among his list of chores around his apartment building. He also came up with several maintenance items related to his blog. Surprisingly, the website required more upkeep than people realized.

While he made notes, he started a separate list, one named Jacob. Soon he was listing everything he knew about Jacob's death, from what he learned on his own and what Quinn and Marci had told him.

Marci, he thought and smiled. He shook his head and refocused on his list of what he learned of Jacob.

What was he missing?

What was everyone missing?

As cars passed by on Monroe Street, Kirby's mind soon touched at a concept slightly out of reach. He could sense it was there but couldn't understand what he was missing. When a newer Lexus pulled up in front of the coffee shop and parked, his mind keyed in on the concept.

Kirby wrote one word on his list and closed his book. He took a final sip of his mocha and tossed the empty cup away. It took only minutes for Kirby to pedal home.

***

Kirby pulled his Toyota to the curb outside Jacob's apartment building.

He walked to the back of the building and looked at the spot marked #4. There was no car parked there.

Kirby hurried inside and walked up the steps to the building. The police tape still crossed the door to Jacob's apartment.

He walked to the opposite apartment and knocked.

Fonda Shay opened the door, wearing her usual frayed denim shorts, a bikini top, and red heart-shaped sunglasses. The smell of marijuana was thick in her apartment. "Strawberry Fields Forever" played in the background.

"Hey, Kirby Kirby Willis," she said, her words slow and labored. "I missed you."

"What happened to Jacob's car?" he said quickly.

"Whoa," she said, pulling back from him. "Why so aggressive?"

"Sorry."

"Is okay," she slurred. "Like you." Fonda turned and stumbled back to her couch. She fell into it before righting herself. The rose-colored glasses sat cockeyed on her face, but she didn't notice. "Didja come for me?"

"Huh?"

"Are you here to make it with me?"

The way the glasses sat on her face disturbed Kirby, so he reached out to reset them. Fonda gently put her hands on his wrists.

"I'm not going to do anything with you, Fonda."

She made a pouty face. "Am I not pretty?"

"You're very pretty," Kirby said. "What happened to Jacob's car?"

"Let's do it, and I'll tell you," she said, her eyes drooping behind the rose-colored lenses.

"I won't do that."

"Then leave!" she said with a flick of the wrist.

Kirby studied her for a moment before starting for the door.

"Wait." Her voice was now small. "Please."

Kirby watched her.

"If I tell you," Fonda said, then took several shallow breaths through her nose, "will you sit for a while? I don't want to be alone."

Kirby slowly walked back to the couch and sat next to her. She slid her hand into his.

"They took it," she said.

"Who took it? The police?"

Fonda rested her head on Kirby's shoulder.

"Who took his car, Fonda?" he whispered. "It's important."

"Tow truck."

"Was it broken?"

She smiled dreamily.

"What happened?"

Fonda started to fall asleep, so Kirby shook her.

Kirby shook her slightly. "What happened to Jacob's car?"

"The bank took it."

"What?"

Before she fell asleep, Fonda said softly, "He wasn't good to me."

* * *

Kirby fell asleep, too. They both remained there for some time with her head on his shoulder. When he awoke, "Lucy in the Sky with Diamonds" was softly playing. A mix of Beatles music was on rotation from somewhere in the apartment.

Before falling asleep, his mind raced at the news the bank had taken Jacob's car. *How could that be?*

Jacob had paid for the car with cash.

After a bit, Kirby realized he only had Jacob's word for it.

Just as he only had Fonda's word that the car had gone to the bank, and she was clearly under the influence of drugs. He could have slipped out when she fell asleep, but he wanted to talk with her while she was lucid.

When his mind cleared from sleep, he checked his watch. He'd been on the couch for a couple of hours, in and out of sleep most of the time. Fonda stirred and turned to look at him. She blinked several times, trying to understand who he was.

She pushed herself upright and looked around. She patted herself, realizing she was still wearing clothes.

"What happened?"

"You asked me to sit with you."

"And you did?"

"Yes."

She put her hand against his cheek. "You're sweet." Fonda climbed off the couch and stretched. "Did we do anything?"

"No," Kirby said.

"Why not?"

"It wasn't appropriate."

A disbelieving smile slowly formed on Fonda's lips. "You didn't want to take advantage of me?"

"Something like that."

"Geez, you really are sweet." Fonda studied him before asking, "How about now? We can roll around for a bit. Might be fun."

"I've got a girlfriend," Kirby said. Marci wasn't his girlfriend, but it didn't hurt to say so at this moment.

"You're too good to be true," she said with a dismissive wave of the hand. She wandered into the kitchen. A moment later, she returned with a bong and lighter.

"Wait," Kirby said and jumped off the couch. "Before you do that. Tell me what happened to Jacob's car."

She stared at him for a moment. "Right. That's why you came by earlier. I remember. The bank repoed it. That's what he said. He came in one day and asked for a ride. I asked him where his car was, and he said the bank repossessed it." She snapped her fingers. "Just like that, and it was gone."

"Why?"

"What do you mean 'why?'"

"I mean why. Jacob told me he paid for the car with cash."

Fonda's faced scrunched in disbelief. "Jacob didn't have any money."

"Jacob had a lot of money," Kirby said.

She laughed. "No, he didn't. He was always over here, trying to borrow money from me."

Kirby looked around. "Where do you get your money from?"

"My dad," she said. "He fronts for me. He doesn't want me living at home, so he pays for my living expenses. It's a pretty sweet deal."

"Before you fell asleep, you said Jacob wasn't good to you. What did you mean?"

Sadness crossed over Fonda's face.

"If you don't want to talk about it, you don't have to," Kirby said.

Fonda glanced at the bong and lighter in her hands before saying, "When I wouldn't give him money, he'd get rough with me. He wouldn't hit me, but he called me names." Fonda stared at Kirby. "Mean and nasty things I bet you'd never call a woman."

Kirby's mouth fell open slightly. "That doesn't sound like Jacob."

"Your friend wasn't a very nice person."

"But you said you guys were together occasionally."

"What can I say? I guess my nice-guy picker is broken."

She lifted the bong to her mouth, but Kirby stopped her from using it. "You might get a nice guy if you didn't do this."

Fonda pulled her hand free from Kirby. "I should have clarified. I want a nice guy *who smokes*."

She continued to light up while Kirby walked out.

***

"Whozzit?"

"It's Kirby."

The magnetic lock released with a buzz, and Kirby pulled open the door. He ran up the flight of stairs to Holly Reese's apartment. She had the door open, waiting for him.

"I've seen you more this week than I did in high school," she said.

"Was Jacob broke?"

"Well, hello to you, too."

"Sorry," Kirby said, walking deeper into Holly's loft.

Holly shut the door and followed him inside. "Was Jacob broke?" she repeated thoughtfully. After a moment, she shrugged. "I don't think so. Why do you ask?"

"Jacob's car wasn't at his apartment complex, so I asked a neighbor of his where it might be. She told me it had been repossessed. She said he was always asking her for money."

Holly briefly frowned. "The last part sounds true."

"I don't understand."

"Remember how I said he always wanted me to pay for things, but then judged me for spending? There were several times he asked for a loan until a check arrived. I never thought much about it."

"He was supposed to be making more than seven thousand a month from his website."

"Really?"

"Yes, really. He also told me he was doing well selling real estate."

"I don't know."

"This doesn't make any sense."

Kirby stood with his hands in his pockets, thinking. Finally, he noticed Holly watching him. "What?"

"You look different," she said.

"Something on my face?"

"No."

"Same guy."

"Huh."

Kirby headed for the door.

Holly called out to him. "Hey, Kirb."

He stopped and turned back. "Yeah?"

"About that dinner."

"Dinner?"

"I mean, if you still want to, that is."

"I'm sorry. I can't."

Holly stared at him.

"I met someone," he said and left without another word.

***

At home, Kirby Skyped his fellow blogger Luke, from *How Now Cash Cow?*

"What's up, buddy?" Luke asked after his image appeared on his laptop.

"You called Jacob a poser the last time we talked."

"Yeah," he said, "I'm sorry. I shouldn't have done that. He was your friend and—"

"Why? Why was he a poser?"

"You knew him. Didn't you see it?"

Kirby thought about it before shaking his head.

"Something wasn't right, Kirby. He was like those guys in college. Those who joined a cause or changed their looks to get a girl but couldn't change who they were inside."

"The boyfriend chameleons," Kirby supplied.

Luke smiled. "Exactly. The boyfriend chameleons. Anyway, that's the way it felt when I met Jacob. It always felt like he was acting. His site was flawless, and his content was way better than it should have been. I envied him for it but, in person, he wasn't right. I felt it at FinCon, and I saw it at that meet-up in Portland a couple of months ago. Tell me you saw it."

Kirby shrugged his shoulders. "I didn't. If he was a fake, I missed it."

Luke said, "It's okay, buddy. If you didn't see it, it's because you're a trusting soul. If he turns out to be what was advertised, then it's because I'm jealous of his quick success. Either way, you're on the side of good."

Kirby lowered his eyes as he thought.

"Hey, Kirb?"

"Yeah?"

"Did you ever take that picture? You know, the one of the police tape?"

"I couldn't. It didn't seem right."

Luke nodded, disappointment on his face. "Don't worry about it, man."

# Chapter 27

"I don't know how I got to this point," Quinn said.

He was sitting at Kirby's kitchen table, a glass of water in his hand. Kirby sat across from him.

"It's fairly simple."

"What do you mean?"

"You weren't paying attention."

He was taken aback by Kirby's frankness. "But I *was* paying attention," he said, weakly.

"Quinn, you came to talk to me about money, which is my favorite subject. The problem with talking about money is that people have so many emotions wrapped up in the subject. Right now, for example, I just heard defensiveness. Usually, there is also guilt and embarrassment mixed in there as well." He held up his hands and wriggled his fingers. "But you have to let it all go. You are where you are, and this is your new starting point."

Quinn felt foolish listening to the younger man. He should be the one offering financial advice. His age dictated that. Age should have made him wiser.

"As I was saying," Kirby prompted, "you weren't paying attention."

"What do you mean?"

"Answer just one simple question for me. It's a question I already know the answer to."

Quinn smiled. "That's an interview technique. It's how we set up suspects."

"I'm not setting you up. I'm helping you learn."

"Okay."

"My question is this, and it's simple: Do you have a budget?"

Quinn sipped his coffee, looked slightly away, and said nothing.

"That would be no. Most people don't. The good news is living without a budget isn't fatal, but you have to know some other things."

"Which are?"

"We're getting to that. Second question. What's your monthly savings rate?"

"What?"

"How much do you save from each paycheck?"

Quinn shrugged.

"Are you saving in an employer-sponsored retirement program? I imagine you have a pension."

Quinn shifted in his seat. "I was saving to it, but then cash got tight, and I pulled my money from it."

"Are you saving anything now?"

Quinn shook his head.

"Final question: What is your burn rate?"

"My what?"

"Burn rate is your negative cash flow. In other words, how much money do you spend every month beyond how much you make? This deals with going further into the hole. I know you use credit cards, we've discussed it. If you're paying off the credit cards every month, then you're at zero. No problem. However, if you're digging that hole deeper every month..."

"I have no idea," Quinn said, the realization settling in that he had no understanding of his own money.

Kirby sipped his water, watching Quinn.

"Do *you* know the answers to those questions?" Quinn asked.

Kirby left the table for a moment and returned with his iPad. A few taps of the screen and a budget application appeared. "This is what I use to track my monthly income versus expenses. Everything is broken down into categories."

"How much time does it take to do this?"

"At first, it took a while, and it took discipline, but once I set it up, it was just a matter of inputting the data and tracking it. It's like riding a bike. You have to learn the skill and then practice it. After a bit, it comes naturally."

"Do you ever go off-budget?"

Kirby laughed. "Like riding a bike, you fall off. But you get back on and start peddling again."

"How did you learn how to do this?" Quinn pointed at the iPad.

"It's easy. It just takes time working with the program—"

"No. I mean the personal finance thing."

"Oh."

"Did you learn it in college?"

"College doesn't teach you how to be an entrepreneur. There's a great quote from Jim Rohn, a motivational speaker who mentored Tony Robbins. Do you know who Tony Robbins is?"

Quinn nodded, glad to finally know an answer to one of Kirby's questions.

"Well, what Rohn said was, 'Formal education will make you a living; self-education will make you a fortune.' College is important, to a point. Too many people believe once they get done with their formal education, they're done with education for good. That's horrible thinking. My real education started after college with the books I found and the mentors I sought out. If a guy like Tony Robbins has a mentor, why shouldn't I? The guy who sold me this building was a big one. He was an elderly investor who wanted to help me understand the game."

"How *did* you buy this?" Quinn asked, waving his hand above his head to indicate the apartment building. He wanted to address the lingering questions he'd had from their first encounter at the property.

"I bought it with a bank loan," Kirby said, "but I didn't have enough for a full down payment. I'd saved up thirty thousand dollars, but I was short the remaining amount. I needed almost a *hundred* thirty thousand for a down payment. I met with the owner, and we hit it off. He toured me through the property and showed me how the various systems worked. His agent and my agent— Paula Fairbanks, you met her—they were very respectful. They saw how we got along and stayed out of our discussion.

"The seller got another offer within a day of mine. My offer was full price but needed him to carry a secondary note for the remaining down payment. The other group jammed him on the price, and they never toured the property, but they didn't need him to carry a contract. He could see what kind of buyers they were from how they made their offer.

"The building had been his baby for a lot of years, and he took great pride in it. The fact that I walked the property with him and took a special interest in it meant a lot. He also liked the fact that I was going to live in the property and take care of it.

"He accepted my offer and carried the second note with low interest for five years. It comes due in two years. By then, I will have put aside enough to pay him off fully."

"He really agreed to that? That seems, well, crazy."

"Why? He wanted to sell the building to someone who would care for it as he did. I explained who I was, where I was going, and what I wanted to do with the building. The answer will always be no unless you ask."

Quinn finished his water, and Kirby got up to get him a refill.

"What do I do now?" Quinn asked.

"I don't know your situation," Kirby said, returning to the table. "Do you?"

"What do you mean?"

"How many outstanding loans do you have?"

"My house and truck."

"Okay."

"I've got a boat, an RV, and a WaveRunner, too."

Kirby smiled.

"What?"

"You just told me you have loans on four depreciating assets. Truck, RV, boat, and WaveRunner."

"What else?"

Quinn stared into his glass. "I have a vacation property, too."

"Like a vacation home?"

"A timeshare. It's a timeshare," Quinn said.

"Do you just buy everything someone tries to sell you?"

Quinn leaned back with a look of defensiveness and crossed his arms over his chest. "I wanted to have a good life and be ready for retirement."

"You already told me you aren't ready for retirement. Are you having a good life?"

Quinn slowly shook his head.

"Too many people equate owning stuff with having a good life. I've never seen that be the case."

Quinn lowered his eyes.

"How many credit cards do you have, Quinn?"

"Three."

"What's the highest limit?"

"Twelve thousand."

"You told me you were cut off."

"They're all maxed."

Kirby said, "You're in your mid-forties, right?"

Quinn nodded.

"I can tell you exactly how you got into this situation."

Quinn sipped his water, an uneasy feeling growing inside him. He had just revealed his entire financial picture to someone for the first time.

"Minimum payments."

Quinn didn't respond, so Kirby continued.

"Albert Einstein said the power of compounding interest is the most powerful force in the universe. You've made the minimum payments for so long that the power of compounding interest finally crushed you."

"What can I do?"

"What do you want to do?"

"You sound like a therapist."

Kirby smiled. "This only works if you want it to work. You have two choices. Either you continue to live the way you do and lose everything, or you fight back, which is hard and uncomfortable. One way you control your destiny. The other way you give up your power. It's up to you."

"I won't like how I feel either way."

"Right now, it probably doesn't feel too good, but when you start tackling your debt and you face your fears, it will be an amazing feeling. Trust me. You'll start to feel some relief, you'll breathe a little easier, and you might even have fun with it."

Quinn rubbed his face.

"If you want my help, I'm here for you."

"Can we keep it confidential? I mean, I don't want Marci to know how bad I am."

"Your finances will be between us."

Quinn watched the younger man for a moment before he asked, "What is it with you and Marci, anyway?"

"What do you mean?"

"I've never known her to go for anyone before."

Kirby tilted his head. "How do you mean?"

"She's never really talked about a guy before. I mean, she's dated, but it usually takes a long time before she likes someone. Then you walk into her life, and suddenly the world makes no sense. I don't understand how she changed because of you."

"She didn't change; she's still Marci." Kirby smiled. "Why do you try to define her to be what you want?"

"What?"

"There was this show called *Life* that I binged on Netflix before I canceled the service. It was eating up too much of my time. Anyway, it was a great show about a former cop who gets imprisoned and then gets out. Ever see it?"

Quinn shook his head.

"Anyway, while this guy was in prison, he studied Zen. It was the thing that kept him together while inside. It fundamentally changed how he thought. During an episode, he said one of the best quotes about life I've ever heard, and I think about it frequently. 'You don't have to understand here to be here.'"

"And this applies to Marci, how?"

"Let Marci be Marci. Celebrate her for who she is. Don't put her in a box that your perceptions have created."

Quinn stared into his cup and thought.

Kirby let him be for a few moments, then asked, "Can I switch gears to Jacob?"

The detective nodded, still staring into his cup.

"I think there was something else going on. Something I didn't see."

Quinn looked up, his eyes refocusing. "What's that? What didn't you see?"

"I think he might have had money problems."

Quinn's brow furrowed. "But his website... He was a money expert."

"I know. I was thinking about his car..."

"The apartment manager said he no longer had a car. That he had given it up."

"He had a car. A Lexus."

"Doesn't that go against what he was blogging about?"

"It was used, and I thought he paid cash for it. Just because you're into personal finance doesn't mean you can't have nice things."

"So, where's his car?"

"Fonda Shay told me it was repossessed. She also told me he used to ask her for money."

Quinn took a moment to think about that. "Do you believe her? She's a bit of a flake."

"It was close to the same thing Holly said."

"The painter?"

Kirby nodded. "She said Jacob also asked her for money. You've talked with her. She's no flake."

"No, she's not."

"I called a fellow blogger who knows Jacob through our circles. He's called him a poser for quite a while. I didn't see it because he was my friend and I looked up to him. I believed him. I was doing to him what you were doing to Marci. I was painting him in a positive light and couldn't see things for what they really were. I still don't know how to get to the truth of who Jacob was, but it's there somewhere."

"I'll look into it," Quinn told him. "That's good info. Now let me ask you something about Jacob. Did he ever mention a guy named Michael Smith?"

Kirby thought about the name for a moment, then said, "No. Why?"

"He was Jacob's partner in the LLC that was buying the property up north. I want to talk with him."

"Sorry, I wish I had heard of him." Kirby looked at the clock on the wall. "If you want to get together this weekend to talk about this further, I'll make myself available. I'll give whatever advice I can."

"I'd appreciate it."

"But I have to ask you to go now."

Quinn's eyebrows raised.

"Marci's coming over for dinner tonight, and there are several things I need to do before that happens."

"I'll see myself out."

# Chapter 28

Quinn drove back to the station. Marci wasn't there. He checked the system, and she had logged off while he was visiting with Kirby. He was going to have to mend that fence.

Meanwhile, he considered the new information Kirby had supplied. Jacob had a car, a Lexus that may have been repossessed. He needed to find it. The computer they had retrieved from his apartment didn't have any personal information on it, so that was no help. He could call every bank in town and still not find out if Jacob had an account there. A teller may not willingly give him that information. Besides, with the advent of online banking, Jacob's bank could be anywhere.

Quinn thought about it for a moment. Where to start finding personal information, specifically? *Go back to the beginning*, he thought.

It took him a moment to find the phone number. She answered on the third ring.

"Hello?"

"Rosanna Tombs?"

"Yes, who is this?"

"Detective Quinn Delaney. We met recently following the death of Jacob Kidwell."

"Oh, yes, Detective. How may I help you?"

"Did Jacob pay his rent by check?"

"Mostly."

"Mostly? What's that mean?"

"When he was on time, he paid by check. It was one of those online checks, the ones that come through the bank. Do you know what I mean? For those months when he was behind, he'd sometimes pay by cash. But mostly, I'd say he paid with a check."

"What was the name of the bank on the check?"

"Let me look quick. I'm doing some paperwork right now, as it happens. PacWest Credit Union."

Quinn sighed.

"Is there a problem?"

"No, no problem. Hey, I heard that Jacob's car was recently repossessed. You told me he gave it up willingly. Were you trying to be nice and save him some embarrassment?"

"Oh, no. He told me he sold his car. Jacob was a very smart young man, and I can't imagine him getting into any sort of trouble where he'd lose it. He was very proud of that car, Detective. He hand washed it every week. He once called it his baby to me. It seems like he wouldn't let something like that get repossessed, but who knows in this world anymore? Up is down, am I right?"

***

It was shortly before closing when Quinn walked into the South Hill branch of PacWest Credit Union. He saw her in the far office and walked back without checking in at the reception desk. Nobody stopped him due to the badge and gun on his belt.

Barbara Delaney focused on her computer screen, not noticing Quinn's approach. It wasn't until he was in her doorway that she turned and looked at him.

"Hey, Babs."

She smiled and leaned back in her chair. "To what do I owe this visit? There've been no social visits since D-Day. Is this *our* business or *police* business?"

Quinn half shrugged. "Police business."

Her smile remained, but the humor in her eyes faded. "Of course."

Quinn stepped into her office and sat in one of the uncomfortable steel and fabric chairs. "I'm working a homicide, and the victim had a bank account with PacWest."

Barbara's smile wholly faded. "If it's that important, you should do a warrant and pull the records you need."

"I know, but it's late Friday afternoon. I figured I could talk with you and find out if it's worth spending time on the paper."

"You want me to look up someone's personal information and tell you what I see? That's a violation of bank policy, not to mention federal regulations. You better give me something better than 'it's late Friday afternoon.'"

"I'm going to lose the house, Babs."

Her mouth opened and closed several times as she seemed to search for the appropriate thing to say. Finally, she said, "I'm sorry."

"It's my fault. I'm seeing that now. Nothing registered before. It's all hitting home. No pun intended."

"I didn't think you'd be joking about it, Quinn."

"I played by the rules, you know? I worked hard and paid my bills on time until a time came when I couldn't. Everything should have worked out in the end."

"Those aren't the rules for success, though," Barbara said. "That's how to scrape by."

Quinn grabbed the steel rails of his chair. "I heard that earlier today from a guy not even thirty years old. He's figured it out. *You* figured it out."

Barbara laughed. "You think I've figured it out? Geez, thank you for believing in me. I need that vote of confidence because I'm still learning every day. I'm trying to make up for a lifetime of bad choices. One of the toughest decisions I ever made was leaving you."

Quinn lifted his eyes to her. "It was that bad?"

"In a way, yeah. A husband and wife should work together to achieve success. If they're at odds, they'll never accomplish anything. It was clear you didn't want to change. I could remain with you and go down with the ship, or I could jump and swim for freedom. You know what I did. It wasn't easy, and it hurt like hell, but I don't regret the choice. I miss you, but I don't miss how we behaved. Not for a minute. In the time we've been divorced, I've already saved more than the two of us ever had combined."

Quinn looked away, fighting back the tears that surprised him.

"I didn't say that to be mean, Quinn. I said that to show you the power of change."

He smiled at his ex-wife, his eyes wet. "I know. You never were mean in the whole process. I was the one who made it that way."

"Just because change is powerful doesn't mean it isn't painful."

Quinn's eyes flicked to the clock on the wall; it was almost closing time for the branch. "Listen, the reason I came, the guy who was killed was a financial blogger."

Barbara's eyes lit up. "Really?"

"Yeah. Why? Do you read them?"

Barbara nodded. "A lot of them, actually."

"The guy's online persona was Frugal McDougal."

"Oh. I've read some of his stuff. He's too arrogant for my tastes, but he has a following. Good for him, I guess. Wait, he's dead? Sorry, I guess there's no good for him coming out of this. He lived in town, though?"

"Yeah. Browne's Addition."

"Small world."

"Anyway, I can't figure the guy out. He was supposed to be this successful blogger with a real estate career on the side. However, it sounds like his car may have been repossessed, and he might have been bumming money from girls he knew."

"He was perpetrating a fraud then, like we used to say back in college?"

Quinn smiled. "Kinda, but I'm not exactly sure yet."

"What's his name? His real name?"

"Jacob Kidwell."

Barbara typed his name into her computer. She gnawed on her lip while she read. Quinn smiled at that effect, as Barbara did it when she was deep in thought. Finally, she spoke while her eyes followed what was on the screen. "Well, he's got three accounts with us—a checking account, a savings account, and a money market account. The checking account has about five hundred in it. The savings account has just over three thousand."

Quinn didn't say anything. He was embarrassed; even though Jacob Kidwell's amount of money in those two accounts was incredibly low, it was more than he currently had in liquid assets.

"The money market account has nearly three hundred seventy-eight thousand dollars in it."

Quinn leaned forward. "What?"

Barbara nodded. "There have been fairly regular deposits every month for the past couple of years. Most of them appear to be transfers out of his checking account. Nothing that seems outrageous. Amounts as small as twenty-five hundred up to ten thousand."

"If a guy has that much money," Quinn said, "why would he bum money off his friends?"

"And why would he let his car be repossessed?" Barbara asked.

# SATURDAY/SUNDAY

## Chapter 29

Kirby woke with a start. He lay quietly in the morning sun that shone through the window. He rolled over and saw the bed empty next to him. Feeling disappointed, he pushed himself upright.

He pulled on a pair of shorts and a T-shirt before shuffling into the living room, wiping the sleep from his eyes as he went. Kirby suddenly stopped when he saw her.

She was on the floor, in her bra and panties, stretching. Marci turned her head and smiled. She let out a final breath and relaxed, straightening.

"I thought you were going to sleep all day. I had to get up and get moving."

He grinned at her. "I was tired. Long night."

Marci stood and walked over to Kirby. She kissed him lightly, then smacked him on the butt as she went into the bedroom.

Kirby walked into the kitchen. He prepared a pot of coffee and returned to the bedroom. Marci had put on the light dress from the previous evening and was fastening the straps on her sandals.

"Are you leaving?"

"In a bit, yeah," Marci said.

She stood, grabbed her purse, and walked into the bathroom. Kirby left her and went back to the kitchen. As soon as enough coffee had dripped, he poured himself a cup and added some creamer.

He opened his book and read. Shortly, Marci walked into the living room.

"As beautiful as last night," he said.

"Trying to get lucky before I go?" She pointed at the cup of coffee. "Got one of those for me?"

Kirby stood and pulled a cup from the cupboard. He poured her some coffee and handed her the creamer.

"I received a text message from Quinn last night," Marci said before sipping her coffee. "Your friend Jacob had a chunk of change in the bank."

"How much?"

She eyed him. "A savings account with mid-six figures."

"Really?"

Marci shrugged. "That's what he said. There wasn't much more in his text. I'll learn more after I talk with him."

"Huh."

"What are you thinking?"

"I expected him to have money like that. Supposedly, he was saving most everything he had and generating a fair amount of money from his blog. That's not including the commissions he made from selling real estate. Jacob never really told me how much money he had, but I suspected a sizeable savings. Although, I'm wondering why he kept that much money in a savings account. It should be in an investment account. Maybe he pulled it out and was getting ready to roll it into the real estate deal. That would make sense. Otherwise, it's kind of stupid to leave that much money in a bank earning so little interest."

"After his death, the things you've been hearing make you question your friend?"

"Yeah. It seems he may not have been the friend or person, I thought. Supposedly, his car was repossessed. He was bumming money from a former girlfriend when they were together and a neighbor whenever it was convenient. He was verbally abusive with his neighbor when she'd say no, which I just can't get my head around."

"Maybe he was just an angry tightwad."

Kirby sipped his coffee. "I guess. There have been stories about people who live such a pauper existence that they become very wealthy. They go to the extreme end of the spectrum, like reusing paper towels, that sort of thing."

Marci crinkled her nose. "That's gross."

Kirby laughed. "I agree. Reusing paper towels is too far, but I wonder if that's what Jacob was doing. I wonder if he had started to develop some of those weird behaviors, some idiosyncrasies, to try to save more."

"Did you see his apartment?"

"Many times."

"The guy hardly had any food in it. There was barely enough in there to survive."

"But he bought a used Lexus. He paid cash for it, at least that's what he told me. That doesn't seem like far-end, pauper behavior does it?"

"No," Marci said. "Do you think he had a new girlfriend?"

"I was wondering about that. I think I would have known, but Jacob has turned out to be a lot more secretive than I thought."

Marci watched him, then said, "Maybe you two were growing apart."

"What do you mean?"

"It happens, you know? You have your life, and he has his. He starts getting involved in new things while you're involved in yours. Before long, you still have some mutual interests, but they seem to be less and less."

Kirby thought about it for a moment. "Not like this. We had very specific interests that overlapped: personal finance, blogging, real estate. We talked a lot about those subjects. Jacob loved being the subject matter expert on personal finance and blogging. I think it bothered him a bit that I owned this apartment building, and he hadn't invested in any real estate yet. However, he worked in the industry and had some decent insights on things. We talked a lot. For a while, I knew everything, even about his relationship with Holly Reese, my dream girl from high school. It used to bother me when he talked about her, but I never said anything to him. We were friends, and we shared that kind of information. However, it's clear now he wasn't sharing everything over the last few weeks, maybe even months."

Marci's eyebrows raised. "Holly Reese was your dream girl?"

Kirby sipped his coffee as he watched the woman across from him.

"Don't mess with me, Willis. I'll choke it out of you."

"Are you jealous, Marci?"

"No, but I'm not exactly the same type of woman as Holly Reese, am I?"

"Why does that matter?"

She thought about it. "I guess it shouldn't, but it kind of does. Maybe it's because you called her your dream girl."

"It was high school."

"I don't care. Is she still your dream girl?"

"It was a mirage, a schoolboy fantasy. She was a pretty girl walking the halls who never paid an ounce of attention to me. I had no idea what a relationship was supposed to be. I'm sure you had a high school crush."

"I've never been anyone's dream girl," Marci said.

He looked into her eyes. "I think you're wrong. I'm sure a lot of men think you're their dream girl."

"What about you, Kirby?"

Kirby laughed. "Me? I'm pretty sure I've never been anyone's dream girl."

\*\*\*

After Marci left, Kirby showered and changed. He had a different mission now. He wasn't trying to find Jacob Kidwell's murderer, he was going to rediscover his friend. The only tool he had at his immediate disposal was Jacob's digital footprint.

Kirby spent an hour scouring *In Frugal We Trust* and the associated social media accounts. Jacob never had any personal social media accounts. He said they sucked up too much energy and didn't provide a decent return on his time. Kirby had almost given up on the social media aspect but remembered how Jacob hadn't told him everything recently.

He decided to check Facebook to see if he had a personal account set up. Several minutes of checking resulted in zilch. The same result came back from his search on Twitter. No personal account was found for Jacob Kidwell.

He jumped to Instagram and, within a minute of searching, found an account for JKidwellWA. It wasn't private, so he could see the photographs associated with it. It was definitely Jacob's account, and it looked to have been started in the early weeks of summer. There were photos of Jacob and a blond woman around town and at landmarks. Kirby had never seen her before. She was beautiful, albeit young. From the pictures, he was guessing she was twenty. There were multiple photos of them on a boat at some lake.

Kirby went to his followers and found her. Madison Collingsworth.

She had no followers, and almost all her pictures were of her and Jacob.

\*\*\*

She agreed to meet him at the Starbucks in Liberty Lake, a small suburban community east of Spokane that had incorporated less than twenty years ago. Even though its population was less than 8,000, it was growing at a quick rate and was one of the top choices for the area's wealthy. It seemed most people wanted to live in a clean, new community around one of the most beautiful lakes in the region. Who could blame them?

When she walked in, her eyes scanned the coffee shop. Madison Collingsworth wore khaki shorts, a black top, and high-heeled brown sandals. Her blond hair was piled on top of her head.

Kirby raised his hand, and she hurried over. She dropped her oversized purse on the floor. Her eyes were wide with excitement.

"This better be good. I don't appreciate Jake ducking me."

"Jake?"

"He can't treat me like some kind of hoochie and think I will tolerate it," she said with a headshake. "I'm not a girl he can just hit and quit. My friends will kick his ass if he continues to treat me like this."

Kirby studied her closer. Her make-up was applied thick and amateurish.

"Why are you looking at me like that? Are you some sort of creeper? I thought you were one of Jake's boys."

"How old are you?"

"None of your fucking business."

"You were going out with Jacob, right?"

"Yeah, but he didn't go by Jacob." When she said Jacob, she air-quoted it and said it with a gay effect. "He went by Jake. Are you crushing on him or something?"

"He was my friend," Kirby said. "And he's dead."

"What?"

"He's dead." He delivered the fact cold and fast and without the remorse he'd had when he told Holly Reese. "The cops discovered his body earlier in the week. I'm trying to find out why he was killed."

"Oh my God," Madison said. The tears started slowly at first, but soon she was weeping. Kirby stood and walked to the counter to grab several napkins. He returned and gave them to Madison. Several patrons in the coffee shop watched the two of them with interest. As she cried, Kirby vacillated between believing Madison was showing real emotion and the thought she was somehow acting on a bad soap opera.

When she got control of herself, she dabbed at her eyes with a napkin. "This is so terrible. That's why he hasn't called. Oh my God, I loved him so much."

She cried some more, and Kirby waited for her to gain control again. When she did, Kirby asked, "How long have you and Jacob—Jake—been seeing each other?"

Madison shrugged. "Beginning of summer, I guess."

"He never mentioned you."

Madison's eyes hardened. "He never mentioned you, either."

"What did you guys do?"

She raised her eyebrows.

"Besides that."

"We did stuff like everybody else. We hung out, mostly on his friend's boat, went to the park, hung out at the lake. We went to some great parties."

"What boat? He had a friend with a boat?"

Madison looked away. "I dunno. Some guy he met at a party, I guess."

"You don't know the name of the friend."

"No," she said, but Kirby wasn't sure he believed the denial. "Do you know the names of everyone you party with? I mean, if you do, you're not doing it right. Ugh. How boring does that sound?"

The more he listened and studied her, the younger Kirby thought she was. "Where did you meet Jake?"

"At my mom's office. He was there working on a deal with her. We had a couple minutes alone and started talking. He was nice."

"Who is your mom?"

Madison's eyes grew suspicious. "Why should I tell you that? I don't even know you."

Kirby shook his head. "Why does it matter? I'm trying to find out what happened to him. If you truly cared about him, you'd want to help."

Madison studied Kirby for a moment before saying, "My mom is Victoria Hayes."

"Hayes Construction?"

She nodded. "You know her?"

"Just the company," Kirby said. "You don't have her last name."

"It's my father's. She divorced him when I was young. Then she married my dad, who passed away a couple of years ago."

Kirby shook his head. "Wait. I'm confused. Your…"

"My step-dad," Madison clarified. "But I don't call him that. He's my dad. He's the one who was there for me."

Kirby nodded. "I get it. So, what was Jake working on with your mom?"

Madison shrugged. "Some real estate deal. I didn't pay attention to it. Real estate isn't my thing. Music and fashion are."

"Speaking of real estate, did Jacob leave his laptop with you?"

"No, why?"

"Doesn't matter. Did your mom know you two were seeing each other?"

Madison's eyes widened briefly, then quickly narrowed. "Nah. She wouldn't care, though."

Kirby smiled. "I doubt that. How old are you?"

"Why's it matter? He's dead."

"Did Jake know how old you were?"

Madison's eyes brightened and a malicious smile crossed her face. "Of course he did."

***

"I doubt she's eighteen. She's one of those tall girls who looks mature for her age, especially with the help of make-up."

They were seated on the patio of The Blackbird, a gastropub on the edge of downtown's Riverfront Park.

Marci stabbed her salad with her fork and held its contents in mid-air. "Quinn told me about a background picture on the computer we have at the department. Said it was with a blonde we haven't been able to identify. I wonder if that's her?"

"I can tell you if I can see the picture."

"Come by Monday, and I'll show you. And I'm going to repeat it: slow down on messing around in this investigation, okay? I don't want you to get yourself in trouble and—"

"I hear you, I hear you."

"You better, Willis. I'm serious here."

"Can I continue my story?"

Marci stuck the bite of food in her mouth and nodded.

"Well, regardless of her age, the girl is trouble. She said she had friends who would kick Jacob's ass if he was breaking up with her. Could they be the ones who did this?"

Marci finished chewing before she spoke. "More than likely, it's a young girl spouting off. Lots of girls, even boys, will say things to sound tough when they're hurting."

"You're probably right."

"I'm like a radio love doctor, Kirby. Seventh caller, you're on with Dr. Marci. Let me mend your broken heart."

Kirby smiled as he cut into his salad. "Oh, I forgot to tell you the big connection from meeting with her."

Marci stopped mid-chew and watched Kirby.

"Madison's mother is Victoria Hayes. She owns—"

"Hayes Construction," Marci said through a mouthful of food.

"Hayes Construction," Kirby repeated.

When Marci finished chewing, she stared at Kirby.

"What?"

"Dude, you lead with that information. You don't hold it back for some big dinner reveal."

"I was going to tell you. I just wanted to tell you the story as it unfolded. It made for better dinner conversation. There is no foreplay if I blurt out 'Hayes Construction' before our salads arrive."

"Hayes Construction as foreplay?"

"You get what I'm saying."

"I think you're dirty, Kirby."

"I was only trying to keep you engaged in the conversation, Ms. Burkett. I didn't want you to think of me as a one-trick pony."

"And what would be the one trick you've shown so far?"

Kirby looked around the patio before lifting his hands to mime a gesture. Even before he could do anything, Marci blushed and said, "Never mind."

# Chapter 30

On Sunday, Quinn awoke to darkness, his mind swirling with worry. He walked over to the blackout curtains and pulled them open, the morning sun smacking him in the face.

He trundled into the kitchen, pulled a Keurig cartridge from its spinner, and snapped it into place within the coffeemaker. After grabbing a mug from the cupboard, he placed it in its proper position. He pressed the brew button and stared into his backyard with its view of the Little Spokane River.

He loved his house. It was everything he had ever dreamed about, but its financial weight was about to crush him. After his conversation with Kirby, he spent most of yesterday, Saturday, in a fog as he wandered around his house, reliving every purchase he'd made. He had discovered various truths about himself.

First, almost everything he had ever purchased, he bought on credit. He couldn't point to one thing inside or outside his house that he had purchased for cash. He hadn't consciously purchased it with credit to earn reward points such as airline miles. Instead, he bought everything because he simply wanted it, and he wanted it *now*.

That was the second truth he'd discovered. He bought almost everything he wanted. He hadn't said no to himself on anything. He was surrounded by so much stuff, even some things he'd purchased on a momentary high that remained unopened when he got them home. On the kitchen table was an unopened Kindle he'd ordered from Amazon. He already had an iPad he used to read digital books, but he thought the Kindle would allow him to read outside in bright light. He bought the Kindle over six weeks ago. When he ordered it, he experienced a momentary euphoric sensation. After it arrived, though, there was no longer any excitement attached to it, so it remained unopened.

Quinn's coffee finished brewing. He grabbed his cup and walked outside to the deck. The morning sun felt good on his face as he sipped the Ethiopian blend.

Kirby had explained to him that he would never get out of the hole he was in by making minimum payments. Quinn could see that now. The system was rigged against people who used credit and made the smallest allowed payments. He could say he was a victim, but there were plenty of people out there who had made smart choices about credit. Quinn wasn't one of them.

He thought about his house. It was five bedrooms and three bathrooms. Even when it was him and Barbara, it was too big. Two people didn't need 3,500 square feet of a house. Now that he was alone, it was a monument to his stupidity, and it was taking him down.

It wasn't just the house, though. Quinn had the truck, boat, RV, and WaveRunner loans that he was making minimum payments on. He also had the timeshare he bought, thinking it was a good investment. He shook his head at his foolishness.

He'd lived his life like a child with a credit card. The wife whom he had loved more than anything in this world couldn't stand to live that way anymore and finally left him. He demanded that he get to keep the toys, and she gladly left them, and the associated loans, with him.

Barbara looked happy when he saw her on Friday. That hurt, not the fact that she looked great and was saving money. Quinn loved her still and wanted her to do well. It hurt that she was not with him. He thought they would have been together forever. He tried to love her the best way he knew.

He just didn't pay attention to the one thing she begged him to change: his financial habits. Now, he'd lost his wife, and he was about to lose his house. If the department found out about the foreclosure and his other financial problems, he could be reprimanded.

His financial ineptitude had crept into every aspect of his life. Quinn sat his coffee cup on the table, leaned forward, and cried.

# MONDAY

## Chapter 31

When Quinn walked into the detectives' office, Marci was waiting for him.

"Where have you been?"

Quinn looked at his watch. "I'm on time."

"Listen, Kirby's coming in this morning."

"For what?"

"He found something over the weekend that could be useful for us."

"Do we need to deputize your boyfriend now?"

"He's not my boyfriend."

Quinn smirked.

"Okay. Maybe he is. I don't know. Whatever he is, it doesn't matter. What does matter, though, is he found something."

"When does he get here?"

"When's who get here?"

Quinn turned to see Lieutenant Brand standing behind him.

"Lieutenant," he said.

Likely still smarting over their previous exchange, Marci only nodded at Brand.

"I need a resolution to the Kidwell case," the lieutenant demanded. "While you two are dragging this case around like an old, worn security blanket, the young bucks, Parker and Johnson, closed two cases last week. Even Nash and Higgins closed one."

Quinn glanced at Marci, who shrugged in return.

"You're holding back my numbers. Close the case. Help me, help you," Brand said as he brushed past them, heading deeper into the detectives' office, probably to give someone else the same speech.

"Help me, help you," Quinn said to Marci.

"Jerry Maguire wannabe," Marci said.

"Help me," Quinn intoned, tapping his chest, "...help you." He pointed at Marci.

She brushed his finger aside. "I should punch you just for repeating him."

"I thought you'd be in a better mood after getting lucky this weekend."

"Don't talk to me that way. I'm a respectable lady."

Quinn laughed.

"It's nice to see you happy again." Marci's phone rang, and she picked it up on the second buzz. A moment later, she hung up. "Kirby's at the front desk."

\*\*\*

"That's her," Kirby said, pointing at the background picture on the computer screen.

"Madison Collingsworth, right?" Quinn said, writing the name into his notebook.

"Yeah."

"And how old did you think she was?"

"I'd guess sixteen or seventeen. If she were eighteen, you'd think she'd tell me. That's the legal age, right?"

Marci nodded. "Legal age is a complicated discussion, but for this situation, eighteen is fine."

The three of them left the computer storage room and headed back to Quinn's and Marci's cubicles. Quinn dropped into his chair and turned to his computer.

"Thanks for coming by," Marci said with a slight smile.

"Anything for you."

"Ugh," Quinn said and stuck out his tongue.

Marci hit Quinn in the shoulder.

"Do you see the abuse I take?" Quinn asked, not taking his eyes off the screen.

"I didn't see anything you didn't deserve," Kirby said.

"My man," Marci said and kissed Kirby on the cheek.

"You two are disgusting," Quinn said. "You know what else is disgusting? Madison Dawn Collingsworth is sixteen years old. She'll be seventeen next month."

"What the hell?" Marci blurted.

"Wow," Kirby said.

Both leaned over Quinn's shoulder and looked at the screen. "She's got several driving entries, a minor in possession of alcohol charge, and two shoplifting entries."

Quinn called up the minor in possession report. He looked to Marci, who was whispering something into Kirby's ear, making him blush. "Hey, partner, pull your tongue out of his ear."

"Are you embarrassed?"

"No. But I've got Madison's address. Let's roll."

***

Quinn and Marci drove toward Liberty Lake. They pulled off the interstate and headed into the gated community known as Legacy Ridge, where the homes quickly passed the million-dollar mark. In Spokane County, that put them clearly at the top. Most of the construction had occurred within the last ten years. There was not a single modest home anywhere in the development.

"These homes are impressive," Marci said.

"I can't imagine the monthly mortgage payments." Quinn's face was passive, but there was hurt in his eyes when he spoke.

"You okay?" Marci asked.

"Thinking about my own home. I'm sinking because of it. That, and other choices."

Marci stared ahead.

"I've never been to your place, Marci. What's it like? It's a condo, right?"

She nodded. "Yeah. I bought it during my second year in the department. Two bedrooms, one bath."

"What's it worth?"

Marci shrugged. "No idea. I bought it for one twenty. Paid it off in seven years. I've never put any debt back on it, so I don't really care what it's worth. It provides a roof over my head and a place to keep my shoes. Besides, I no longer have a mortgage payment, so that makes me happy."

Quinn stole a couple of glances at her.

"What?"

"You don't have a mortgage payment?"

"No."

Quinn shook his head. "I can't imagine that."

Marci watched the passing scenery, not responding.

"Life would be so different," Quinn said, his voice trailing off.

"I talked with Kirby about it this weekend," Marci said. "It's weird. I've talked more about money with Kirby in just a couple of days than I ever have with anyone in my entire life. Anyway, we talked about mortgages. He said most people get into a routine of regular house payments and car payments. It goes on for their whole lives, even into retirement. They don't know anything different. I'm not even sure they can imagine doing anything differently. I never thought about getting ahead when I paid off my mortgage. It was never some personal finance mission like Kirby is on. I just didn't want the payments forever. After talking with Kirby is when I realized I sort of lucked into my reality. I mean, how can anyone get ahead when they're always making minimum payments?"

Quinn pulled the car to the side of the road.

Marci unbuckled her seatbelt and started to get out of the car. She paused when she saw her partner sitting behind the wheel in a daze. "Quinn?"

He looked at her and turned off the car. "I realize how far I've put myself behind the eight ball with how I've lived my life."

"Worry about it later. We still have a homicide to solve."

Quinn nodded and slid out of the car.

They rang the bell at the front door. A female voice broadcast through a speaker in the doorbell. "Yeah?"

"Spokane Police Department," Quinn announced. "We're here to speak with Madison Collingsworth."

"She's not home."

"Please open the door."

"I'm not Madison."

"Madison, if you don't open the door, we're going to call your mother and get to you that way."

The speaker was silent for a moment, then the door unlocked and opened. A blond teenager stood in the entry.

"Good morning, Madison."

The girl shook her head. "I don't know who you're talking about."

Quinn glanced at Marci. "It's the girl from the photo, right?"

Marci smiled. "Oh, yeah. The same."

"What photo?"

"Last chance, Madison," Quinn said. "We need to ask you some questions."

"I'm not this Madison person you're looking for."

"Let's talk with mom. We'll handle it that way."

"Sounds good," Marci said with a grin at the young girl. "Then we can arrest her for obstructing. Looks like she can use a night in juvie."

The detectives turned and walked down the sidewalk. They were near their car when Quinn said, "I thought she would have broken by now."

Marci shrugged. "She's trying to be tough. After mom weighs in, we'll see how tough she is."

*** 

"You are not allowed to talk with my daughter," Victoria Hayes said.

Marci glanced at Quinn before settling her eyes back on the owner of Hayes Construction. They were seated again in the overly large conference room. This time, however, Victoria Hayes had lost any pretense of being accommodating.

"We think she may be material to this investigation," Marci said.

"I don't care."

"She lied to us when we asked who she was."

"The police in this nation, especially in this part of the country, do not have the best reputation. Why should she talk with someone who puts her in fear?"

Quinn smirked at Marci, which he saw her catch out of the corner of her eye. Her cheeks flushed, and her eyes slanted, focusing more attention on Victoria.

"We understand your position, Ms. Hayes. Thank you for your time."

Quinn's face flattened. "Huh?"

Marci stood and stuck out her hand. Victoria followed suit, and they shook hands.

"Just to let you know," Marci said, "I'm going to approve the press release about the assault that took place in your parking lot. Although, I'm going to tweak it slightly and say we were following up on a crime involving an employee of Hayes Construction. I'll make sure to note that you were not cooperative in our follow-up."

Victoria tried to jerk her hand free from Marci, but she held it firmly.

"You can't do that," Victoria said through clenched teeth.

"Oh, but I can. Perception is reality, Ms. Hayes. You told us that. I'll make sure that the news perceives just how uncooperative you were and that you fully supported the actions of your employee."

Victoria quit pulling her hand and stared at Marci. "You're quite the bitch, aren't you?"

Marci released Victoria's hand then. The two women stood for several moments, staring at each other. Finally, Victoria sat and waited until Marci did the same. When she did, Victoria asked, "What is it you want to know?"

"Were you aware your daughter was dating Jacob Kidwell?"

Hatred flashed through Victoria's eyes.

"I'll take that as a yes."

"I never said that."

"You didn't have to. Your sixteen-year-old daughter was running around with a twenty-seven-year-old man."

Victoria sneered at Marci.

Quinn leaned forward. "If you don't realize it, Victoria, you've just given us *motive* for Jacob's murder."

Her eyes widened, and she looked between the two detectives. "I didn't... I wouldn't..."

Marci smiled. "Your employee, Douglas Rafferty, was outside Jacob Kidwell's apartment. He assaulted a friend of Kidwell's. He even assaulted me when we came looking for him. That looks suspiciously close to *means*. I could easily see Douglas Rafferty assaulting Jacob Kidwell, couldn't you, partner?"

Quinn nodded, his eyes focused on Victoria, who suddenly looked frightened.

"All we have to do is figure out *opportunity*. It wouldn't be hard to paint a picture that you told your thug employee to assault Jacob Kidwell for messing around with your underage daughter."

"That never happened."

"No? Then what did happen?"

Victoria looked from Marci to Quinn, then back to Marci. "I told Madison to stay away from him, or I would call the police."

"Why didn't you? Call the police, I mean."

"Because she said she told him she was nineteen."

"You didn't want the bad press, did you? Perception and all?"

"I'm not a bad mother."

"We need to talk with your daughter. We need to know what she can tell us about Jacob Kidwell. We also need to know what you told Douglas Rafferty."

"Nothing. I never told Mr. Rafferty to do anything, nor did I condone his actions. I swear."

"That's fine," Marci said. "Now, about your daughter."

***

The presence of her mother did not lessen Madison Collingsworth's defiance.

"I don't have to tell you shit," she said.

"Madison!" Victoria shouted. "Tell them what they want to know, and they'll be on their way."

"Mom, it's not the first time I've dealt with the cops. They can't make you do anything you don't want to do." She curled her lip. "I'm not scared of juvie."

Quinn stepped forward and studied Madison. He didn't say anything, just looked closely at her. Marci moved back as she knew what Quinn was doing. They had done it before with different suspects. Some suspects responded better to those of the opposite sex. Sometimes the suspect had mother issues. Occasionally, it was that they just liked talking with members of the opposite sex. Marci and Quinn didn't need to explain the plan to each other. They'd worked it enough to know immediately.

Madison smirked at Quinn. "You can try to be all hard. I'm not buying it."

"I wouldn't expect you to. When did your father leave?"

"What?"

"Your father. When did he leave?"

"You think I've got daddy issues?"

Quinn shrugged. "I dunno. I'm not a psychiatrist."

"Well, I'm a woman," Madison said. "I don't need no man."

"Yet you hooked up with Jacob Kidwell."

"That was for kicks. It doesn't mean I'm some cliché fucked-up girl."

"I didn't say you were. I just asked when your father left."

"He didn't leave us. My mom left him."

"I didn't leave—" Victoria interjected, but Marci grabbed her arm. After a silent exchange, she escorted Victoria out of the room.

"How old were you when they divorced?"

Madison remained silent for a moment but finally said, "I was two. A baby. It didn't affect me none."

Quinn nodded.

"I don't miss him."

"I didn't say you did."

"I miss my dad, though."

"The guy who owned the construction company?"

"Yeah. Robert. My mom married him when I was three. As far back as I can remember, he had always been in my life."

"What happened to him?"

"He had a heart attack. About two years ago."

"My dad died of a heart attack when I was about your age."

Her eyes searched Quinn's. "Really?"

"For real. My mom died a couple of years later when I was in college. Life sucks sometimes."

Tears formed in Madison's eyes.

"What was the deal with Jacob?"

She crossed her arms and blinked away the tears. "It was fun. He liked me, and he took me to nice places. We spent a lot of time at the lake. I think he liked seeing me in a bikini." A sad smile appeared on her face.

"Did he know how old you were?"

She shook her head. "Nah, Jake thought I was nineteen. He said he felt like he was robbing the cradle, but we were having fun together, so he let it slide. I couldn't tell him my real age, or he would have dumped me for sure. He was a good guy. Whenever he introduced me to people, he'd tell them I was twenty. I even went through my online accounts and dumped all my high school friends. I couldn't have him friend me online somewhere and find out how old I really was. I never put my age on those accounts anyway, but well, it's like my mom always says, right? Perception —"

"—is reality," Quinn finished.

Madison nodded. "Yeah. She loves saying that shit. So stupid."

"Did your mom tell you to break up with him?"

A tear rolled down her cheek.

"Did you?"

Madison gave a barely visible shake of her head. "I wouldn't do what she told me. That was part of the fun of being with Jake. It pissed her off so much. That's why I bought everything for us when we were out."

"What do you mean?"

"She gave me a credit card. I paid for everything when I was with Jake. I bought his gas, paid for dinner, even paid for a hotel room a couple of times. I had to get cash advances for that. Hotels would want to see an ID, know what I mean? Had to think ahead for those times."

A murmur came from the other room.

"I don't think my mom even looks at her credit card bill. She didn't care what I was doing. Why would she? I was a reminder of my father, and she hated him. She never let me forget how much she despised him."

"Do you know anyone that would want to hurt Jacob?"

She wiped her eyes with the palms of her hands. "Not really, no. But he was worried about that real estate deal he was working. He said he thought people were following him. He was getting paranoid about it. He was going to make a lot of money on it."

"Who was following him?"

"I dunno. He never told me, and I never saw them. I think it was in his head."

"Do you know a man named Douglas Rafferty?"

"I don't think so."

Quinn studied Madison's face.

"What about Michael Smith? Have you heard of him?"

"Who's that?"

"Jacob's partner."

"Partner? You mean, the guy who I met at the coffee shop?"

"No, that was a friend. Michael Smith is somebody different. He would have been working with Jacob on the real estate deal."

Madison frowned and looked down. "Haven't heard of him. Sorry."

Quinn was unsure if she was telling the truth about Rafferty and Smith.

"What about Jacob's car? Did you ever ride in it?"

Madison looked up and smiled. "His Lexus? Hell, yeah. It's nice. He used to let me drive it."

"Why was it repossessed?"

Madison's eyes narrowed. "What? Who said it was repossessed?"

"We were told the car was repossessed. That the car was towed away."

She snickered. "He just told people that so he could hide his car without people asking where it went."

"Hide it? Where?"

"In a storage unit. He put some other stuff in there, too."

"What other stuff?"

"I don't know. Records and things."

"Music records?"

"What? No. Like files. You know, folders with papers in them. That sort of thing."

"Did he show you where this storage unit was?"

\*\*\*

The storage unit was on Highway 395, also known as the Pullman Highway. Madison was in the backseat of the detectives' car. Victoria Hayes had followed them in her white BMW.

Quinn walked inside to find a man in his late twenties standing behind the counter. He was heavy with thick hair and dark-rimmed glasses. He wore a black polo shirt and blue jeans. The name tag on his shirt read *Burt Mankins*. "May I help you, sir?"

"Hey, Burt, I'm Detective Delaney with the Spokane Police Department." Quinn pointed at the badge on his belt.

Burt's polite smile changed to one of excitement. "Sir?"

"Did Jacob Kidwell lease a storage unit here?"

"I'm not supposed to release that type of information."

"I'm investigating a homicide. I need to know if Jacob Kidwell has a storage unit here."

Burt's smile never left his face. "Yeah, he has a unit. I'll get you the number." He turned to his computer. "That Jacob guy is kind of popular, huh?"

"What do you mean?"

"A few days ago, some other guy showed up wanting me to let him into Jacob Kidwell's storage unit. I told him I couldn't do that since I don't have a key to the unit. Besides, we're under off-site video surveillance, and I'd get in trouble for doing that. He left after that."

"Do you have a video of the guy?"

"Oh, no, we don't have cameras in here, just outside in the storage areas. Guess the owners figure it's more important to protect other people's stuff than it is to protect their employees." Burt chuckled at his joke as he continued working on the computer.

"Do you remember what he looked like?"

"Yeah, sort of." Burt pointed at the computer screen. "Jacob Kidwell's unit is in building two, unit seventeen."

"I'll be back with a warrant."

When Quinn returned to the car, Marci, Madison, and Victoria were talking together. "It's confirmed," Quinn said. "Thank you for your help, Madison."

She looked at her mom.

"Detectives, are we done?" Victoria Hayes asked.

Quinn and Marci nodded in unison.

*** 

Back at the station, Quinn settled behind his computer. Marci leaned against his cubicle wall. "What do you think we'll find in his storage unit?"

"His car."

"What else? What if we find a head like they did in *Silence of the Lambs*?"

"I hope not."

Marci hunkered over and rubbed her hands together. "Maybe there will be gold in there."

"What?"

She ended her pantomime and straightened up. "Come on, man, where's your sense of adventure?"

"Marci, I need to get to work."

"You're taking all the fun out of a storage unit. It's like a treasure hunt."

"It's paperwork, Marci. And in this relationship, I know my strengths and your strengths. Yours are not warrants. So stop talking and let me type."

She stuck her tongue out at him before ducking into her cubicle.

# Chapter 32

When Kirby had finished caring for the lawn, he put the mower and string trimmer away. After locking the storage shed, he stood at the edge of the lawn to survey his work. He took great satisfaction in how it looked.

He returned to his apartment, showered, and changed into clean clothes. Kirby needed to write a blog post for the week, but his heart wasn't in it. The past week had thrown off his habits. The death of Jacob and the subsequent hunt for his killer had been more exciting than fixing toilets, writing blog posts, and worrying about his current finances. Adding Marci into the mix had mixed up his world, so now nothing felt normal.

It was a nice feeling, but also an abnormally unproductive state to be in. That left him uncomfortable and slightly anxious. Mowing the lawn helped. It gave him a sense of normalcy and accomplishment.

He wanted to return to the blog, but it seemed stale for the moment. Even the management of his social media accounts had grown tedious. He didn't want to engage with anyone in the digital world. Kirby Willis wanted to be involved in life—*real* life.

That didn't mean blowing up his financial picture by any means. Far from it. He was still focused on the bigger prize, but he was anxious. He was reminded of a concept from Eckhardt Tolle, the author of *The Power of Now*: all negative emotions come from either the past or the future. Anxiety was negative, for sure, and he certainly didn't feel in control now.

Instead, he felt like a raft on the ocean, drifting along. Kirby hated that feeling, but banging out a blog post didn't hold the allure it had previously.

A knock at the front door brought him out of his thoughts.

He opened it, and a woman stood there, her eyes wide with anticipation. She looked vaguely familiar.

"Kirby Willis?"

"Yes."

"I'm Amy Tillerson."

Kirby looked outside, beyond Amy. Not seeing anyone else, he asked, "How'd you find me?"

"I'm a real estate broker, Kirby. It's my job to find people, and you're not particularly hard to locate. Besides, you left me your phone number. I figured you wanted to talk."

Kirby thought about that for a brief second and put it away for further reflection. He also thought about asking her into his apartment, but he remembered how she wouldn't come out of her office for him. He knew it was petty and spiteful, but he decided to ignore that social norm. "I would have come to your office."

"It's okay," Amy said, looking past Kirby into his apartment. When she realized she wasn't going to be invited in, she asked, "What did you want?"

"Do you know anyone that would want to hurt Jacob?"

"Is that all you wanted?"

"What about the deal he was working on Queen? The twenty-four houses he had under contract? Were you aware of that?"

Amy forced a smile. "I'm his designated broker. Of course, I knew."

"I think that deal got him killed."

"I doubt it."

"What do you mean?"

"That deal was shaky from the beginning," she said. "The numbers never made sense." She didn't sound convincing.

"Wouldn't you buy those houses to control a full neighborhood next to the mall and the best retail corridor in the city?"

"Maybe," Amy said with a shrug. "I don't know."

Kirby didn't believe her. "Did you know who Jacob was working with?"

"No. He wouldn't tell me. Supposedly, his client wanted to remain anonymous."

"How did that sit with you?"

"Not well." Amy bit her lip before asking, "Did he leave his laptop at your house?"

Kirby's heart raced. *She's after the computer, too,* he thought.

"More than likely, it was in that stupid backpack he carried everywhere. Did he leave that here, by chance?"

Kirby's pulse pounded in his head, and his breathing shallowed.

"I need to find it."

"Why?"

"Jacob was working several deals on my behalf," Amy said as she looked past Kirby into the apartment. "He had documents that were never sent to me. I'd like to get those documents, or those deals will die." Again, she didn't sound convincing.

"It's not here," Kirby said.

"You're sure?"

Kirby nodded.

Amy studied Kirby's face for several seconds. "Thank you for your time."

Kirby watched her walk down the sidewalk and climb into a white Porsche Macan. When it sped away, Kirby closed the door.

Kirby drove to Jacob's apartment in Browne's Addition. He hurried into the building, past the landing where Jacob was found, and up the stairs. His eyes darted to the apartment where the DO NOT ENTER tape was still crisscrossed over the door.

He turned left and hurried to apartment #3. She opened the door after several raps. When her eyes focused on him, Fonda Shay smiled slowly and said dreamily, "Kirby Kirby, you've come for me."

He shook his head. "I've come for the laptop."

Fonda blinked several times, and her smile drooped slightly. "The what?"

Kirby pushed past her into the apartment. His eyes scanned the apartment. "Where is it?"

"Whereswha?" Fonda said, swaying next to Kirby.

"The backpack. I saw it here."

Fonda put her hand on Kirby to steady herself. "Nopackback."

Kirby turned to her and grabbed her by the arms. "Fonda. I saw the backpack. I'm sure it was his. Was his laptop in it?"

Fonda's eyes rolled back in her head, and she repeated, "Nopackback."

Kirby shook Fonda. "Where did you put it?"

She started to cry.

"Fonda, where did you put it?"

"WhydonyoulovemeJake?"

Kirby struggled to hold her as she collapsed to the floor.

\*\*\*

She slept for two hours on the couch. During that period, Kirby searched her apartment. It was a violation of someone else's privacy that he'd never experienced before. At moments, it was scary, and, at others, it was exhilarating. He went through every nook and cranny of the apartment. When he was done, he hadn't found the backpack. It was no longer there.

That led him to second-guessing himself. Perhaps he hadn't seen it. Maybe it was all in his imagination. Finally, he told himself to trust his gut. He had seen the backpack. It had been out of place, so he hadn't recognized it as familiar. Not until Amy brought it up, and it suddenly fit within his memory.

Kirby found a glass and filled it with water. He drank it rapidly and then refilled it. He thought about leaving the apartment, but he wanted to be there when Fonda awoke. He wanted to ask her questions about Jacob's death. She knew something. He believed it now.

When Fonda awoke, she stirred and moaned. She sat upright and looked around. "Guh," she said and walked to the restroom, passing Kirby without a word.

Behind closed doors, the toilet flushed, and she remained there for several minutes. When she came out, her face was freshly washed, and her hair pulled back with a scrunchie.

She opened the refrigerator door and removed a bottle of coconut water. She twisted off the cap and drank deep. When she was done, she smiled at Kirby. "You keep coming back. I'm starting to think you may like me or something."

Kirby remained silent.

"How long was I out?"

"A couple of hours. You almost hit the floor when I got here. I caught you before you did."

"My hero," Fonda said and took another long drink of the flavored water.

She walked over to the couch and sat, pulling her legs underneath her. "It's nice to see you again."

"The first time I met you, there was a black backpack," Kirby said and pointed to the space next to the Papasan chair, "right there. Where is it now?"

Fonda sipped her water. "I don't own a black backpack."

Kirby thought for a moment. "I saw it."

Fonda shrugged. "I've never owned a backpack like that."

"You're answering a different question. I never asked if it was yours. I was asking where it was. I believe it was Jacob's."

Fonda shook her head.

"It was, wasn't it?"

Fonda sipped from her bottle.

"How did it get there?"

"I dunno."

"Come on."

"Really. I swear. Jake might have left it after he visited one time. Or maybe he brought it in and put it there. I don't know. One day it was there, and the next Jake was dead."

"Then, where did it go, Fonda?"

"You need to leave, Kirby."

He nodded. "Okay, but I'm going to let a couple of detectives know what I saw. I'm sure they'll be in touch."

Kirby turned and took several steps toward the door.

"Wait."

Fonda untucked her legs and leaned forward.

"He didn't hurt Jake."

"Who has the backpack, Fonda?"

*** 

The offices of Sonnen Development were open and vibrant. The brick building was in the University District and had originally been a warehouse built in the early 1900s. Now, its wood beams had been sandblasted clean. Spiral ducting had been brought in to distribute heating and cooling throughout the space. A few offices were built on the outer ring, but most of the work was conducted in an open format. It made for a lively and creative environment.

Kirby waited at the front desk as Craig Sonnen was located. Sonnen was a large man, standing roughly six and a half feet tall and weighing easily two hundred fifty pounds. His bald head and weightlifter's physique gave him an imposing demeanor.

Sonnen appraised Kirby as he approached him, running him up and down with his eyes. He didn't offer his hand when he introduced himself. "I'm Craig Sonnen," he said, his voice deep.

"Mr. Sonnen, I'm Kirby Willis. Can we speak in private?"

"What's this about?"

"Fonda."

Sonnen looked around to see if anyone was in earshot. "Follow me."

Kirby trailed the big man through the open floor plan to a back office with windows overlooking Martin Luther King Boulevard and the suspension bridge leading to Sherman Avenue.

Sonnen's office had several pictures of him and Fonda in various locations. One of them looked to have been in Paris when Fonda was younger. Another photograph appeared to be the two at an Aztec ruin. Kirby stopped when he saw Sonnen and a blond woman standing with surfboards on a beach. "You surf, Mr. Sonnen?"

"I tried it once, but we're not here to talk about my vacation habits. You said you wanted to talk about my daughter."

"She's in a bad way. I'm sure you've seen it."

"Her drug use, you mean?"

Kirby nodded.

"I've tried to push her into a program, but she won't go," Sonnen said. "Her mother left when she was thirteen. Fonda changed after that. She started using drugs and acting out. She even took her mother's maiden name, to spite me. I've tried helping her, but she doesn't want it."

"The last couple times I've been over there, she's passed out. I'm worried something bad will happen to her."

"I appreciate your concern, Kirby, and I'll check on her when I leave tonight. How long have you been friends?"

"We just recently met," Kirby said. "I left my backpack over at her house a few days ago, and she said you might have picked it up by accident."

Sonnen's face darkened. "Your backpack?"

"Yeah. It's black and about this big." Kirby gestured its size.

"I don't know who you are, guy, but that wasn't your backpack."

"Okay," Kirby said with an embarrassed laugh, "you got me. It's not my backpack, but you have it, right?"

"I don't know what you're talking about."

"Of course, you don't."

Sonnen moved quickly from behind the desk. Kirby scrambled out of his chair, sending it scuttling to the side, but he wasn't quick enough to escape Sonnen. The big man grabbed Kirby by the shirt and pinned him to the wall.

"You'll get hurt if you continue to push this," Sonnen said, his lips close to Kirby's ear.

Kirby turned to look through the glass wall at the employees in the common area. No one paid any attention to Sonnen and him.

Sonnen leaned back slightly to study Kirby's eyes. "Understand?"

The big man punched Kirby in the stomach before dropping him to the floor to suck for air.

"Stay away from my daughter. She doesn't need a friend like you."

\*\*\*

Marci Burkett's condo was on the South Hill near Manito Park. Kirby parked in a visitor spot and bounded up the steps two at a time. He rang the doorbell and waited.

She opened the door, wearing a yellow summer dress and white sandals. Kirby stared at her.

Her eyes narrowed. "What's wrong, Willis?"

"I'm taking it all in. You look fantastic."

She leaned in and kissed him. "You're going to get lucky. You don't have to start sweet talking me now."

"I'm not sweet talking."

Kirby walked in, and Marci closed the door behind him. "There's not much to see. It's pretty small but make yourself at home. Want a beer or something?"

"I'm good," he said.

"The sauce is simmering, and the salad is made. All I've got to do is drop the pasta in the water when you're ready to eat. I'm not the best cook in the world, but spaghetti is pretty hard to screw up."

"It sounds good to me."

"How was your day?"

"Productive."

"How so?"

"I know where Jacob's laptop is. At least, I think I do."

"What do you mean?"

"First, Amy Tillerson—you know her, right?"

"Yeah, Kidwell's boss."

"His designated broker, right? She came to my apartment."

Marci crossed her arms. "Why would she do that?"

"She said it was because I left her a message wanting to talk about Jacob, but what she wanted was his laptop."

"His laptop? Huh. Interesting."

"Yeah, I thought so. She said something, though, that reminded me where I might have seen it. She said the laptop might be in Jacob's backpack. That's when I remembered seeing Jacob's backpack in Fonda's apartment the first time I met her. Right after his death."

"How did it get there?"

He shrugged. "Fonda said she didn't know. She said maybe Jacob left it there a couple of days earlier when they hooked up, but she couldn't remember. Regardless, it wasn't there when I went back."

"Where did it go?"

"Fonda's father took it."

"Her father? Who is he?"

"Craig Sonnen. The owner of Sonnen Development."

"Let me guess. He wants the city block that's under contract, too?"

"That's my guess."

Marci made a sour face. "Your friend was involved with the daughters of two developers looking to cash in on this deal. I'm not impressed with him."

---

"Neither am I, as it turns out."

"Quinn and I will contact Sonnen in the morning."

"That's good. The only thing is, I already did."

Her eyes flared. "You know you shouldn't be involved in this investigation, Kirby. At least, not anymore. For a lot of reasons."

Kirby nodded. "Yeah, I know."

Marci touched the side of his face. "Don't get hurt, and don't screw anything up for us, okay?"

"About that."

"What happened?"

"I asked if he took the backpack from Fonda's apartment. I told him it was mine. He slugged me for asking."

Anger flashed across Marci's face. "What?"

"Stomach punch. It dropped me to the ground. He's a big guy."

"Oh, I'm definitely going to talk to this guy tomorrow."

"But that's not the really interesting thing about the meeting."

"That wasn't the interesting part? Pray tell, what was the most interesting part of the contact?"

"On his wall was a picture of him and a woman on vacation. Guess who the woman was?"

"I don't want to guess."

"C'mon, take a guess."

Marci put her hands on her hips and stared at Kirby.

"Someone doesn't want to play."

"Oh, I want to play. Just not that game."

"Fine," Kirby said. "Take the fun out of it, why don't you? Anyway, the picture on his wall was of Sonnen and Amy Tillerson."

# TUESDAY

## Chapter 33

Even though Detective Quinn Delaney was behind the wheel, it was clear his partner was in control of the car.

"Turn left," Marci said.

"Are you going to tell me where we're going?"

"Not yet."

The smile on her face did a poor job of hiding the fact she knew something.

"Your poker face sucks, Detective."

"I got laid last night."

"I don't want to hear that."

Marci made a face. "Whatever, man. You guys always talk about your sexual exploits. Why can't I talk about mine?"

"First of all, we don't talk about our sexual exploits once we get past twenty-something. We keep that stuff to ourselves. Second, when we did talk about it, we were talking about the same thing, sexual exploits with women. I don't want to hear about you and some dude. Third, I know the guy is Kirby, and I like him. I don't want to think about you two doing the dirty."

"The dirty?"

"The horizontal mambo. Is that better?"

"You might as well call it the spank and tickle for what we were doing. Seriously, it was amaz—"

Quinn jerked the wheel to the right and back to the left, bouncing Marci's head off the passenger side door.

"What the shit!"

"I told you I didn't want to hear about it."

Marci rubbed the side of her head. "Damn, you're aggressive this morning."

"I spent last night starting a budget. It tends to put you into a weird space."

"Whatever. You can tell me about it over lunch."

Changing lanes in traffic, Quinn said, "I brought my lunch today. It's in the back. I'm happy to eat with you wherever you want to go."

Marci looked into the backseat. "You'll bring a sack lunch inside Jimmy John's and sit with me?"

"I've got to turn my financial ship around. It starts with baby steps like this. Have you heard of a guy named Dave Ramsey?"

Marci looked directly at Quinn.

"What?"

"You're kidding me, right?"

"No. Why?"

"Everyone's heard of Dave Ramsey."

"I hadn't. I just started listening to him. The guy makes a lot of sense."

"Of course, he makes sense. That's why he's famous."

"Don't make fun of me, Marci. I'm trying to clean up my mess."

Marci nodded. "You're right. I apologize. This is serious, and I'm glad you're finding guys like Ramsey. Keep listening. And you should talk with Officer Kemper."

"Tony Kemper? Swing shift officer, right?"

"Yeah," Marci said, still rubbing her head. "Remember his wife was on the department about ten years ago?"

"I forgot about her."

"She was cool. I liked her. Anyway, they got heavily involved with the Dave Ramsey program. They paid off their personal debt and then their house. Then she quit the department to raise their kids."

Quinn glanced at Marci. "They're living on a single officer's income now?"

"I guess it's not hard if you make the right choices, especially if you make them early in life."

Quinn was silent after that, letting the thoughts of Officer Kemper and his wife overwhelm his thinking. He turned whenever Marci told him to, but otherwise she remained silent as well.

Finally, she said, "Pull over here."

They were in front of Home Town Realty.

"What are we doing here?" Quinn asked.

"We need to follow up on a couple of things." Marci released her seat belt and reached for the door handle. "I'm lead. You stand back and look handsome."

"I can do that."

*** 

The bell tinkled when they entered the office. Helen Erwin looked up from her computer as Quinn and Marci walked in. Amy Tillerson was in her office on the telephone.

"Detectives, how may I help you?"

"We'd like to speak with Amy," Marci said.

"I'm afraid she has an appointment in a couple of minutes."

"It will have to wait. This is more important."

Marci walked away toward Tillerson's office. Quinn stood, staring at the dumbfounded receptionist. He pointed at Marci. "She's lead today. I'm just supposed to follow her around and look handsome." When Helen didn't answer, he turned and walked after his partner.

Marci pulled open the door just as Amy finished her phone call. "Detective? I'm sorry I don't have time this morning. I have a client coming in. He's here now."

Quinn looked over his shoulder, and a man who appeared to be in his late thirties to early forties was standing in front of Helen. He seemed irritated as the receptionist explained he'd have to wait. Quinn turned his attention back to Marci and Amy.

His partner said, "This will only take a minute, Ms. Tillerson."

"Please, make it fast."

"Why do you want Jacob Kidwell's laptop?"

Amy looked between Marci and Quinn before returning to Marci. "I... well... he was working on some projects with me, and he never emailed me the work. I'm trying to get the information from that computer."

"We'd like to see that computer as well."

"I didn't know that."

"Now, you do. If you come across it, you'll be sure to call us, right?"

"Of course."

"When we were here last, there was a frame turned upside down on the corner of the desk where these folders are." Marci put her hand on some folders stacked on the desk's corner. They wobbled slightly under the pressure of her hand.

"I don't know what you're talking about," Amy said.

"When my partner asked how your vacation was, your eyes went to the frame, and you said it wasn't what you hoped."

"You've got a pretty good memory."

Marci smiled. "I'm a homicide detective. I wouldn't be one if my memory were poor." She reached under the folders and pulled a picture frame free. She turned it over and put it on top of the desk. The picture was of Amy Tillerson and a tall, physically fit man in his mid-fifties. They were on a beach holding surfboards.

"Was this taken during your vacation?"

Amy shook her head. "That was from Christmas."

"Where was it taken?"

"Maui."

"Maui," Marci said, then looked to Quinn. "Maui. Very nice." She looked back at Amy. "Why didn't this latest vacation go as well as Christmas?"

"I thought he was going to propose."

"But something else happened," Marci said.

Amy nodded. "He broke it off at the end of the week. He said our relationship wasn't going the way he expected." Tears formed in Amy's eyes.

"This is Craig Sonnen, isn't it?"

Quinn looked at Marci with a questioning look. He mouthed the words, "Who is Craig Sonnen?"

Marci waved away his question and turned her focus back to Amy, who was wiping away the tears from her eyes. "Why does Craig want Jacob's laptop, Amy?"

"The same reason as everyone else."

Amy looked into the lobby. "It looks like my appointment has left." She called for Helen, who hurried back to the office.

"Yes?"

"What happened with the appointment?"

"Mr. Smith said he would call to reschedule."

"Great," she said, not bothering to hide the sarcasm.

Helen backed up, then hurried to her desk.

Amy shrugged. "Well, it looks like my next half hour is free."

"Smith?" Quinn asked. "That wouldn't happen to be Michael Smith, would it?"

"How did you know that?"

Quinn looked at Marci before focusing on Amy. "That's Kidwell's partner."

Amy stared at Quinn.

"You knew that already, didn't you? He wants the laptop as well and has contacted you. It's starting to make sense. You two are working together."

"We're not working together. He only told me it was missing. I had no intention of giving it to him if I found it."

"Craig knows about the laptop as well," Marci said.

Amy's brow furrowed.

"He hit a friend of mine when he asked about it."

"That doesn't sound like Craig."

"When did you learn about the missing laptop?" Quinn asked.

Amy looked down. "Helen called me after you came in about Jacob."

"We didn't tell her the laptop was missing then. We didn't know about that for some time. Did Smith call you later?"

Amy nodded.

"What did he say? Did he tell you about the laptop?"

"Not at first. At first, he called to ask about the purchase and sale agreements and what would happen if they weren't assigned before Jacob's death. I told him I'd get back to him and called Helen. I asked her to pull the files so we could review them over the phone."

Quinn and Marci glanced at each other, then turned to glare at Amy.

"Yes, Detectives, I lied about learning of the missing files when you first came to my office. What was I supposed to do?"

"Tell the truth," Marci blurted.

"We could charge you with obstructing an investigation."

Amy's face whitened.

"You better come clean now," Marci said.

The real estate broker bit her lower lip before speaking. "When I called Smith back, I told him the files were missing and that Jacob had taken them. He knew Jacob had his own copies since he'd reviewed them and worked with them. He said Jacob had hidden them because he was trying to extort him for a bigger position in the deal. The way he told the story, it sounded plausible. Jacob had become sort of greedy about this deal. Walking around like he was a big shot, understand? Anyway, he said Jacob had a backup of everything on his computer, and it was linked to some cloud-based file service, like Dropbox, but not. The gist of Smith's pitch was we needed to find the laptop. Unfortunately, Smith told me that the cops—you guys—took both computers, and we were out of luck."

"So why did you suddenly think Kirby might have it?" Marci asked.

"Smith called me on Saturday night and said he was starting to believe maybe the cops didn't have the laptop. He thinks he knows where the files are and maybe the laptop is there, too. I figured I should keep my eyes and ears open for any opportunity to find it. None of this may matter, though. The whole deal is probably dead before we can even get a crack at it. We're not going to be able to assign. We have to wait for it to fall completely apart and then try to re-create the wheel. Think about how hard that's going to be. We're probably on a fool's errand with this."

"Did he tell you where he thought the files might be?" Quinn asked.

"No, he was playing it close to the vest. I don't blame him."

"Do you think Craig could have overheard your conversation with Smith?"

Amy looked up at the detectives. "The first one. Yeah. He was sitting next to me while on vacation. At that point, I didn't think there was any reason to hide anything from him. The second call came on Saturday after Craig and I were done. If Craig is searching for the laptop, I have no way of knowing why."

Quinn glanced at Marci before asking, "Do you have a phone number or any other way of contacting Smith?"

Amy opened her cell phone, grabbed a Post-it Note, and quickly jotted some information. She handed it to Quinn. "I've got a phone number. That's all I've got."

"If he calls you again, please schedule a meeting with him and then call us."

\*\*\*

Back in the car, as they reentered traffic, Quinn asked, "Going to explain to me what just happened in there?"

"Like I was saying, I got laid last night."

"Don't make me jerk the wheel again."

Marci laughed. "Okay, okay, geez, you're temperamental. Kirby came by last night and said he found a lead for us to follow."

"You could have told me that before we walked in there."

"How would that be fun?"

"Partners don't keep stuff from each other."

"So, you *do* want to hear about the sex?"

Quinn jerked the steering wheel.

\*\*\*

The offices of Sonnen Development were bustling when Quinn and Marci walked in. The young receptionist smiled at Quinn, ignoring Marci. "How may I help you?"

"We'd like to see Craig Sonnen."

She nodded and picked up the phone.

Marci smiled at the receptionist, who continued to disregard her. When she finished with her call, the receptionist hung up and said to Quinn, "Craig will be right out."

"Thank you."

"You're welcome."

"Yeah," Marci said, finally getting the receptionist's attention. "Thank you."

The receptionist looked irritated by Marci and turned back to her computer.

Quinn pulled Marci to the side. "What the hell is going on?"

"That girl never even looked my way when we checked in."

"That doesn't mean you have to go psycho on her."

"Listen, I expect misogyny from men, but when I get it from women, it pisses me off."

Quinn nodded. "I can see that."

A tall man walked out of a back office and approached the receptionist's desk. His tight black T-shirt highlighted his sculpted physique. He smiled at both Quinn and Marci. "I'm Craig Sonnen. How can I help you?"

Quinn pointed at himself. "I'm Detective Delaney. This is Detective Burkett. We'd like to talk with you."

Sonnen smirked. "Is this about the guy I punched yesterday? Listen, I was out of line, but it doesn't need a two-detective response, does it?"

"Actually, it does. We believe you have a laptop that may be pertinent to a homicide investigation."

"You're wrong."

Quinn nodded. "Why don't you come to the station with us, and we'll talk about it down there."

"No, I mean, I don't have the laptop. I want it, but I don't have it."

"You took the backpack, though?"

Sonnen nodded.

"Where is it?"

"My office."

"Let's go get it," Quinn said.

They followed Sonnen back to his office. When he stepped behind his desk, Quinn followed him closely to make sure he wasn't reaching for a gun. Sonnen grabbed the bag and handed it to him. "It was personal finance books and notepads. That's why I thought there might have been a laptop in it."

"Did you take anything out of here?"

Sonnen shook his head. "I wanted the laptop. Not a bunch of books and random scribblings."

"Why did you take the bag, then?"

"It was in my daughter's apartment. I asked her about it, and she told me who it belonged to. He always had his laptop with him, and I figured it was in the bag. It had a small combo lock on it. Why would you put a combo lock on a backpack? The paranoid little freak. Anyway, I couldn't get into it until I got back here." Sonnen grabbed his trash can, reached in, and pulled out a small combination lock that had its metal loop cut. He laid the now worthless lock on the corner of the desk.

"So, you knew Kidwell?" Quinn asked.

Sonnen's face flushed slightly. "Yeah. He hung out with my daughter."

"I take it you weren't a big fan."

"Not really, no, but I'd imagine it's probably how most fathers feel. I think it's universal."

"Why do you want the laptop?" Marci asked.

"Really?"

"Humor me."

"The kid put together the best real estate deal I think I've ever heard of in my entire career. I've never seen anything like that done." Sonnen dropped heavily into his chair. "I wish I was part of it. I really do, because I want that deal more than any deal ever. I can make that project into something special. He was tight-lipped about who was in the project with him. He made it sound like he was going to put the deal together first, fully cook it, so to speak, then bring in the money partners to get it across the goal line. The more I hear about the project, the more I realize it was a line of bullshit. He had a partner from day one.

"Anyway, I was brought in early because of my former girlfriend. She worked with the kid. He was sort of a fart in a skillet if you know what I'm saying. Sort of amped up and all over the place. He wanted me to bid out the project to make sure it made sense. It did. Surprisingly, it wasn't skinny, either. There was enough meat on the bone to make it attractive to everyone involved. We were a month or so into this when I started hearing rumors the kid was flirting with Victoria Hayes over at Hayes Construction. I don't know who else he might have looped into the conversation. We were both running it as if it was our own. I think he wanted to see what each of us would do with it if we were part of the deal. Pissed me off."

Quinn asked, "This sounds like a substantial investment to pull off. How could Jacob do that if he didn't have that kind of money?"

Sonnen smiled. "Detective, real estate is an idea game. You don't need money if you can see things others can't. I'll be the first to admit I never envisioned this project until the kid put it in front of me. Frankly, no one else had either. Jacob Kidwell put lightning in a bottle. If the kid wanted a minority partnership in the project, I would have handed it to him in a heartbeat to do the deal. Just for his idea and for tying up all the properties. That's why I figured the laptop was so important. We need to know where everything is. I overheard my ex talking with her receptionist, and she said Jacob had removed all the files pertaining to this deal from the office. The whole thing was in danger of disappearing into the ether."

"If it falls apart, why not put it back together again?"

Sonnen shrugged. "Maybe we could, but it's highly unlikely. Look at it this way. Jacob went out and put together twenty-four separate purchase and sale agreements, each interlocking the next so they all had to close or none of them could. It was ingenious.

"What's more ingenious is he kept it quiet until they were all under contract. If the deal falls apart, that information is already out into the world. Everyone knows about it. Developers like Victoria and me will descend on that block in a hurry, and we'll tear it apart just trying to control it. The houses will be overpriced, and we'll stop the other from getting full control of the block. Nothing will ever happen in our lifetimes. It will all be lost because everyone now knows what can be done. I'm not saying this is a once in a lifetime opportunity, but it sure as hell feels like it. That's why that laptop or those files are important to someone like me."

"And Amy Tillerson," Marci said, tapping the photo on the wall.

"What?"

"Amy stopped by Kirby Willis's apartment. She was looking for the laptop as well. Kirby's the guy you punched yesterday."

---

Sonnen shook his head.

"Guess you shouldn't have broken up with her on vacation, huh?"

"She told you that?"

Quinn nodded. "Did you break up with her because of this deal?"

"What? No. Not at all. She wanted more from the relationship, and I wanted more freedom."

"Ouch," Marci said.

Sonnen shrugged. "Listen, when you get in your mid-fifties, life either gets really into focus or you start to fade out. I'm very focused on what I want now. Being tied down is not one of them. If Amy finds the laptop or files before me, good for her. She won't know what to do with the project, though. She's good at what she does, but she clerks deals. That's it. She doesn't develop."

"Maybe she'll deliver the laptop to Victoria Hayes."

"If she does, she does," Sonnen said. "I'll still be free and can continue to live my life the way I want to."

"Mr. Sonnen," Quinn said, "if you find any of Jacob's materials, we need to see it first."

Sonnen sighed. "Yeah, okay."

"I'm serious," Quinn said. "It's material evidence in a homicide. Not turning it over is a felony."

"All right. I get it."

"I hope so." Quinn grabbed the backpack and broken lock from Sonnen's desk and followed Marci out of the office.

Outside at the car, Quinn put on a pair of latex gloves and removed the contents of the backpack. Inside were several personal finance books and a science fiction book written by Ray Bradbury. There were also a couple of different notepads, each with a variety of notes. Quinn shoved the contents back into the bag along with the lock and tossed the bag into the trunk.

"The bag was a bust," Quinn said.

"No, it wasn't," Marci corrected him. "We've found out several people are hunting for that laptop. It means we're on the right trail."

"Let's get the search warrant signed for the storage unit, then head over there."

# Chapter 34

Kirby Willis drove around town for a few hours. The Tuesday morning Uber fares were not lucrative, but it gave him something to do to keep his mind active and away from Jacob's murder. He wanted to help, but he didn't know where to go next.

He picked up a fare from the Davenport Grand Hotel and took her to the airport, dropping her off at the Delta Airlines gate. The woman spent the entire trip texting on her phone. Occasionally, she giggled, but she never engaged Kirby in conversation even after he'd tried when the trip started.

On the drive back to the city, Kirby's mind drifted to the past week. So much had changed in such a short period. Jacob had died, and he'd discovered new things about his friend. He'd also found a new romantic interest in Marci. It was a great feeling, and he wished Jacob had been around. He would have told him about it. He wondered why Jacob hadn't told him about Madison Collingsworth. Was it because he knew she was underage? He couldn't imagine Jacob continuing the relationship if he had found out. Jacob had always told him about previous girlfriends, even the one-night stands. Jacob liked to brag about his conquests, but he kept Madison a secret.

He kept the deal in north Spokane secret. He kept leaving Home Town Realty a secret.

Kirby Willis took the Maple Street exit and headed south to the Dream Living offices.

\*\*\*

Paula Fairbanks smiled when she walked out.

"Kirby, I haven't seen you this much in a long time. You keep giving me hope you're going to buy another property."

"What happens when a broker leaves his office?"

"Straight to business. No pleasantries. That's unlike you."

"I'm sorry," Kirby said. "My mind has been elsewhere lately with this Jacob thing."

Paula reached out and patted his arm. "I understand. I do. What was your question?"

"When a broker leaves an office, what happens to the deals in progress?"

"Technically, the deals belong to the real estate firm. If the broker leaves during the middle of them, the deals are finished with the firm. The agent will still get his portion of the fee, but so does the firm. The agent simply can't take them with him."

"The deal stays even though the broker goes?"

Paula nodded. "Does this have something to do with Jacob's death?"

Kirby didn't answer as he was hurrying out the door.

*** 

Kirby walked into the office of Home Town Realty. Amy Tillerson was alone in the building. Her receptionist had gone to lunch. Amy looked up from her desk. "Kirby Willis?"

"You terminated Jacob's contract, right?"

"That's none of your business."

"If you've terminated his contract, you will still be the broker of record for any deals in progress, correct?"

Amy stared at him.

"Jacob couldn't proceed with his deals without hanging his license elsewhere, because he would be unlicensed. Even then, he'd still have to work whatever deals he had previously in progress through your firm."

"Technically, yes."

"Normally, would you have the agent complete the deal, or would you take it over?"

Amy shrugged. "It depends on the deal, I guess."

"What's that mean for the Queen and Lidgerwood deals?"

Amy crossed her arms. "We can't complete the deal. We don't have the files. Jacob removed them."

"Why did you terminate him?"

"Because he wasn't performing."

Kirby shook his head. "Most of your agents pay a basic desk fee and never come in. You couldn't care less if he ever stepped foot in here. It was something else."

Amy stared at him.

"Why did you terminate his contract?"

"You need to leave."

"You hooked up with him, didn't you?"

Amy's face flushed. "No! I would never do something like that with Jacob."

"What did he do? Did he say something? Did he ask you to do something?"

"Get out!"

Kirby started to leave and saw the frame in the trash can. It was the picture of Amy and Craig at the beach. He turned around and faced Amy. The color in her face faded.

"It was because he was hooking up with Fonda, wasn't it?"

Amy didn't say anything. She stared at him, her lower lip trembling.

"Her father knew about them and put pressure on you, didn't he? He wanted you to press him to stop messing around with his daughter."

Amy lowered her head.

"You terminated Jacob's contract because he was sleeping with your boyfriend's daughter?"

Amy lifted her head and set her jaw before saying, "I did what he asked, but it didn't change anything for anyone."

"Except Jacob. Did you tell him?"

"What?"

"Did you tell Jacob why you were firing him?"

"I did," Amy said, her eyes reddening. "I liked Jacob, but I loved Craig. I told Jacob I couldn't keep him around because of his relationship with Craig's daughter."

# Chapter 35

"The geeks say the number we got for Michael Smith is registered to a burner phone," Marci said.

Quinn shook his head. "Geez, they help you fast."

"Say it."

"What?"

"It's because I'm good."

"No. They adore you."

Marci punched him in the shoulder. "Say it, Delaney."

"You're pretty."

Marci whispered, "Say it, or I'll punch you again."

Quinn laughed. "You smell nice."

"Delaney, you're a dog in heat," Captain Ackerman said as he passed by their cubicles. He was on the way out of the detectives' office. "Why is it that I'm always asking Burkett if she feels harassed by you?"

Marci shrugged. "Bad timing, Captain. We were in a funky-smelling house, and I wanted to make sure I still smelled okay."

Ackerman looked at Quinn with suspicious eyes. "Give her that answer with less enthusiasm next time."

Quinn nodded. "Yes, sir."

The captain turned and headed down the hallway. Marci spun and punched Quinn in the shoulder.

"Damn!"

"Serves you right, you perv. 'You smell nice.' Who says that in front of a captain?"

Quinn chuckled. "Don't make me talk to the lieutenant about you. I'm sure he'd love to write a report about the mental harassment I take from you."

"You wouldn't dare."

"Oh, try me. I'll make up some weird stuff that people will be wondering about for years."

Marci gave him a sideways glance. "Okay, truce. I don't know if you're playing or not. Should we call Smith's number now or wait?"

"We only get one shot to call him. If we misplay it, he tosses the phone and moves on to a new one."

"We're in no hurry, right?"

"Right. Let's do the search warrant first and figure out the play from there."

\*\*\*

Burt Mankins read the search warrant with great delight. His lips moved slightly as his eyes scanned over the page, his fingers occasionally adjusted the thick-rimmed glasses on his face. He was bent over the counter, his elbows supporting his weight. When he finished reading, he stood upright, tucked his orange polo shirt into the back of his jeans, and said, "Everything looks in order."

Quinn said, "I'm glad you approve."

"You read a lot of search warrants?" Marci asked as Burt grabbed a pair of bolt cutters from the corner of the room.

"No, why?"

"Just making conversation."

The heavyset man led the way out the door, his gait buoyant with excitement. Marci grinned at Quinn, who shook his head in amusement. The walk to building 2, unit 17 took only a few minutes. Burt opened the bolt cutters, stuck the loop of the lock through them, and applied pressure. His face purpled as the exertion was more than anticipated. It took a couple of attempts before the metal relented, and the lock snapped. Burt grabbed the lock and twisted it free.

"There you go, Detectives. Let me know when you're done, and I'll come back to lock it up."

He turned and sauntered cheerfully back to the office.

Quinn and Marci both watched him go.

"That's a happy guy."

"Good for him, right?" Marci said.

Quinn crouched and grabbed the handle for the roll-up door. With a quick yank, it clattered up, revealing a silver Lexus. Marci stepped inside and opened the driver's side door. The car keys were on the seat. She sat inside and repositioned the seat for her size. The car started on the first attempt, and she pulled it straight out of the unit, allowing them more room to work.

Behind the car, along the back wall of the storage unit, was a wall of white banker boxes. Quinn walked over to them. He opened the top one. The file inside was a thick folder with paperwork relating to the sale of a house on 4th Street. Quinn put the file aside and grabbed the next record. The address was listed on Sullivan Avenue. The dates on the files were from the previous year. "These are his old real estate files," Quinn said. He put the top back on the box and returned to the car.

Marci opened the back door and examined the backseat. "Nothing here."

With the car keys, she opened the trunk. As the trunk slowly popped open, they saw various files stacked upon themselves. On top of the files was a laptop with a power cord.

"And there it is," Quinn said.

Both detectives grabbed a file and opened it. "Lidgerwood," Quinn said.

"Same," said Marci. "These are the files for the purchase of the city block."

Quinn examined the two different types of folders, manila and brown. The tabs on the manila folders were handwritten while the brown folders were typed. He discovered the same addresses on folders of different colors. When he opened them, they contained the same paperwork. Quinn held both folders up. "Jacob's copies and Amy Tillerson's copies."

"Why would he take them from Amy? She could have gotten them from the title company like you did."

"He was upset, right? Not thinking clearly. He grabbed them to show he had some power after his contract was terminated."

"What was he going to do with them?" Marci asked.

"I don't know. He hid them here, with his car, because he was paranoid. He was afraid he was being followed."

"Well, Douglas Rafferty *was* following him."

Quinn thought about that for a moment, then said, "We never got a clear answer on who hired him, did we?"

\*\*\*

Douglas Rafferty leaned on the table with one elbow while his head rested in his hand. His eyes drifted up to Detective Quinn Delaney as he entered the jail interview room.

"Why am I here?"

"We never got a clear answer to one of our questions."

Rafferty looked bored when he said, "My lawyer should be present."

"Listen, I'm not here for the assault on my partner." Quinn leaned in, lowering his voice. "If you want me to get your attorney, I'll do it, but I'd rather leave the women out of it if we could."

Rafferty grinned. "Works for me. They tend to clutter up a conversation, anyway."

Quinn leaned back in his chair. "When we first met, you said you were hired to keep an eye on Jacob Kidwell."

"I didn't kill the man," Rafferty insisted.

"I'm trying to believe you."

The two stared at each other for several seconds before Rafferty admitted, "I roughed him up a bit, but that's it."

"Who was it for?"

"I did that for myself."

Quinn shook his head. "Well, that doesn't sound true."

Rafferty shrugged. "I don't need more trouble."

"Did you kill him?"

"No."

"See, that's what I care about. If you didn't kill him, that's a win in this discussion. If you gave him a beating for some reason and he lived to tell about, let's call it good, okay? I care about the bigger picture."

Rafferty squinted.

"I'm not jerking you around, Doug. Your attorney isn't here, right? I'm totally out on a limb. Anything you tell me won't be admissible in court, even if I tried. What did you do to Kidwell, and why?"

Rafferty ran his tongue across the front of his teeth as he thought. "You only care about the murder, right?"

Quinn said, "That's it."

He pushed his lips out while he thought. Finally, he said, "I broke his fingers."

Quinn tapped the table. "That finally answers one of my riddles. I appreciate the honesty. Who told you to do that?"

"No one. I did it for myself."

"Okay, why?"

"I told him to get rid of them."

"The files?"

Rafferty shook his head.

"What did you want him to get rid of?"

"Imagine a greedy asshole was dating your teenaged daughter."

"Victoria Hayes hired you?"

Rafferty shook his head. "You're missing the point."

"What point is that?"

"Imagine that greedy asshole dating your daughter wanted leverage over you. What might he use?"

Quinn studied Rafferty until he understood. "Shit."

"Exactly. I asked him nicely. He told me to fuck off. That's when I broke his fingers."

"Why would you do that? Were you hired to do that?"

Rafferty said, "No, but I liked the girl even if she is messed up. Her stepfather was always good to me. He was a good man, worked his way up from the bottom. You can get behind a guy like that, know what I'm sayin'? The old lady's a ballbuster, which is why I don't have much loyalty for the company no more, but when I found out the asshole had photos of her, I stepped out of line."

"How did you learn about the photos?"

Rafferty scrunched his face together.

"I'm not trying to jam you up, Doug. I'm trying to catch a murderer."

"Whatever he did, he did. I mean, if he did it. I don't know nothin'. I'm just sayin' I didn't have nothin' to do with it. I was only paid to keep an eye on Kidwell after he started goin' squirrely."

"Who told you about the pictures? The guy who hired you?"

Rafferty stared at Quinn.

"Who hired you? Craig Sonnen?"

"Guard!" Rafferty yelled.

"Smith? Was it Michael Smith?"

The interview room door opened, and Rafferty looked past Quinn to the guard. "I'd like to go back to my cell now."

"Tell me, Doug. Who hired you?"

"I ain't no rat. I've said enough to cover my ass. That's enough."

***

Marci was in her cubicle, working on a report when Quinn walked in. When he tapped her on the shoulder, she said, "How'd the chat with Rafferty go?"

He jerked his head away from the detectives' office and said, "Let's walk."

As they roamed the hallways of the department, Quinn laid it out for her.

"In respect to Kidwell's murder, we've always believed two physical items were missing."

"The laptop and the cell phone."

"The laptop and the phone, exactly. We know why everyone wanted the laptop. Supposedly, there's information on it about the real estate deal, right?"

"Tell me something I don't know."

"So, why was the phone taken?"

"Who knows why anyone would take anything? A crime of opportunity. They took it because it was there."

"Jacob Kidwell was taking pictures of Madison Collingsworth."

Marci shrugged. "So? They were going out."

"Rafferty said they were photos of the inappropriate kind."

Marci grabbed Quinn's arm and stopped him in the hallway. "He was taking nude photos of a sixteen-year-old?"

"I'm going on the word of the guy who assaulted you, and nothing is confirmed yet."

"Do you believe him?"

Quinn nodded. "He said he broke Jacob's fingers to force him to delete the pictures."

"Did he tell you who hired him?"

"He said he assaulted Jacob on his own volition. But we know he was keeping an eye on Kidwell for someone. He still wouldn't say for who."

"Who do you think it was?" Marci asked.

"I don't know, and he refused to say more. He said he wasn't a rat and only gave me enough to get himself away from Jacob's murder."

"Huh."

Quinn shoved his hands in his pockets as he thought. Finally, he said, "What if the cell phone was what we should have been concentrating on this whole time?"

*** 

Quinn pressed the doorbell and waited for the speaker to announce her intentions not to speak with them. When the door opened, Quinn was mildly surprised.

"What?" Madison Collingsworth said, crossing her arms. "I thought you had everything you needed."

"Just a couple follow-up questions," Quinn said.

"Are you guys here to play bad mommy, good daddy with me again?"

"You need your mouth washed out with soap," Marci said.

"Was Jacob Kidwell taking photos of you?" Quinn asked

A small, mischievous smile formed on the teenager's lips. "He took photos of me all the time. He said I was beautiful."

Quinn studied her eyes when he clarified, "Did he take *nude* photos?"

The smile turned malicious. "I knew what you were talking about."

"You were okay with it?"

"Why wouldn't I be?"

Marci stepped forward. "Because those photographs are forever. They could end up on someone's website. Somebody could use them to hurt you."

Madison shook her head. "First, Jacob wouldn't do that to me. Second, I look good. I may never look this good again in my life. I want some pictures of me looking hot before I grow old and bitchy like my mother. Or you."

Quinn grabbed Marci's shoulder to hold her back.

"Did Jacob send those pictures to you after he took them?" he asked.

"No," Madison said with a shrug. "He showed them to me, though. They looked nice. We were getting good at taking them."

\*\*\*

"She didn't even care about the photographs," Marci said, staring out Kirby's kitchen window. "I can't believe it."

Using a wooden spoon, Kirby moved the shrimp and vegetables around the wok as she spoke.

"Have you ever taken those types of pictures?" Marci asked.

Kirby shook his head. "Nope. I don't want to be naked on anyone's camera."

"No, you dork. I mean, have you taken them of a girlfriend?"

267

He turned off the stove and removed the wok from the burner. "That's a tough question, Marci."

Marci playfully punched him in the arm.

"Ouch," he said and exaggeratedly rubbed the impacted area. "What did you do that for?"

"Because you're a dirty dog and now a drama queen."

Kirby laughed. "I didn't say I did take pictures. I said it's a tough question."

"It sounds like you're a politician. What's that mean?"

Kirby stepped back out of striking range. "There may have been a time that a phone was out when... well, you know. When the moment passed, the photo was deleted. So a picture was taken, but it wasn't kept beyond that time. Get it?"

Marci nodded, not happy with the answer. "Yeah, I get it."

# WEDNESDAY

## Chapter 36

She was leaning back in an oversized chair, sipping a cup of something and reading a paperback version of Stephen King's *The Shining*.

Kirby had texted her and asked if they could meet. She said she was at the Rocket Bakery on First and would be there for an hour or so. If he could meet now, they could talk. If not, she was unavailable until the next day. For someone who lived her life on a trust fund and did only the things she wanted, Holly Reese had little time for others to interrupt.

Kirby dropped into the oversized chair next to her. Holly caught the movement, checked the page she was on, and closed the paperback.

"How's the book?" Kirby asked.

"You didn't ask to meet so we could start a book club, Kirby."

"No, I didn't."

"Ask what you want. I'm on a schedule today."

Kirby nodded once and said, "Did Jacob take photos of you?"

Holly stared at him.

"Not regular photos, but—"

"I know what you mean. Why do you ask?"

"Since his death, I've been learning a lot about Jacob. Who he was and how he lived his life. I thought he was my friend and that I knew him. As it turns out, I didn't know him as well as I thought. This detective I've started seeing told me—"

"You're seeing a detective? What's that mean?"

"Going out with."

"Really?"

"Yeah. Anyway, she said Jacob had been taking—"

"Is she the dark-haired detective that came to my apartment after Jacob's death?"

"Maybe. Why?"

Holly shrugged. "No reason."

"She said Jacob was taking pictures of—"

"What's her name again? Marsha?"

"Marci."

"Marci," Holly said, softly.

"What I was saying was Marci found out Jacob had taken pictures of his previous girlfriend. Inappropriate ones."

"I know what you're talking about, Kirb."

"He was assaulted because of these photos. His cell phone is missing. He used it to take pictures of this girl."

Holly's face went pale, and she turned to look out the window.

"So, he took pictures of you, too," Kirby said softly.

Holly remained silent for a minute before saying, "He said he deleted them after he took them. When we broke up, he texted me one of the photographs and said, 'Good times.' That's when I went to his apartment and painted *die* over the picture I created for him. I didn't care if he had that painting or not. Until that moment, I didn't care if he had those photos of me or not. I was cool with it, I really was, but when he sent me a picture with that tag, I realized who Jacob was as a person. I couldn't tell anyone about it. I kept my mouth shut. There was a part of me that believed he would show up at my doorstep one day demanding money to keep quiet about the pictures or he would post them somewhere."

"I'm sorry," Kirby said.

Holly shrugged. "You didn't know."

"He's not the person I thought he was. There were good parts of him, I know, but I'm starting to lose sight of them."

"Jacob could be charming and loving when he wanted to be. That was the person I fell for, but there was another side of him that was cold and calculating. It was that side that hurt."

"I never saw that in him," Kirby said.

"Then, you were lucky."

They sat quietly for a moment, each lost in their thoughts. Finally, Kirby slid forward in his chair. "Thank you for giving me some time this morning, Holly."

She smiled.

As Kirby turned to leave, Holly said, "She's pretty."

He turned back. "What?"

"Marci. She's pretty."

Kirby nodded, and Holly opened her book to continue reading.

\*\*\*

Fonda Shay was seated on the front steps of the apartment building when Kirby arrived. He'd parked in front of the building and was walking up the sidewalk when she recognized him. She waved and said, "What are you doing here?"

"I came to see you," he said and sat next to her.

A smile grew on her lips, and she leaned her head on his shoulder. "You're a nice person."

"Can I ask you a question?"

"Sure. You can ask anything, Kirby Kirby."

"It's about Jacob… Jake."

She sighed and, with resignation, nodded twice.

"Did he take pictures of you?"

Fonda lifted her head from his shoulder and stared straight ahead. Kirby looked at her and could see the unhappiness on her face.

"You didn't want him to, did you?"

She looked down at her hands and began picking at her cuticles.

"I'm sorry. I'll leave it alone."

"The first time he did it, I woke up to it. I'd passed out, and he was standing over me, taking pictures. He said it was because I was…"

"Beautiful," Kirby suggested.

"He used that word when he wanted something." She rubbed her hands together. "He would come over when he wanted to… you know. We'd smoke, and I'd let him." Tears filled her eyes. "After a while, I quit arguing about the camera."

"I'm sorry, Fonda."

"I told him once that I didn't want to be with him anymore, and he said if I wasn't nice to him, he'd show the pictures to my dad. I didn't believe him until he showed me a picture of my dad and him at a city function. A couple weeks ago, he came over. It started out like it always did. He said nice things to get his way, and I gave in like I always do, then he got physical. I mean rough. Do you understand? He blamed me for getting him fired from his job. He said everything he had worked for was falling apart. I asked him to stop, but he didn't."

Kirby sat silent.

"I'm glad he's dead," Fonda said.

"Fonda, did you…?"

"Did I kill him? No." Fonda rested her head on his shoulder again. "I wish I had, though."

\*\*\*

The receptionist told Kirby that Craig Sonnen was in a meeting. He waited in the front office. It was at moments like this he thought about Eckhart Tolle's book. Tolle made the argument that Kirby should be so fully engaged in the Now that he wasn't waiting, he was simply being. It was a wonderful book, and the goal of learning how to be alive in this moment was one of his highest priorities. Unfortunately, he was anxious to talk with Sonnen, and he had trouble keeping his thoughts in the present. He paced the waiting room, fighting the urge to grab the door and just walk back and interrupt his meeting.

The glass door to Sonnen's office opened, and a man walked out, his head held high, and shoulders pulled back. His hair was cut short on the sides and left slightly longer on the top. His blue T-shirt and jeans were crisp and clean. Kirby had seen him before, and he struggled to place him. The man was in his late thirties and had a purposefully grown five o'clock shadow. He made eye contact with Kirby as he passed the reception desk and winked. Kirby turned and watched him leave.

"Who was that?" Kirby asked the receptionist.

She shook her head. "He wouldn't say. He came in with a file for Craig. Said he had some photographs for him to look at."

Kirby ran to the door, yanked it open, and looked into the parking lot. A black Cadillac Escalade pulled out of the lot and sped away. He turned and walked past the receptionist's desk.

"If you wait a moment, I'll call Craig," she said.

When Kirby didn't stop, she hurried after him, her high heels clicking on the stained concrete floor. "Sir! Sir, you can't just walk back there."

Kirby stopped at Craig Sonnen's office. Leaning on his desk, his head in his hands, the big man was crying. Underneath him was a closed manila folder.

The receptionist stopped talking when she saw her boss. Kirby looked at her and nodded. He stepped inside his office. "Mr. Sonnen."

When he didn't look up, Kirby repeated, "Mr. Sonnen."

Craig Sonnen looked up with tears in his eyes. The sadness was replaced with rage, and he stood quickly from behind his desk. Kirby lifted his hands into a defensive posture and said, "Wait. I'm not with him."

Sonnen stood in place, tears in his eyes.

"I know what those are," Kirby said. "Fonda told me what Jacob did."

The big man dropped into his chair and shook his head. "I wish I could kill him."

"I know."

"I want to hurt someone."

"I know that, too. That man, did he tell you his name?"

Sonnen shook his head, then tapped the folder. "He said this is just a sampling of the pictures. He said those pictures would go public with a description including 'daughter of Sonnen Development.'" He used two fingers to air quote *daughter of Sonnen Development*. "He said I could stop the pictures going public if I give him a hundred thousand dollars."

"You need to call the police."

Sonnen shook his head. "No. He said if the police are involved, he will upload the pictures, and they'll be out there."

"Mr. Sonnen, I'm not a police officer, but even I can see what he's going to do. You'll give him the money, and then he'll ask for more. He'll keep asking until you say no. The day you do, he'll upload the pictures."

"Get out."

"Mr. Sonnen—"

"Get out!"

Kirby turned and walked out, the entire office staff watching him in silence.

# Chapter 37

"Did he say why he wanted to meet?"

Marci shook her head as she turned the wheel.

"How are things going with you two?"

"We just started. Why are you interested?"

"Making conversation."

Quinn's phone buzzed. He looked at the screen, saw the North Carolina area code, and silenced it.

"Barbara?"

Quinn shook his head. "It's a creditor."

Marci glanced at him.

"That's who all the calls have been from that I've ignored," Quinn said. "I'm behind on all of my loans, so I've been getting calls."

Marci opened her mouth to say something but remained silent as she drove.

"It's humbling to be in this position," he said.

"Financially?"

"Yeah, but it's more than that. I've been thinking about it. Do you think I'm a good detective?"

Marci nodded. "One of the best."

"I've had a good career. I've been involved with some big cases. Been involved in a shooting and survived. Never had an actual sustained complaint. I've played by the rules and excelled."

"You've had a solid career."

"I've taken decent care of my health."

"Mr. Stud Runner Man," Marci said.

Quinn smiled. "I don't drink to excess. I don't gamble. I've never taken drugs. I don't mess around with women I'm not supposed to when I'm not supposed to. I've lived right."

"Your point being?"

"I played everything like I was supposed to, yet I'm broke. Worse than that, I'm in the hole. A huge hole. I'm still wrapping my brain around how I got here."

They drove in silence for a few blocks before Marci said, "People don't get fat overnight."

"Huh?"

"It takes time and effort. Well, lack of effort, but it still takes time. You get what I'm saying. There's only one way to lose weight—eat less and exercise more. Simple. Or to put it another way, consume fewer calories than you burn."

"The solution to my problem is to consume less money than I earn?"

"Pretty simple, right? Even when you make more money, you still have to spend less than you make. It's the only way to get out of the hole. There are all sorts of fancy things you can do to make new money or cut expenses, but when it gets down to it, that's as simple as it is—consume less money than you earn."

They listened to the sounds of the passing road for a couple of minutes before Quinn asked, "Why haven't we talked about money before?"

"We've been taught it's impolite," Marci said.

"Why?" Quinn asked. "We both know exactly how much we each make. We're civil service employees. Our pay scales are public knowledge. Hell, the newspaper subpoenas our salaries every year and posts them to their website, but for some reason, we don't talk about money. I've never talked about investing or saving with anyone, not even Barbara."

"There are some in the department that talk about it. I told you about Kemper and his wife. They had a group working on the Dave Ramsey program when I was on patrol."

"Were you part of it?"

Marci shook her head. "No, I don't want people knowing my business."

She pulled into the parking lot of Sonnen Development and parked near the entrance.

Kirby stood behind his Toyota Prius and watched them enter the lot. He waited for them after they exited their vehicle.

Marci kissed him when she neared him.

"Get a room," Quinn mumbled under his breath.

"What have you got?" Marci said to Kirby, smiling at her partner's uncomfortableness. "You said it was important."

"After you told me about the photos with Madison Collingsworth, I stopped by Holly Reese's to ask if she'd ever had that happen. She said Jacob had taken photos of her, and she was okay with it until their breakup when he texted her a photo. That's really why she went to his apartment and wrote *die* on the painting she gave him."

Marci and Quinn glanced at each other.

"He was doing the same thing to Fonda Shay but without her permission. She didn't want him to take more pictures, but he was using the ones he already had as a threat. He said he'd show them to her father if she stopped him. She was very upset that he'd taken those photos."

"Okay, that's good information, but why are we here?"

"Craig Sonnen is in there with a folder full of pictures. When I walked in, he was crying. The guy who was there just before me looked familiar, but I couldn't place him. He told Sonnen not to call the police and to pay him one hundred thousand dollars, or the photos would end up online. Sonnen refused to call you guys, so I did."

Quinn nodded and headed toward the door.

Marci grabbed Kirby's hand. "Thank you, Kirb. We'll take over."

***

The receptionist was calling for Craig Sonnen when Marci walked in. She glanced at Quinn, who shrugged.

The receptionist hung up the phone and said, "He was here just a minute ago. He came out front, saw what was going on in the parking lot, and went back to his office."

Quinn looked into the parking lot and saw Kirby's Toyota backing out of its stall. He turned to Marci and said, "He saw us talking with Kirby."

Both hurried back to Sonnen's office, the receptionist behind them. It was empty. Quinn turned to the receptionist. "Is there another way out?"

"There's a back door," she said and pointed toward the corner of the building. Quinn led the way with Marci close behind. He shoved the emergency bar, and the heavy metal door swung open to the outside. A quick look around showed no one nearby. A sidewalk wrapped around the building. Quinn followed it while Marci went back through the building.

An engine roared from the parking lot, and Quinn quickened his pace. As he turned the corner, a burgundy GMC truck bobbed out into the street, took a hard right, and raced away.

Marci exited the building and caught up with Quinn. "Was that Sonnen?"

"Yeah."

"Who do you think showed him the photos?"

"If I had to guess, I'd say Michael Smith. He keeps popping up everywhere we've been."

# THURSDAY

## Chapter 38

The cell phone vibrated, waking them both. Kirby lifted himself onto an elbow and watched as Marci answered it.

"Uh-huh," she said. She listened for a moment, then said, "Got it. I'll be there in twenty minutes."

When she hung up, she flopped back into the bed and stared into the darkness.

"What's going on?" Kirby asked.

"Homicide," Marci said and sat upright.

Kirby reached over and turned on the bedside light. "You okay?"

Marci looked over her shoulder at Kirby as she buttoned her blouse. "I don't like call-outs, but it's my job. This should be an easy one."

"How so?"

"Convenience store robbery gone bad. The clerk had a gun. One of the robbers is dead. Clerk is wounded. Second suspect got away. It's on camera." She looked at the clock. It was shortly after 3 a.m. "It's going to be a long one, but we'll wrap it up today. Reports and all."

"Wow."

Marci pulled on her pants. "Exciting, huh?" she said, her voice lacking enthusiasm.

"Sort of."

"Don't be fooled. Most of this job is what's going to happen now. We know everything from the get-go. We just document it and file it. Most homicides aren't mysteries. We don't solve crimes as much as we catalog them."

Marci pulled her shoes on before leaning over to kiss Kirby.

"Go back to sleep. Stay out of trouble."

\*\*\*

When Kirby awoke, he updated his website, did a new post, and handled his Buffer accounts. He then went to Jacob's personal Instagram account and called up the photos that were there. This was a part of Jacob's life that was a mystery to him. He'd never heard of these moments. Why would he even post them here?

Most of the pictures were with Madison Collingsworth. Why did he publicly share his relationship with her but not talk to Kirby about it? He must not have known how old she was. Kirby was convinced of that now. As much as he was let down and disappointed in the person he thought was his friend, he couldn't imagine Jacob willingly dating someone who was sixteen years old, let alone broadcasting to the world that he was seeing her.

A queasy feeling hit him when he saw the man in the background. He was at the helm of the boat, smiling, while Madison posed at the forefront of the picture, in a bikini, with her arms thrust into the air. This is where he'd seen the man before.

Kirby knew the man was the key to the mystery now. He needed to find the boat.

\*\*\*

Madison Collingsworth's convertible Volkswagen Beetle pulled into the parking lot. She had the top down, and her hair pulled back. Kirby walked over to her car as she turned it off. She opened the door, climbed out, and leaned against her car. It was all about the show, and she had perfected the display.

"I'm only meeting with you because you aren't the cops," Madison said, crossing her arms. "I'm done getting dragged into this bullshit."

"Jacob's dead. I thought you wanted to help."

"He's gone. Ain't nothing I do is going to change that, and I still have a life to live. You know what I'm saying, right? The cops hassling me isn't part of my equation."

"I'm not hassling you."

"Yeah, whatever, you're sorta cool," Madison said, "for a square."

Kirby held a hand in the air, silently admitting to Madison's accusation. "You said you hung out on a boat that belonged to Jacob's friend."

"Yeah," she said with a wistful smile. "Good times."

"Whose boat is it?"

"Why would I tell you?"

"Was it Michael Smith's?"

Madison's smile faded.

"I think he killed Jacob."

"He wouldn't do that," Madison said. "He's cool."

"Not really. He's got Jacob's phone, and he's blackmailing the father of another girl Jacob had been with. How long do you think it is before he shows up at your mom's office showing her photos of you?"

A wicked smiled grew on Madison's face.

"If it doesn't bother you about the photos, think about Jake's murder, okay? He's going to get away with it if we don't do something."

Madison thought for a moment, before saying, "I don't know how to tell you how to get there, but I can drive you to it."

"Okay, I'll follow."

"Why don't you get in?"

Kirby hesitated.

"I won't bite."

Kirby's Toyota chirped when he pressed the lock button on his key fob. Madison smiled as Kirby walked around the car to the passenger side. He pulled his cell phone from his pocket before he slid into the seat.

"Have you ridden in a convertible before? No? You're going to love it," Madison said with a giggle as the Beetle lurched forward.

# Chapter 39

The body had been removed from the crime scene.

Quinn was reviewing his notes when his cell phone buzzed. He pulled it from his pocket, saw the out-of-state area code, and silenced it. For a moment, he realized he wasn't irritated, frustrated, or annoyed by the phone call from the creditor. He was taking the first steps to clean up his financial position, and he felt like he had some control back in his life. He refocused his attention on his handwriting.

He disliked easy cases like this. They were boring. It reminded him of his days on patrol when he responded to collisions. Even before he arrived, he could determine the type of crash just by where it occurred. There was no challenge to it.

Being a police officer was about pushing himself. That's why he loved being a detective. He didn't want easy cases. He wanted difficult ones that required him to work, think, and hustle.

Marci walked over to him and hit him in the shoulder with the back of her hand. "Look at this," she said, holding up her phone.

It was a text from Kirby Willis. HEADING TO COEUR D'ALENE. CHECKING ON LEAD.

There was a second text. WITH MADISON. GOING TO BOAT TO FIND SMITH. SHE KNOWS HIM.

"I told him to stay out of trouble," Marci said, her voice tight with concern.

She pressed the call button and waited. She muttered, "Damn it," and a moment later said, "Kirby, it's me. Call me when you get this."

The look on Marci's face worried Quinn. "Text him," he said.

"I did."

"No response?"

"None."

Marci looked at her phone again. Her worry was something Quinn had never seen. They'd been partners for several years, and he never once saw her fear anything or anyone—until this moment. She suddenly appeared trapped. She looked more dangerous than ever.

"I'm leaving," she said.

"What?"

She quickly stepped to him and kept her voice low. Quinn fought the urge to step back from her. "Dude, this is a slam dunk," she said. "You can catalog this shit in your sleep. You don't need me."

"You're my partner, Marci."

"Give me a break. This is a nothing case," she said and turned to leave.

"It's more than that, Marci. Someone's dead."

She spun around and yelled, "Don't you think I fucking know that?" Marci immediately realized what she'd done and glanced at the other officers on the scene, including the on-duty lieutenant, who stood near the shift sergeant. Several of them were looking in their direction now. Marci moved back near Quinn. "Don't you think I know that?" she said again, her voice lowered this time. "Kirby's found Smith. He's the lynchpin in our investigation. We should be out there with him."

"And where is *there* exactly?"

Marci stared at Quinn. From the corner of his eye, he saw her clench her fists. His partner had found an edge he didn't know was possible.

"They're in Coeur d'Alene, Marci, and they're going to a boat. Do you know how big the lake is? How many places can a boat be docked? How are we going to guess where they are?"

Marci's face reddened.

"Worse, maybe Kirby said Coeur d'Alene, but they're really in Hayden. Lots of people do that since they're next to each other. That's a huge lake as well. More places for a boat to be docked, right?"

Marci inhaled deeply but kept her eyes fixed on Quinn's.

"Maybe the boat isn't even docked. Maybe it's roaming the lake."

He waited for her to say something, but she didn't. Finally, Quinn said, "If you go, I'll go as well."

"Why?"

"Because you're my partner."

Her brow furrowed.

"You're on tilt, which makes you out of control."

Marci's hands opened, and her jaw relaxed.

"If you want to go," Quinn said, "I'll call Brand, and we'll request the next two detectives get sent out and finish this for us. I'll take the heat."

He could see he'd gotten to her. She glanced around the scene. Other officers had stopped what they were doing and were now watching the exchange between the two of them. Even the patrol lieutenant and sergeant were carefully observing the dialogue between the detectives.

"Otherwise, let's buckle down on this and knock it out, okay?"

Marci looked back at her partner. She studied Quinn's eyes before nodding.

"He'll be okay, Marci."

"He better be," she said and walked back toward the convenience store.

# Chapter 40

Madison Collingsworth pulled into the Coeur d'Alene Resort boat launch and parked. She climbed out of her car without hesitation. "I think the boat is up here," she said.

Kirby watched her, an uneasiness growing in his stomach.

She started toward the pier and turned back when Kirby closed the car door. "C'mon. Let's go find Mick," Madison said.

"Aren't you worried at all?"

Madison shrugged. "You've got it all wrong. He's cool."

Kirby stood still, his mind working to comprehend the moment.

"Don't be a pussy," Madison said before hurrying up the pier. Her head never turned to examine any boats as she passed them. After she had gone some distance, she turned back around and raised her hands. "Are you coming or what?" she hollered.

Farther down the dock, a man jumped off a boat. When he turned to look in their direction, Kirby recognized him immediately.

Michael Smith yelled, "Madison? What's going on, baby?"

She looked over her shoulder for a moment and then turned back to Kirby. Even at that distance, Kirby could see her grin. She spun and ran down the pier toward Smith. When she got to him, she pointed back at Kirby. It only took a few seconds before Smith sprinted toward Kirby.

It was like watching a movie for Kirby. He realized Smith was running, but he didn't immediately understand the reason. When he did, Smith had covered half the length of the pier and was quickly closing on Kirby. He spun and ran from the parking lot.

He had a head start, but it wasn't much. Kirby ran toward downtown. He knew he could lose Smith among the various restaurants and eclectic stores. Unless the older guy was a runner, Kirby could keep running for some time. So that's what he did.

Kirby made it to the road and ran, zig-zagging through the streets. After a while, Michael Smith was no longer there.

When he was alone, he continued running through residential neighborhoods, doubling back when he could. Eventually, he found a quiet spot in the Calypsos Coffee Shop and texted Marci.

\*\*\*

When she arrived an hour later, Kirby didn't even need to hear her words to know she was upset. She stood in the doorway, made eye contact with Kirby, and turned around. She walked back to her car, which was double-parked in front of the coffee shop.

He'd just stepped out onto the sidewalk when she turned and yelled, "What the hell were you thinking?"

"I thought—"

"You were? You were thinking? It sure as hell didn't look like you were thinking when you went after Smith by yourself. You realize he's a suspect in your friend's murder, right?"

"I do. Listen—"

"No, you listen, Kirby," she said, slapping the hood of her car. "I don't want to worry about you doing something stupid. You can't put yourself into these situations and expect someone to come rescue you."

"I'm not an idiot," he said.

"You acted like one today. What you did wasn't smart. It was stupid. Coming here with Madison was dangerous, and you don't even seem to realize it."

"I do realize it was dangerous, but I was trying to help."

Marci slapped the hood of her car again. "We don't need your help. I need you to be safe."

Kirby stared at her.

"Get in the car," she said.

Kirby shook his head.

"Get in the car, Kirby," she repeated, her voice a little softer, but still stern.

"I'll get another ride home."

"What?" Marci said.

"I'm sorry I worried you. I didn't mean to. I would never want that." He shoved his hands in his pockets and bowed his head as he searched for the correct words. When he looked up, Marci was watching him. "Regardless of what I did, I don't want to be talked to that way."

Marci thought about his words, then nodded once.

They silently stood as passersby watched them with interest. One car honked at Marci for being double parked. She ignored it.

Finally, she said, "I'm sorry for yelling."

"Yeah," Kirby said.

"Please, will you get in the car?" she asked, her voice soft.

He thought about turning and walking away, but he needed a ride home. Besides, he liked Marci. He didn't know how to handle what was occurring, but he could think about it another day. Right now, he just wanted to get back to the safety of his regular life.

He opened the door and dropped into the passenger seat. Marci climbed into the driver's seat and gently closed the driver's door. The car eased away.

They drove in silence through Coeur d'Alene. When they made it to the interstate, Marci said, "Kirby."

It was so soft he almost missed it. "Yeah?"

"I'm glad you're okay."

# Chapter 41

Victoria Hayes looked up from her desk when the receptionist, Tommi, escorted Quinn Delaney back to her office near the end of the workday. The detective took a seat across from her.

"I'm guessing this isn't good news," Victoria said, laying her pen down.

"Your daughter may be mixed up in the death of Jacob Kidwell."

"I can't believe that."

"It's possible, not definite. What is definite is she's involved with Michael Smith."

"My daughter is not mixed up with Smith," she said dismissively.

"You know him then."

"I don't personally know him, no. As I said before, I know him by industry reputation."

"He's in our system for methamphetamine possession. How does his reputation fare in your industry?"

Victoria leaned back in her chair and crossed her arms. "He was a former commercial real estate broker who went to jail for drugs. He was burning the candle at both ends and thought he was untouchable. I guess he needed something to keep himself up. It was all a bad combination, which led to his downfall and losing his business."

"Somehow, he got tied in with Jacob. That connection led him to Madison."

"I don't believe you," Victoria said. She picked up her pen and returned to making her notes.

"Jacob had a habit of taking photographs while with his girlfriends."

Victoria looked up from her paper and stared at Quinn. "Those types of photos can tend to be graphic."

Her eyes softened.

"He took those types of photos of your daughter and many others. One of the girls is the daughter of Craig Sonnen. I imagine you know him?"

"We're competitors," Victoria said, no hint of malice in her voice.

"We believe Michael Smith is now in possession of Jacob's phone, which has all of those photographs on it. He printed some of them and took those pictures to Sonnen as blackmail. If he doesn't get paid, he's going to start releasing those photos of his daughter. He said he would make sure to put Sonnen's company name with each photograph."

"Oh, my God."

"Your daughter is part of this."

Victoria's brow furrowed. "How?"

"She is with Smith now. They're together. She lured a civilian witness who was looking into what occurred with Jacob out to Smith's boat. Smith tried to attack him, but the witness ran away. When officers responded to the boat to find them, they were no longer there."

Victoria stared at the pen in her hand.

"When they get desperate enough for money, they'll come at you with those photos. Know that your daughter is part of the scheme. She knows Jacob took those photos of her."

Victoria shook her head in disbelief.

"We don't have a line on Michael Smith yet, Mrs. Hayes. We will alert the local agencies to be on the lookout for them, but can you think of anywhere Madison might go to hide? Does she have friends who would take them in? Do you have a lake cabin somewhere?"

Victoria lifted her eyes. "Not a lake cabin."

Marci leaned her head against the headrest and closed her eyes. "How did Victoria take the news of her daughter running around with a blackmailer and possible murderer?"

"As well as can be expected."

When Marci didn't ask a follow-up question, Quinn glanced over. She had fallen asleep, and her mouth was slightly open. He smiled and drove in silence.

They were headed to a cabin at 49 Degrees North Mountain Ski Resort, located in Chewelah, a community almost sixty miles north of Spokane. They were expected to meet local deputies upon arrival.

Marci woke up twenty minutes outside of Deer Park, about ten miles south of their destination. Marci looked over at her partner and blinked several times. "How long was I out?"

"Thirty minutes."

"Damn," she said, rubbing her eyes with the palms of her hands. "I'm sorry I conked out. Do you want me to drive for a bit?"

"We're almost there."

They rode in silence for a couple of minutes before Quinn asked, "How's your boyfriend?"

"He's all right."

"You don't sound all right."

"I laid into him pretty hard. I was worried. He didn't take it well."

"No one takes that well, Marci."

"Yeah."

Marci watched the nighttime scenery pass by her window. Quinn left her to her thoughts.

After a few minutes, she said, "I like the guy, you know?"

"Yeah, I know."

"I don't want him hurt."

"I'm sure he knows that."

Marci kept her eyes focused on the window outside.

When they arrived in the small town of Chewelah, they pulled into the parking lot of NAPA Auto Parts. Two Stevens County Sheriffs were waiting outside their black-and-white Ford Interceptor SUVs. Their uniforms were light tan shirts, green cargo pants, and black boots. Both deputies were young, big, and serious. They looked startlingly similar.

As Quinn approached, he could see they had the same name tag on—*Simmons*.

"I'm Detective Delaney. This is my partner, Detective Burkett."

"Deputy Simmons," said the first hulk when he shook hands.

The second was friendlier. "I'm also Deputy Simmons. If you haven't figured it out yet, we're brothers."

"I make it at as twins," Quinn said.

"Proving you're a detective," the first Simmons said without a smile. "I'm John. This is Paul. Our father was a big Beatles fan. I think he was hoping for two more boys. Unfortunately, we were it."

"Lucky for the son who wasn't born Ringo," Quinn said.

Marci glanced between the deputies and raised her eyebrows. "How do we tell you apart?"

Simmons #1, John, said, "I smile a lot. He frowns." Both Simmons brothers' faces remained passive.

Marci looked at her partner and shrugged. "Whatever."

Quinn quickly laid out the situation to the deputies.

When he was done, Paul said, "We're happy to help, Detective. Just follow us, and we'll lead the way."

*** 

They formed a short line as they drove up to the ski resort, which was sleepy when the snow was gone. There were opportunities for mountain biking and hiking, but it didn't bring in the kind of tourist traffic that skiing did.

Victoria Hayes owned a condo at Alpine Lodge. The keys for the unit were in Quinn's pocket, courtesy of Victoria. He was hoping there wouldn't be the need to break any doors down.

The two sheriff's SUVs pulled to the side of the road at the entry point to the community. Quinn tucked his patrol car behind them. Both detectives got out and met up with the deputies.

Before leaving, Marci had changed into a long-sleeved black T-shirt, blue jeans, and low-top combat boots. Her badge and gun were on her waist. Quinn was in jeans and a button-up shirt.

Paul pointed down Nelson Creek Road. "Your girl's building is second on the left."

John walked away toward the gate, pressed a key, and spoke into the pad. The other three waited patiently. A moment later, the gate opened, and John walked back toward them. "Good to go," he said.

Without further word, they got into their respective vehicles and entered the resort community. Quinn and Marci followed the deputies until they parked in the unassigned lot. When they arrived at the building, Quinn applied Victoria's key fob to the underground parking garage door, and the four of them entered.

"That's the convertible Volkswagen Kirby told me about."

"It's Madison's, right?" Quinn asked. "We don't know what Smith drives, so we can't be sure if he even has a vehicle here. Not sure if it would be parked down here, anyway."

"Should we head up to their condo?" John asked.

"Let's think about this," Quinn said. "If we knock, we lose the element of surprise. Smith can destroy whatever evidence he has in there—*if* he has any evidence in there. If we walk in, who knows what the hell happens? They may have a weapon inside. The level of danger with that move is extreme."

"But didn't you say the girl was underage?" Paul asked.

"She is," Marci said. "But she's cooperating with Smith. He may technically be in possession of child pornography, but she's not upset about it."

"Okay, that's the problem, then. How do we get them to come out?" Quinn looked at Marci and then to each of the deputies. "We don't want to give them a warning and give them a chance to destroy evidence."

"I've got an idea," Marci said.

"What is it?"

"We need to think outside the box."

***

Twenty minutes later, Marci walked back into the garage with Paul at her side. Quinn and John had waited in place in case Madison Collingsworth or Michael Smith returned to their cars.

"It's all set," Marci said.

"Of course it is," Quinn said with a playful smirk.

"What do you mean?"

"It's because you're pretty. They wouldn't have done it if I had asked."

"I did it on the phone. Ask Simmons."

Quinn nodded. "Uh-uh."

"They can't tell I'm pretty when I'm on the phone. They did it because I was nice."

Knowing it would aggravate Marci, Quinn exaggeratedly rolled his eyes. "Oh my God, whatever."

She cocked her hand back, ready to punch him in the arm when the fire alarm went off.

\*\*\*

Quinn and John hurried to the third floor to keep a watch on the room. No movement came from condo unit A-33. They could hear a fire truck arrive almost immediately with its sirens running.

Marci and Paul had remained outside to meet the firefighters when they arrived on the scene. It was only a few minutes before Marci silently hurried up to where Quinn and John were. The other Simmons brother was waiting in the garage, in the unlikely event Madison and Michael got around them.

Two firefighters made a show of walking down the hallway, banging on doors that had not exited. There weren't many people staying in the building at this time of the year, so the show of precaution was not met with many answered doors.

When the firefighters got to condo A-33, they banged loudly on the door. It took only a moment for Madison to open. Her hair was messy, and she had a blanket wrapped around her. "What's going on?"

"Ma'am, you need to exit the building," the taller of the firefighters said.

"Why?"

"There's a fire alarm, ma'am."

"No kidding. Really?" Madison said, her voice full of sarcasm. She stuck her head out of the door and looked up and down the hallway. "Is this a drill?"

"It's never a drill until we know for certain." The fireman then pointed upward as the blaring from the alarm continued. "You need to go now. Is there anyone else in the room?"

The door closed, and the firefighter glanced back to the corner where Quinn and Marci were hiding. He banged on the door again. A moment later, Madison stepped into the hallway with Michael Smith. He wore only a pair of khaki shorts. He had a handful of clothes with him.

The two of them hurried down the hallway and entered the stairwell. The firefighters moved to another door and continued their ruse.

*** 

In the parking lot, they stood together, looking back at the structure. Smith held the blanket up as a screen while Madison continued to put on her clothes.

The two of them were so engaged in their conversation that they didn't hear the four approaching figures behind them.

"Where do you think the fire is?" Madison said.

"I don't know, and I don't care," Smith said. "I don't like being out in the open like this."

"Relax, Mick," Madison said. "Nobody knows about this place, and why would they care about us?"

When she was dressed, Smith dropped the blanket and grabbed her hand. "Let's go," he said and yanked her to follow. When he turned, he stood face-to-face with

Detectives Quinn Delaney and Marci Burkett as well as two Stevens County Sheriff's deputies.

***

Quinn restrained Smith and put him in handcuffs. He had a cell phone in his back pocket and one in his front.

"Two cell phones," Quinn said. "You must be an important guy."

"They're for work."

Quinn pressed a button on the first cell phone, lighting it up. The background screen was a picture of Madison. "You can't do that," Smith said. "That's my phone."

When he grabbed the second phone, he started that phone as well. Another picture of Madison popped up. "You can't do that," Smith repeated.

"Yeah, you said that." Quinn pulled his cell phone from his pocket and opened his notebook. He found a number and dialed. The phone Michael had been carrying in his front pocket lit up. Quinn opened an app and took a quick look at the photos before powering the phone down.

Quinn then looked up at Smith. "You're under arrest."

His face contorted. "What the hell?"

Quinn smiled. "Madison's sixteen."

Smith laughed. "So what? That's the age of consent in this state. You better read your own laws."

"Oh, you're not under arrest for having sex with her. I'm arresting you for possession of child pornography. That's a Class B felony. One charge for every single picture on this phone."

Smith looked at Madison standing nearby, then turned back to the detective. "She said she was nineteen."

"She lied."

Victoria Hayes answered on the second ring. "Hello?"

"Mrs. Hayes, this is Detective Delaney. I'm sorry to bother you, but we've located your daughter at your condo." Quinn briefed Victoria on what had occurred to that point. "We need to keep her for questioning. We're going to have—"

"I don't want her home. Do what you have to do."

"Victoria, I don't know how involved she is, we just need to question—"

"I don't want her home," Victoria repeated. Quinn heard the tears then. "I don't want her back here. Something needs to wake her up. Maybe this will be it."

Victoria ended the call. Quinn stared at his cell phone for a moment before walking over to Marci. She was sitting in the back of one of the deputy's SUVs.

"How did the call with mom go?"

"She said to keep the daughter. She doesn't want her home."

"Ouch."

"Yeah."

"So, what do we arrest her for?"

"Let's book her for rendering criminal assistance," Quinn said.

"To what?"

"Possession of stolen property. He had Jacob Kidwell's phone. She helped him."

"That's weak."

"I know, but we need to buy ourselves some time with her."

"How about obstructing a criminal investigation? We could go back to some of our previous contacts with her and prove it."

Quinn thought about it for a moment. "Let's do them both. Not much more paper, but it will give a justifiable reason to hold her. You want to do the honors?"

Marci walked over to Madison. "Turn around."

"Why?"

"You're under arrest."

"I didn't do anything," the teenager blurted.

"Oh, yes, you did. You're under arrest for rendering criminal assistance and obstructing a law enforcement investigation."

"What are you talking about?"

Marci spun Madison around and pushed her against the patrol car. She grabbed Madison's right arm and pulled it behind her back. "Jacob Kidwell's cell phone."

"I didn't take it. Mick had it. He stole it."

"Exactly. You knew about it. You were with him. Therefore, you're getting booked on it as well."

Marci grabbed Madison's left arm and brought it behind her back, securing it quickly into the cuff.

"I swear I didn't know about it."

Marci turned Madison around to face her.

"Oh, my God. This can't be happening. I didn't do anything." Tears quickly formed in Madison's eyes. Suddenly, the girl who passed for twenty barely looked a frightened thirteen. "I was only with Michael because I was afraid of what he would do to me. He scared me. He threatened me. You have to know that." Tears ran down her face. Her voice rose in hysterics. "He raped me in that room, and you're arresting me because he stole a phone? That's not fair. I'm the victim here. I loved Jacob. He was my life. Michael tortured me. He hurt me."

Marci stared at Madison evenly.

"It was mental torture," Madison whined.

Marci continued to stare.

"You've got it all wrong." Madison exaggeratedly shook her head. "Why are you such a heartless bitch? Can't you see he's playing you like he played me?"

"Listen, kid. This act you're pulling? I've seen it before. A lot. And from better actors than you."

Madison's face reddened, and she stared at Marci. Without warning, she spat at Marci, who turned at the last moment, catching most of it on her cheek and hair. Deputy John Simmons grabbed Madison and yanked her away from the detective.

"That's assault," the deputy said. "You just made your night worse."

"I didn't mean to do that," Madison cried to the deputy. "I was only talking loudly, and spit came out of my mouth."

Simmons shoved Madison into the back of his patrol car. When he had her secured, he turned to Marci. "You good?"

Marci wiped her face with the sleeve of her shirt. "Yeah. Been hit with worse."

"That kid is a peach."

"That's putting it nicely."

***

The two deputies transported both Michael Smith and Madison Collingsworth back to the Spokane County line, where a couple of Spokane Police Department officers met them. They transferred the prisoners to their vehicles and then drove them to the department. There was no protective barrier in a detective's car, so transporting prisoners was forbidden.

It was late, almost one in the morning, when they arrived at the department. Quinn was tired, and Marci had fallen asleep again during the last twenty minutes of the drive.

He argued with himself about the best course of action. He could take Smith into an interview room and try to break him down on the murder of Jacob Kidwell. But he was tired and nowhere near his best.

Or he could book him into jail, write the affidavit of probable cause, and have him held for forty-eight hours. That would be enough time for him to get some decent rest, reset his thoughts, and go at Smith in the morning.

They could also do the same with Madison Collingsworth.

Quinn debated it, but he knew what his body was telling him.

When they pulled into the department parking lot, Quinn woke Marci. The two patrol cars were behind them, waiting for direction.

Marci looked at him, her eyes slightly out of focus.

"Let's book them and come at them in the morning."

Marci silently nodded.

"Book the girl for rendering criminal assistance and assault of an officer," Quinn suggested. "I'll book Smith for possession of child pornography, along with possession of stolen property. Then let's get some sleep and come back in the morning."

Marci nodded and slowly climbed out of the car.

# Chapter 42

Knocking awoke him from his sleep.

He sat upright, struggling to get his bearings. A quick check of his phone showed it was almost 2 a.m.

A second knock came on the door. Maybe someone was having a problem in their apartment. He hadn't had that occur before, but it was something he knew would happen someday.

At the door, he checked the peephole before opening it.

Marci stood there with tired eyes and an apologetic smile. "Can I come in?"

Kirby stepped out of the way, allowing her in. He closed the door after her.

They faced each other for a moment before she said, "I'm sorry for biting your head off earlier."

Kirby wiped the sleep from his eyes and ran his hands through his hair. "You were worried. I get it."

"You're not mad?"

"I was then, but I got over it. Life's too short to worry about that stuff."

"We caught Michael Smith."

"Did he confess?"

"Not yet."

"Then what's the plan?"

"To go to bed."

"Sleep is important," Kirby said and headed toward the bedroom.

"Kirby," she said, causing him to stop and turn back to her. "I didn't say anything about sleep."

# FRIDAY

## Chapter 43

Lieutenant Brand quietly stood over Quinn's shoulder while he finished the search warrant for both Jacob Kidwell's and Michael Smith's cell phones.

"Good work, Detective."

Quinn looked up and nodded.

"Where's Burkett this morning?"

"It's not even eight-thirty yet, sir. We had a late night. She'll be in soon."

"Your dedication is outstanding. Have you thought about taking the sergeant's test?"

"I like being a detective."

"If you don't like the idea of the job, think about the extra money. It's a great bump. It would go a long way in getting ready for retirement."

Quinn's fingers hovered over the keyboard. "More money won't solve most problems," he said, quoting something he'd read a couple of days before, "it only amplifies the personal faults that are already existing."

"You can just say no, Delaney," Brand said with an element of disgust. "You don't need to preach."

Quinn raised his eyebrows as the lieutenant walked away.

\*\*\*

When Marci walked in, Quinn was at his computer.

"Hey, partner, what are you working on?

"Finalizing the warrants for the phones."

"Damn. How early did you get here?"

"About eight."

"I thought we agreed to go home and get some sleep."

Quinn looked at her. "Doesn't look like you got much."

"Well, I got into bed."

"Keep your dirty talk to yourself."

"Bah," Marci said and turned to her computer.

"Hey, partner, I need you to do me a favor."

\*\*\*

When Quinn returned with the executed search warrants, Marci was at her desk writing a report.

"Did you get what I asked for?" Quinn asked.

She nodded. "Both of them gave positive identification."

Quinn tapped the top of his desk with his fingers. "That's perfect. Then let's look at these phones."

He unlocked his bottom drawer and pulled out an evidence bag. They walked into an interview room and closed the door. The last thing they needed was someone not connected with the case walking by, seeing potentially inflammatory pictures, and then commenting to the brass. The department had been an old boy's network in the past, but it was doing everything it could to change its reputation. A Human Resources complaint about detectives viewing sensitive material in the open was sure to be dealt with harshly.

From the evidence bag, Quinn removed two smaller bags. The first was marked *Kidwell*. The second was marked *Smith*. Quinn slid the phone out of the Kidwell bag. He powered it up. It still had roughly forty percent battery.

It was an iPhone, and Quinn located the Photos application. He tapped it and called it up. The photos were organized into albums which were labeled with the names of women. Holly, Fonda, and Madison were there. So were more than twenty other women Quinn and Marci had never heard of.

"You're kidding me," Marci said, looking over his shoulder.

"Who do we start with?" Quinn asked, his voice an almost apologetic whisper.

"Start with Madison."

Quinn opened the album labeled *Madison* and was met with a variety of pictures. Some of them were partially clothed, most were fully nude. A lot were posed, but a couple of them had been taken during intercourse.

"I wish he were alive so we could bust him for this," Marci said.

Quinn went to the folder for Holly Reese next.

"Why'd you pick that one?" Marci asked.

"Because she didn't care that he had these until he sent one after the breakup. I want to know why."

The photos with Holly were all nude and posed. None of them were during intercourse. Quinn closed the album and moved on to the one labeled *Fonda*.

"Shit," Marci said.

"Yeah."

None of the pictures were posed. Some were during intercourse. There were also half a dozen videos on there.

"Play a video," Marci said.

"You sure?"

"Dude, if you treat me like a fragile woman now—"

"Touchy," Quinn said and started the last video. The picture was crystal clear, and Kidwell had held the camera while he and Fonda engaged in sex. The camera panned Fonda's length during the act. She appeared to be feeling the effect of some drug but was still coherent.

Kidwell's voice filled the room. *"Should we show Daddy this video?"*

*"No,"* Fonda said.

*"Are you sure?"* Jacob said, his words taunting her.

*"Okay,"* she said softly.

*"Okay, what?"*

Fonda said, *"Show him."*

Kidwell spun the camera on his face and smiled. *"Hi, Daddy."* He turned the camera back to Fonda. *"Say hi to Daddy."*

Fonda closed her eyes and forced a smile for the camera. *"Hi, Daddy."*

Kidwell's pace quickened. *"Open your eyes and say it again."*

Fonda opened her eyes. *"Hi, Daddy."*

Quinn stopped the video. "What the hell was wrong with that guy?"

"I need a shower," Marci said. "This is what sex crimes deal with every day?"

"I think this is mild compared to what they deal with."

"No wonder they're messed up."

Quinn put Kidwell's phone back in the appropriate bag and then slid the phone out from the bag labeled *Smith*. It was a Samsung phone.

The only nude photos in there were under a file labeled *Madison*.

"Do you think," Marci said, "he was trying to be like Kidwell?"

"I don't know."

Quinn tapped on the file and was exposed to a variety of photos and videos of Madison Collingsworth. Most of them were posed in and out of her bikini on his boat. Madison was smiling broadly in each picture. None of them were taken during intercourse.

"You're kidding me," Marci said.

Quinn thought for a moment and backed out of the file. He went to the Gallery folder.

"What are you doing?"

"Just checking something."

The Gallery folder opened. It was full of a variety of pictures—some of buildings, boats, and scenery. However, the latest item was a video recorded the previous night.

He pressed the start button on the video and turned the phone to see the video in full size. Madison Collingsworth was in front of the camera in shorts and a tight T-shirt. Michael Smith was talking to her from behind the camera.

Quinn raced forward a bit. Madison and Smith were soon naked and engaged in intercourse. Quinn dragged his finger along the video time bar to speed it up.

"Ugh," Marci said.

"Yeah," Quinn said and pushed the video further.

The camera was now above Madison as she lay on her back.

*"Let's say hi to Mommy,"* Smith said.

Madison giggled. *"Oh, God, let's!"*

Smith turned the camera on himself. *"Hi, Mommy,"* he said with an exaggerated smile and a wave. The camera turned down his body and up Madison's until he got to her smile. She laughed when she said, *"Hi, Mom! Guess what I'm doing—"*

The sound on the video was interrupted by the sound of a fire alarm.

Barely heard above the blaring was Smith saying, *"What the hell?"* as he rolled off, the camera spinning wildly over the room. The video ended after that.

Quinn closed the video and tucked the phone back into an evidence bag.

"It was gross up until the fire alarm, but I liked the ending," Marci said.

***

Juvenile Detention's yellow brick building sat directly west of the Public Safety Building across a narrow strip of the parking lot. At Quinn's request, Madison Collingsworth had been escorted to the detectives' office and placed in an interview room. Marci called and notified Victoria Hayes of the scheduled interview time and the reason for the interview.

Madison wore the burgundy jumpsuit of a juvenile inmate and sat at the table, her hands in her lap, and her head down.

When Quinn and Marci entered the room, Quinn moved toward the seat across from Madison, and Marci sat in a chair to watch them. He laid a file and a notebook on the table.

"Good morning, Madison," Quinn said.

She looked up, her eyes red and filled with fear.

"As you know, I'm Detective Delaney, and that is my partner, Detective Burkett. This interview is being recorded both by audio and video." Quinn pointed to a red light in the middle of the wall above Marci's head. "That red light shows we're being recorded. If it goes off, we're not being recorded. Do you understand?"

"Yeah."

"Madison, we called your mom," Quinn said.

The girl's eyes brightened.

"She declined to come to this interview."

Tears began to fill Madison's eyes. "Why?"

Quinn shrugged. "She was hurt by what you did."

"It never stopped her from being here before."

"You can only push people so far, even family, before they pull away."

"I'm only a kid." Her voice raised, and fear was now clearly in it.

"You can't have it both ways," Quinn told her. "You can't be an adult to get into trouble and then claim to be a kid to get out of it."

Madison lowered her head and sobbed.

"Before we get started with my questions, I must do this," Quinn said and pulled a card from his file. "Have you heard your Miranda warnings before?"

Madison nodded.

"You have the right to remain silent," Quinn read from the Miranda Warning card. "Anything you say can and will be used against you in a court of law. You have the right at this time to talk to a lawyer and have him present with you while you are being questioned. If you cannot afford to hire a lawyer, one will be appointed to represent you before questioning if you wish. You can decide at any time to exercise these rights and not answer any questions or make any statements."

Quinn looked up from the card.

Madison's head was bent, and tears rolled down her nose. He flipped over the card to read the juvenile warning. "If you are under the age of eighteen, anything you say can be used against you in a juvenile court prosecution for a juvenile offense and can be used against you in an adult court criminal prosecution if you are to be tried as an adult. Madison, do you understand each of these rights I have explained to you?"

She nodded and sucked for air amid her sobs.

"Having these rights in mind, do you wish to talk with me now?"

She nodded.

"Madison, my boss is a stickler for paperwork. Would you put your initials on this card right here in the 'Yes' boxes and then sign it?" Quinn handed Madison a pen. She took it, glanced at the card, initialed the boxes, and signed the card. When she was done, she slid both the card and pen back to Quinn.

"How did you meet Jacob Kidwell?"

Madison sat up straight and, with the back of her hand, wiped the tears from her eyes. "I met him at my mom's office."

"What was he doing there?"

"Some sort of real estate deal. I don't know much about it."

"Who initiated contact, you or Jacob?"

"I did. He was cute, and he didn't know who I was. We were in the lobby. He told me his name, and I told him mine. I said I was there for a job interview. I Googled his name later that day and found his cell number, so I texted him. It was a goof, you know? To see if I could get the older guy interested."

"It worked?"

Madison smiled. "Yeah. We just traded a lot of texts at first. Finally, he invited me over to his place."

"Did you tell him how old you were?"

She shook her head. "I told him I was nineteen. As soon as I started texting him, I deleted everything from my accounts. I didn't want him to see anything from school, you know?"

"Your accounts?"

"Instagram, Snapchat." Tears ran down Madison's cheeks. "He was pretty worried at first. I mean, I look nineteen, but most guys are scared about the age thing. They don't want to get in trouble."

"You did this before Jacob?"

Madison nodded.

"How many times?"

Madison shrugged. "I dunno. Three, maybe. Something like that. Just like for a night, not as boyfriends."

"Three?"

"Four."

"How did you finally convince Jacob?"

Amid the tears, an impish smile spread on Madison's lips. "The way you convince all guys. They'll believe anything at that point. After we do it, I could tell them I'm Beyoncé, and they'd believe it."

"So, Jacob quit asking about your age?"

"He'd make comments, but as long as I was taking care of his needs, he didn't really care anymore."

"When did Jacob start taking pictures?"

Madison shrugged. "I don't know. The second time, maybe. Or the third. I don't remember, really, but it was quick. It was like his thing. I could just tell, you know?"

"You were okay with him doing it?"

The young woman smiled. "Why wouldn't I be? We sexted, and I sent him pictures when we were apart. I wanted him to be thinking of me. I didn't want some hoochie getting between us. Jake was going to be something special, and I wanted to be a part of it. Did you know he had his own website? He was a good writer."

"There were videos on his phone of you two having intercourse."

"You mean sex? Yeah, so?"

"Weren't you concerned about those pictures and videos getting out?"

Madison laughed. "You're not famous until you have a sex tape. I don't understand the big deal, anyway. Everybody has sex. Why do we pretend we don't?"

"When did you meet Michael Smith?"

"Jake took me to his boat."

"How was Michael introduced to you?"

"He's an investor. Jake was working for him."

"When did you and Michael hook up?"

Madison stared at Quinn.

"I'm not judging, Madison. I'm trying to understand what happened."

"Mick was after me like a dog with a bone. Do you know what I'm saying? The first time we were on the boat when Jake went down below to use the bathroom, Mick asked me for my number."

"Did you give it to him?"

"Yeah. He started texting me like right away, even though he knew I was Jake's girl. I wasn't into him at first; he's way older than most guys I've been with, but he's persistent and charming, you know? He said he'd wait for me until I got tired of Jake. We got together a couple of times before Jake's accident because we were both getting worried about him. Jake was totally getting paranoid about someone following him. I knew then Mick wanted me, but I was like trying to stay loyal to Jake. I thought he was going to be special. When I found out about what happened to Jake, I called Mick right away. I went out to his boat and told him the news. He was upset. He liked Jake like a little brother, I mean, even though he had a thing for me. It's complicated, you know? Anyway, we were both really upset, so we got high and did some drinking. Then one thing led to another and well, you can understand, right? We were like dealing with our grief."

"Did he ever say anything about wanting to hurt Jacob?"

"No. Not really. I mean, he was jealous of me and Jake."

"He said that to you? Does he get mad easily?"

"Not really, but he got super mad once, like crazy mad, when I told him he could take pictures of me like Jake did."

Quinn glanced over to Marci.

"He got over it, though," Madison said.

"Did Michael know how old you were?"

"Not at first, then he snooped through my wallet. He saw my driver's license."

"What did he say to that?"

"Nothing."

"Nothing?"

"Nope. He just tucked it back into the wallet, put it in my purse, and kissed me. He loves me. Age doesn't change that."

Quinn wrote something on his notepad. "Did he tell you how he came into possession of Jacob's cell phone?"

"Yeah," she said with an attitude that was supposed to make Quinn feel stupid.

He ignored it and asked, "Well?"

"Mick said he went to Jake's apartment after he died. He broke in, found it, and took it. He said he didn't want the police to find it and have my pictures out there. I don't care if they are, but he's sort of jealous about things like that. That's when he found the pictures of the other girls."

"Do you know he was blackmailing the father of one of the girls on the phone? If the father doesn't pay him, he'll post the photos on the Internet."

"Sucks to be them, I guess."

"You're okay with him doing that?"

Madison shook her head. "I didn't say that. You're putting words in my mouth."

"Jacob's phone was never in his apartment after his death. It was missing from the moment his body was found. We thoroughly searched it. We even searched for it a second time to make sure. The apartment was never broken into."

Madison stared at the detective.

"What we're saying is Michael killed Jacob," Quinn said.

Her brow furrowed, and her eyes grew intent. Quinn watched her working it out. He remained still while she struggled with the truth. When the realization hit her, she slowly smiled. "You mean he killed him for me?"

A sourness turned Quinn's stomach. "Did he tell you he would do that?" Quinn asked.

"If he had, I wouldn't have talked with you."

"What do you mean?"

Madison's eyes turned hard, and her lip curled. "I want a lawyer."

Quinn looked down at his notepad.

"I want a lawyer," Madison yelled at the red light on the wall.

"I heard you," Quinn said, collecting his file and notepad. Marci waited near the door as the young woman glared at the two detectives.

*** 

Outside the interview room, Quinn stood with Marci as a patrol officer handcuffed Madison. She yelled at Quinn, "I'll have your badge, Detective. I saw the way you looked at me in there. You're a dirty old man. I'm going to get you. I know your type. You were trying to seduce me."

The patrol officer tugged on Madison, pulling her away from the detectives' office and down the hallway. As she walked away, Madison continued to yell.

"That girl is all sorts of messed up," Marci said.

Quinn remained quiet, watching the young woman as she was escorted down the hallway.

"What's wrong, partner?"

"Did I get everything I could?"

"You did fine. It was a solid interview."

"It got away from me when she realized Smith might have killed for her."

Marci shrugged. "On another day, it could have just as easily had the opposite effect."

"I saw what was happening. There was something in her eyes when she said he loved her and their ages weren't going to change it."

"Pride?"

As the officer turned the corner and disappeared with Madison, Quinn turned to his partner. "It wasn't pride. It was control. She had control over him, and she knew it."

"At sixteen?"

Quinn shrugged. "It's what I saw in her eyes."

# Chapter 44

Michael Smith sat in the same chair as Madison Collingsworth had. His attitude was distinctly different than the young woman's, however. He leaned back in his chair with his arms crossed. His orange jumpsuit stretched tight around his biceps and chest.

When Quinn sat in the chair on the opposite side of the table, Smith immediately said, "Should I call my lawyer?"

"Would you like to?"

Smith studied Quinn's face before shaking his head. "Not yet. Let's see how this plays out."

Quinn pulled out the Miranda Warning card from the previous night. "Do you remember the Miranda Warnings I read you last night?"

Smith nodded. "You didn't ask any questions, though."

"It was late. I figured we were both tired. Why not start fresh?"

Smith smiled. "Want me to initial that, I suppose?"

Quinn pushed the card and pen across the table to Smith, who quickly initialed where appropriate. He slid both items back to the detective.

"This interview is being recorded, both by video and audio." Quinn pointed to the red light on the wall. "If that light is red, it means we're being recorded. Understand?"

Smith nodded. "Completely."

"Let's start with Madison Collingsworth."

"No. If you start with her, I'll call my lawyer. Let's talk about something else. Anything else."

Quinn knew it was a power play, but one he decided to let happen. "How did you know Jacob Kidwell?"

"He was my real estate agent."

"What was he doing for you?"

"We had a sweet deal put together. Twenty-four homes. An entire city block next to the mall. When the kid came to me with the idea, I didn't think it was possible. I coached him on how to put it together, and he pulled it off. It was extreme. Have you ever heard of anything like that being done in this town?"

"No, but I'm not a real estate guy."

"It would have been incredible. Let me tell you."

"What happened to the deal?"

"He died."

"So, the deal died when he did?"

Smith clicked his tongue against the back of his teeth. "Unfortunately."

"Couldn't it have been assigned? You were part of the LLC, right?"

"It could have. It should have, but I made the mistake of letting him put the contract in his name. I should have controlled the deal. Instead, I let the kid do it, and it went down the tubes. It's a damn shame."

"Why did you let him do that? Put the deal in his name, I mean."

"My name isn't the best after my… troubles."

"You mean your drug arrest?"

"Like I said, my troubles."

"Why would he hide his car? His files and laptop were inside. Even the ones from his brokerage firm."

"Who knows? He was a weird guy."

"We were told he became paranoid. That he was concerned about people following him. Maybe you were the reason."

"Maybe the boogeyman was the reason. I think you're grasping, Detective."

"Madison showed us where he kept his car."

"And?"

"That means you knew."

"That doesn't mean anything."

"Why does it matter if you hold that back from me?"

Smith thought about it before saying, "She told me she showed you."

Quinn opened his file and removed a montage of six photographs. There were two rows of three pictures each. The photos were booking photos of men with similar features of Michael Smith, who was in the bottom left corner of the page. Marci had prepared a couple of montages earlier and ran them out for witness review. Quinn laid this montage on the table and faced it toward Smith.

"An employee at the self-storage yard identified you as the man who'd tried to bribe him into opening Jacob Kidwell's unit."

Smith's eyes flicked to the paper and then up to Quinn. "I didn't do that. It could have been anyone."

"You knew his files were in the car. You knew the laptop was in there as well."

"How would I know that?"

"Madison told you."

"Again, I think you're grasping."

"Did Jacob get greedy?"

"Jacob was stupid. He didn't know what he had. He didn't know how to be greedy."

"Then why did he get paranoid? Why did he hide the files?"

"Maybe he didn't want me to have them."

"Why?"

Smith gnawed on his lower lip as he thought.

"Madison," Quinn supplied. "He knew you were interested in her. She was driving a wedge between you two."

"I said, don't talk about her. I'll end this interview."

Quinn lifted his hands in mock surrender. "Did it bother you that the deal died upon his death?"

Smith shrugged. "The deal of the century comes along every week. Was it something very cool we were doing? Hell, yeah, this was going to be one of the best deals ever done. It would have easily been the best deal I'd ever seen or been a part of. Twenty-four simultaneous closings? Ridiculous. It was legendary. In the end, though, it's just a deal, and we'd do another one tomorrow or the next day. Deals come and go."

"When did you find out Jacob Kidwell had sexual relations with Fonda Shay?"

Smith shrugged. "I knew about it early on. Once, when I stopped by his apartment, he was talking to her out front. I asked who the girl was. He said she was a friend with benefits. This was while he was already running around with Madison. I couldn't believe it. He already had the perfect girl but was messing around with a woman like that. Jake told me Fonda was part of the Sonnen Development family. That piqued my interest, of course, but I was still pissed at the guy for what he was doing to Madison."

"Speaking of Sonnen Development," Quinn said and opened the folder on the table. He pulled out another six-pack. He again laid it on the table facing Smith. Smith's picture was circled. Initials and the date were next to the picture. "Craig Sonnen identified you as the person who came to his office and demanded one hundred thousand dollars or naked pictures of his daughter would be released on the Internet and sent to his clients."

"That could have been anyone. I look like a lot of people. There are five guys on this piece of paper who look surprisingly like me."

Quinn tucked the piece of paper back into the folder. "We arrested you last night with a phone in your possession that belonged to Jacob Kidwell."

"He gave it to me."

"Kidwell gave you his cell phone?"

"Yes."

"He was a real estate agent. His livelihood came from that phone."

"Maybe he got another one. Who knows why people do what they do?"

"On that phone were naked pictures of Craig Sonnen's daughter, Fonda Shay." Quinn opened his folder and removed two photographs. "These are just two of more than seventy pictures of Fonda that were found on that camera."

"I didn't know those photos were there."

"These are some of the same photos you delivered to Craig Sonnen when you demanded he pay you a hundred grand."

"That wasn't me," Smith said with a shrug. Quinn didn't believe the effect. Despite the carefree shrug, Smith's eyes betrayed him. He was now worried.

"We saw texts on Jacob's phone from last night to some of the other women who had photos on that phone. Those texts demanded money from them, or their photos would be released."

The color ran from Smith's face. "I don't know what you're talking about."

"We've contacted those women," Quinn continued evenly. "We explained the situation, and they've all agreed to press charges. That's five additional women who will be seen as victims by the court. That will be a hell of a scene in the courtroom. I think you can already imagine that."

Smith parted his lips like a fish out of water, struggling to breathe.

"Either you wrote those texts last night or Madison did."

Smith's eyes darted around the room, looking for a get-out-of-a-jail-free card. "She did. Madison wrote them."

"Why?"

Smith was silent for a moment before he whispered, "Because we were going to run. We needed as much cash as we could put together. She was even going to try a push on her mom for some, but if it failed, we would have left anyway. We were going south."

"Why run?"

Smith stared at him until Quinn understood.

"You knew how old she really was."

"She's older than her years," Smith said. "I love her. She knows how to twist that."

"How did you come into possession of the phone?"

"Jake gave it to me."

"He gave it to you?"

"Yes."

"You didn't think you would get caught, did you?"

"I don't know what you mean."

"You didn't delete any of the text messages on Jacob's phone. You deleted them from your phone, though."

Smith blinked several times as he realized what Quinn's words meant.

"On the night of Jacob's death, you texted him at 11:47 p.m., asking if he was awake. He answered that he was. You asked if you could stop by for a quick meeting. Initially, he said it was late and you guys should meet in the morning. You pressed, though, and said it was an emergency. You said it would only take a minute. He agreed to meet, and that was the last text. There was no further activity from Jacob's phone until last night when you or Madison texted the other women about blackmail money."

Smith didn't look up. He'd sucked his lips into his mouth as he thought.

Quinn leaned forward, studying Smith's face as he spoke. "To solve any crime, Michael, I need to find three things: opportunity, motive, and means.

"I've got you at the scene the night Jacob was murdered. Even without you admitting anything to it, I'll place you there. Your own words put you there. That's *opportunity*. I'm going to check the box.

"Now, let's talk about *motive*. Legally, we don't need motive to convict; it's irrelevant. However, it matters to juries—a lot. Do you know what's great about that? You had not one, but two reasons for killing Jacob Kidwell. You had a real estate deal that would have made you millions, but you were head over heels for Madison, the girl who had been with Jacob. I think that's your bigger motive, don't you? Regardless, that's two reasons for murder, and I think a jury will see it that way as well. That's motive in a big way. Let's check that box.

"All that leaves is *means*, or in other words, would you be able to kill Jacob? You're a felon, but not a violent one. I'll give you that. Would you be able to graduate to murder? That's the question, right? Then I realized, this isn't stabbing a man in the heart or shooting him face-to-face. This is sort of a gray area when it comes to a violent assault. You see, Jacob was thrown down a flight of stairs. It might not have even been that much; it could have just been a push. Yeah, let's call it that. Let's call it a push. Anyone can push someone. Little kids push each other around on the playground all the time. Imagine that, just a simple push killed Jacob."

Smith's eyes widened.

"Well, it probably had to be more than a push, right? Let's call it a shove. Not quite thrown down the stairs but shoved down them. Doesn't sound so bad, right? Except the resulting impact broke his neck, and he asphyxiated to death. The coroner thinks it took him up to twenty minutes to die. That's a horrible way to go, don't you think?"

Smith swallowed as he rubbed his hands together.

"Anyway, it could all be an accident, you know what I mean? Yes, Jacob had injuries consistent with a fight, but the catalyst for this death, the push down the stairs, could be something different. That's for a defense attorney to figure out. However, I'm more than confident a prosecuting attorney can paint the picture that a former felon was able to beat up a skinny real estate agent and shove him down a flight of stairs. So, do we have enough to check that box?"

When Quinn finished speaking, Smith's face was completely slack.

"That wasn't a rhetorical question, Michael. Do I have enough to check the box for means?"

It was barely perceptible, but Smith nodded with his eyes closed.

When Smith reopened his eyes, Quinn held up three fingers. "Means, motive, and opportunity. We've got them all, and we'll let a jury decide. What do you think?"

Michael Smith bent his head down, his eyes darting as he thought. Quinn waited patiently. He'd been here before many times. Time was now his ally. He'd given Smith both the reality of the situation as well as a route for escape. However, the path for escape was a mirage and would only ensnare Smith more. In Quinn's mind, Smith had only one option: be silent. To open his mouth and say anything—deny, lie, or admit—would only paint him further into a corner.

"It was an accident," Smith said finally, his voice regaining its strength.

"How so?" Quinn asked.

"I did meet with Jacob that night," Smith said, nodding as if he remembered the story for the first time. "The deal was proceeding fine for the houses, but Jake had gotten squirrely about it. He didn't want to talk with me anymore. Our relationship had devolved to a point where he was threatening to poison the well with some of the sellers so the whole deal would tank. Quite frankly, I didn't care anymore."

Smith blinked several times before continuing.

"I approached him about Madison. He wasn't good for her. I could see it. Madison told me things. I mean, I heard it in the things she said when we talked. She was hurting, and he was the cause. I wanted it to stop."

Quinn wanted to ask questions, but to do so would interrupt Smith and his confession, even if it was likely a modified version of the truth.

Smith put a hand on the table and tapped a couple of times while he worked out his thoughts. "Jacob met me at the door when I got there. I told him it was time he left Madison alone. He laughed at me because it was the first time he had something on me. Until then, I always had the upper hand, but now he had the power. He had the girl I wanted."

Smith remained silent for a couple of moments until Quinn softly asked, "What did he say?"

"He said, 'She'll never be with you, old man.'" The line sounded stilted, and Smith seemed to realize it. "Or something like that. Anyway, I tried to play it off, that it wasn't about my feelings for her, but he knew better. He made a couple more wisecracks, and I hit him. Then I hit him again. He didn't know how to fight, so it went quick. It was only a couple of punches. He didn't fight back.

That was who Jacob was. He was more of a talker than a fighter. When it was done, I told him to stay away from her. I turned and left, figuring it was over. He grabbed me at the end of the hallway and tried to hit me with his one good hand. His other hand was bandaged up for some reason. I didn't do that, by the way, hurt his hand. That was messed up before I got there."

Quinn watched him, not saying anything.

"Anyway, he had no business fighting me. His punches kept landing on my arm, so they didn't hurt. I shoved him to get him away from me.

"I didn't realize we were at the top of the stairs. When he hit the landing, it was hard. I knew it was bad. I was scared and never bothered to check on him. I ran down the stairs and out of the building. I never looked back."

The two men sat in a silence broken only by the hum of the fluorescent lights. Quinn made a couple of notes, knowing he would be able to review the recording of the interview later for actual quotes.

"Did she ask about me?"

Quinn looked up from his paper and studied Michael Smith. "What?"

"Did Madison ask about me?"

He nodded.

"What did she say?"

"She seemed happy you killed Jacob for her."

A smile grew on Smith's face. Then he realized what he'd done and looked at the red light on the opposite wall.

"I almost believe your story," Quinn said.

"What do you mean?"

"You forgot to account for Douglas Rafferty."

"Who?"

"He said he was hired by you to keep an eye on what was going on at Hayes Construction over this project."

"He wouldn't say that."

"Of course he would. He's in lock-up. We've had him for days. He admitted to assaulting Jacob and breaking his fingers. He said he threatened him so he'd get rid of the videos of Madison."

Michael licked his lower lip but didn't say anything.

"He said Jacob bragged to the wrong guy about those photos. And he was right, wasn't he? Jacob bragged to you, and you spouted off to Rafferty, not knowing how everything was going to fall apart from there."

"I don't know what you're talking about."

"Maybe it was in a moment of trying to impress you, but what he didn't know was you were infatuated with Madison. The idea of those photos twisted you up inside. You probably told Rafferty to get the photos, but what you couldn't have known was Rafferty's partiality to old man Hayes. He felt a certain loyalty to the guy. He didn't want Jacob Kidwell to have naked photos of the sixteen-year-old Madison, but he didn't want you having them either. So he bullied Jacob into destroying them, which we both know he didn't. When he came back, he told you he didn't get the phone, but he told the kid to delete them. That must have pissed you off, right? Especially since Jacob knew Rafferty had to come from you."

"I want my attorney."

"Now? Now you want your attorney?" Quinn raised an eyebrow at him. "I won't ask you any more questions, but give me a minute to play this out, just so you can see how I'm reading it. You were mad when you arrived at Kidwell's place. It wasn't about the deal. I see that now. You no longer cared. Everything revolved around Madison and those photos. You probably beat him right away and took the phone. Yeah, that's how you got the phone. Because you couldn't leave his apartment without the phone, without those pictures. You had to have taken it by force, right? By the look on your face, I know I got that right. And that's why he ran after you down the hallway. It wasn't to continue to fight. I mean, why would a skinny guy like that, who just got his ass kicked by you, want to continue to fight? Your story didn't make sense. Unless, of course, it was to get back something that meant a lot to him. That's when you shoved the guy down the stairs. You might not have meant to kill him, but you did. How's that sound? I think I'm pretty close. That's first-degree burglary, robbery, and murder—three class A felonies."

Smith was breathing heavily now.

"Oh, by the way, it's only a class B felony, but I should let you know I'm going to add sexual exploitation of a minor to your charges for the video you took of Madison last night."

"Attorney. Now!" Smith yelled, his face red.

# Chapter 45

Kirby Willis was on his knees with a wire brush, scraping flaking paint from the deck of his apartment building. It was slow, tiresome work, but it allowed him time to think.

He'd written a new blog post earlier in the morning and gone for a short run through the neighborhood. He could feel his routine starting to fall back into place. Life was returning to some sense of normalcy for him after the death of Jacob Kidwell.

For a moment, he dwelled on his friend, and who he was and who he wasn't. After a bit, though, Kirby pushed Jacob from his mind. He needed to move on. Resenting Jacob and what had occurred would only hold him back in his own life. Kirby knew he needed to focus on now and what needed to get done. Life was about immediate moments—not yesterday that had already been acted and tomorrows that might never be played.

The scraping of the brush caused Kirby to miss the sound of the footsteps ascending the staircase. "Looks like a tough job."

Kirby looked over his shoulder. Holly Reese leaned on a pillar, watching him.

He dropped the wire brush and stood.

"I like your knee pads," Holly said. "Makes you look like you're doing roller derby."

Kirby tapped his knuckles against the hard-plastic pads.

"How are you doing?"

Kirby shrugged. "Fine. You?"

"I'm good. I was a little freaked out when I got a text from Jacob demanding money."

"I can imagine," Kirby said.

Her eyes challenged Kirby as she spoke. "I'm not worried about the photos, you know? I'm okay with them. Really. I'm proud of how I look. It's that those photos were taken in confidence. They were from a specific time. For someone to give them to the world violates a trust. I'm not ashamed they exist."

"Why are you telling me this?"

"Because you looked at me differently the last time you saw me."

"I did?"

Holly nodded.

"And if it's because of the pictures, I can't take that back, but I also won't be sorry for them."

"I'm not asking you to be. I didn't realize I looked at you differently."

They stood in the quiet of the morning before Holly turned to leave. She hesitated and looked back. "Kirby, what took you so long to come and see me?"

Kirby stared at her, not having an answer.

She turned and walked down the steps, not waiting for him to reply.

# Chapter 46

Quinn and Marci were both bent over their computers, writing reports, when Lieutenant Brand walked into the office.

He glanced over Quinn's shoulder to read his words. Quinn knew he was there but chose to ignore the man. Not getting any recognition from the detective, Brand moved to Marci's desk.

As he looked at her computer screen, Marci's face reddened. Still, she contained herself, following her partner's example.

Finally, Brand said, "You misspelled *photograph*, Burkett. I don't think the suspect had a cell phone full of naked *phonographs*. That would make for an embarrassing day in court, don't you think?"

Brand laughed to himself as he walked away from their desks.

Marci turned to Quinn, who was staring at her with wide eyes. Her face was a purplish red as she struggled not to yell at the lieutenant. She finally inhaled slowly through her nose and let out a measured exhale through her mouth. When she regained her composure, she said in a low, husky voice, "Before he retires, I'm going to dick punch that man. I swear to God."

Quinn turned back to his computer without a word.

\*\*\*

When the final report was done, Quinn sat alone, reviewing his work. Marci had clocked out late in the afternoon. She said she wanted to get in a workout before seeing Kirby.

Quinn had watched her leave the department. It was only after she was gone he realized he was smiling. *Good for her*, he thought. Then he shook his partner from his thoughts and focused on the report.

Michael Smith's booking charges would be upgraded to 1st Degree Murder, 1st Degree Robbery, 1st Degree Burglary, and Sexual Exploitation of a Minor. Quinn made sure he had all the elements of the various crimes in his report, as well as the updated charging affidavit.

The Rendering Criminal Assistance charge against Madison Collingsworth was weak and had been intended only to hold her. Frankly, so was the Assault of an Officer charge. Quinn was sure she'd be out quickly and cause problems again. He believed they hadn't seen the last of Madison. She was only beginning to discover her power over the opposite sex. She'd exerted some control of Jacob Kidwell, but it wasn't as strong. Her understanding of power probably hadn't blossomed until she was with Smith and in that interview room.

Quinn closed the file on Smith and Collingsworth. After he walked Smith's upgraded charging affidavit over to jail, he would call it a day.

# Chapter 47

Marci dropped onto the couch next to Kirby. "Where's your head tonight?"

"What do you mean?"

"You seem sort of out of it."

Kirby shrugged. "Maybe. I don't know. I guess I'm thinking about where I'm going."

"What do you mean?"

"Before this happened—this thing with Jacob, meeting you, everything—I had a nice plan in place. I had it all figured out—a road map. It was all a function of numbers. You know what I mean?"

"I think so."

"Then I was running around, searching for clues, trying to find answers for questions I hadn't even thought of yet. It was..."

"Exciting?"

"Yeah. I love what I've been doing. Don't get me wrong. But I don't think there's a whole lot of excitement in my side hustles."

"I don't know, Kirby. I think owning an apartment building sounds damn scary. Every time I'm at your place, I'm impressed that you bought it and that you take care of it. I think you've gotten so accustomed to it that you've forgotten how hard it is for most people to do."

He thought about her words for a moment. "Maybe you're right. It was intimidating when I first got it."

"I'm not saying not to try something different if that's what you want to do. Just don't forget how hard things are when you first start."

He nodded.

"What have you been thinking about doing?" Marci asked. "Want to go to the police academy?"

Kirby smiled. "Not a chance."

Marci feigned offense.

"I don't want a real job," he told her. "Just because I'm feeling a lack of excitement in my day-to-day activities doesn't mean I want to start reporting to someone. Looking around at the world, I'll be the first to admit I'm fortunate with how I've set up my life."

"Okay, so no police academy. What else then?"

"I don't know. Maybe I should start a business. Or like you said, buy a new building. Whatever it is, I don't think the safe way is really what I want."

"You're not going to start spending money like a drunken sailor, are you?"

Kirby laughed. "No. The principles are there. They'll stay in place. I guess I want some new challenges in my life."

Marci climbed into his lap. "Is that starting tonight?"

Kirby kissed her. "Would that be such a bad thing?"

# Chapter 48

Quinn Delaney was bent over his kitchen table, reviewing the document.

He liked seeing the numbers, even if he hated the story they were telling. It had been a week's worth of nights preparing the spreadsheet. Though the numbers totaled correctly, the history they told showed poor financial sense. That had been the truth that was exposed. As a detective, he appreciated the honesty the process taught him. As a man, he was embarrassed at the history of bad choices it revealed.

However, his budget now pointed him in the direction he needed to go. He had talked about it with Kirby over coffee. He couldn't ignore his responsibility for his financial stability any longer.

His new plan was simple. He needed to simplify his life before he could move forward.

Quinn's home was about to be foreclosed, yet the housing market was hot. Therefore, he called the bank and told them his plan to place his house immediately up for sale. The contact at the bank said they would forestall the proceedings for a short period. Quinn would have to agree to remain in touch with the bank during the entire sale process. At Kirby's recommendation, Quinn contacted Paula Fairbanks to list the house for sale. They had scheduled a meeting for tomorrow to discuss how to move forward.

Quinn also contacted the lot who sold him his RV. He had done some homework online and found out the value of his RV was roughly what he still owed on it. He asked the lot if they would take the RV back. It was clean (Quinn had taken good care of it and rarely used it), and the lot agreed to consider Quinn's offer upon inspection. Quinn would bring the RV in on the weekend. If he could give the RV back, that would remove a monthly payment immediately from his back.

After he dumped the RV, he'd be free to figure out what to do with the truck. Looking at it through frugal eyes, Quinn realized he had bought it with child-like impulse. It was big and burgundy and super cool. However, the payment was almost $500 a month. The insurance payment was another chunk of cash. Quinn planned to approach the dealership on it and figure out something. Trade it in, maybe. He'd still need a car, and in his present financial condition, it would require payments. There was no way around that, but if he could cut the monthly payment in half, it would be a huge win.

The WaveRunner was worth more than he owed on it. Quinn had taken pictures of it so he could post it on Craigslist later in the evening.

Quinn thought about the various other items he would soon put on Craigslist to sell. He had a pinball machine in the basement that he and Barbara once bought on a lark. They played it for one summer, then it sat quietly for the past several years, collecting dust. That was also going up for sale.

Quinn also had various guns he'd purchased over the years. As he bought the different pistols and rifles, he rationalized it was a "cop thing." However, Quinn didn't hunt, and he didn't shoot when he wasn't at work. Instead, the guns sat locked up in a costly gun safe in the basement. Next to the silent pinball machine, Quinn mused. He knew a local gun dealer who would eagerly buy the guns and the safe.

He shook his head when he realized his house was full of items he rarely touched and didn't need in his life. It would take time to deal with it all, but Quinn felt a new mission, a sense of purpose to his life that he hadn't felt in a long time.

He thought about calling Barbara and inviting her over for dinner to talk about it. Instead, he decided to put on a different pair of shoes and go for a run.

A jog through the neighborhood wouldn't cost him a thing.

# Afterword

The characters of Jacob Kidwell, Luke Jennings, and Kirby Willis—along with their respective websites (*In Frugal We Trust*, *How Now Cash Cow?*, *and New Fashioned Hustle*)—are fictitious. Their personal finance journeys were created to further the narrative.

However, to provide depth and realism to the story, there were many actual personalities and websites mentioned. There is a wealth of available knowledge that can help change a person's life. If you or someone you know is struggling with personal debt or their finances, below is a list of books and websites that can provide valuable insight.

## DEBT
*Financial Peace* by Dave Ramsey (daveramsey.com)
*Making Sense of Cents* (makingsenseofcents.com)
*The Money Peach* podcast (moneypeach.com)
*Mr. Money Mustache* (mrmoneymustache.com)
*Rich Habits* by Tom Corley (richhabits.net)
*Rockstar Finance* (rockstarfinance.com)
*You're Broke Because You Want to Be*
    by Larry Winget (larrywinget.com)

## REAL ESTATE
*Bigger Pockets* (biggerpockets.com)
*Coach Carson* (coachcarson.com)
*The Real Estate Guys* podcast
    (realestateguysradio.com)
*Rich Dad, Poor Dad* by Robert Kiyosaki
    (richdad.com)

## LIFESTYLE DESIGN
*The 4-Hour Workweek* by Tim Ferris
(fourhourworkweek.com)

While not necessarily concerned with personal debt or finance, this book was referenced in the story.

# Did You Like the Book?

I love when friends and family recommend a book for me. I'll often give it a read just because the recommendation came from someone I trusted. That's probably how we all are.

If you enjoyed this story, I'd truly appreciate it if you would tell your friends and family or leave a review at where you got the book.

All writers need feedback on their work—not only to help other readers discover them, but so they know they're delivering the goods with their stories.

Thanks for reading and I hope to see you again!

# About the Author

Colin Conway is the creator of the 509 Crime Stories, a series of novels set in Eastern Washington with revolving lead characters. They are standalone tales and can be read in any order.

He also created the Cozy Up series which pushes the envelope of the cozy genre. Libby Klein, author of the Poppy McAllister series, says *Cozy Up to Death* is "Not your grandma's cozy."

Colin co-authored the Charlie-316 series. The first novel in the series, *Charlie-316*, is a political/crime thriller that has been described as "riveting and compulsively readable," "the real deal," and "the ultimate ride-along."

He served in the U.S. Army and later was an officer of the Spokane Police Department. He has owned a laundromat, invested in a bar, and run a karate school. Besides writing crime fiction, he is a commercial real estate broker.

Colin lives with his beautiful girlfriend, three wonderful children, and a codependent Vizsla that rules their world.

Find out more about Colin at colinconway.com.

Made in United States
North Haven, CT
08 March 2024

49672877R00214